*She heard a voice. "Elizabeth, Elizabeth, awaken,
it's Michael." She struggled to follow the voice through
the caliphony of sounds and kaleidoscope of images which
flooded her mind. "Follow my voice. Here, take my hand,"
the gentle voice lovingly directed.*

*Elizabeth timidly inquired, "Am I dead? Are you God?"
She began to see a glowing, smiling face before her
and a dim recognition crossed her mind.*

*"No, no," the voice said, almost chuckling. "I called you
in the night of your forgetting and you are awakening.
Rest, let your mind clear and your thoughts become still.
Do not depend on what you think, but rather on what
you know and all will become clear."*

Ships of Song
A Parable of Ascension

Ships of Song
A Parable of Ascension

Patricia *&* Stanley
Walsh-Haluska

DESTINY PRESS

For information:
Destiny Press, Inc.
P. O. Box 1906
Birmingham, AL 35201-1906
Phone: (800) 601-9970
        (205) 930-1775
Website: www.destinypressinc.com

ISBN: 0-9668872-0-4
Library of Congress: 99-90745
Printed in Canada.

*Dedicated to
humanity's eternal search
for the truth.*

Alpha

In the night of my forgetting,

the consciousness of All That Is called to me

to awaken from my slumber,

to greet the Eternal Dawn of self-awareness and recognition.

Dawn

Chapter One

Day Break

In a dimension in which neither time nor space has meaning, where everything is eternal and present, Michael carefully maneuvered the great ship toward the mountaintop. Hearing the distress of his friends in his mind, he knew the recent years had been difficult for them. The responsibilities and cares of providing food and shelter for nearly one hundred fifty refugees had taken its toll on them. Both hope and time seemed to be running out for his friends on the planet below.

The darkness of night began to disperse as the light of the sun sought to penetrate the blanket of pollutants and debris that encircled the planet. A dismal excuse for a dawn peered through the intruding clouds which threatened Earth's increasingly fragile ecosystem.

"Time is, indeed, running out for them," Michael whispered to Miriam. "In fact, time will soon be no more." She nodded in agreement as they gazed out over the ancient mountains of the Appalachian range. Michael could tell from her pained expression that sadness filled Miriam's heart. He enveloped his mate of a thousand millenniums in his arms and whispered, "All soon will return to what was originally intended."

"Your embrace always reassures me," she murmured, glancing at the planet below. "I wish I could hold them close and reassure them."

Michael understood Miriam's sadness. All on board the ship had wished the exploration of All That Is could have been more joyous. Sometimes, Michael thought, the greatest pain comes during the healing process. So it seemed for humanity. On the eve of the fulfillment of a promise made millenniums before, humanity reeled in response to Earth's convulsions and humanity's creations of chaos.

A multitude of ships from throughout the universe now encircled the planet to guide and welcome their friends home. Michael knew that humanity's destiny with All That Is would rise as a phoenix from the ashes of humanity's mistakes. Those on the ship knew it to be humanity's greatest moment—the labor pains of a new era of awareness; for those on Earth—their greatest tribulation and challenge.

Every eon or so, the universe takes a great step forward in awareness. Today would be one such galactic event—one prepared for since the beginning of time.

∞

On the planet below, Elizabeth's dreams tossed her in a devilish parade of nightmarish images. The overwhelming burden and the often futile attempts to alleviate the suffering of those who wandered into the encampment weighed heavily upon her very being.

The restless wind rattled the window panes, stirring Elizabeth from her fitful sleep. Caught in the limbo between sleep and wakefulness, too fatigued to rise and too anxious to sleep,

Elizabeth struggled vainly to comprehend what had happened to her life, her sanctuary in the mountains and her world.

The cold wind knifed through the encampment. The fear of not surviving yet another winter in what was becoming a desolate world was beyond her ability to bear. The torment she experienced was the internal struggle between hope and hopelessness and it was tearing her to pieces. Even more confusing, deep within the darkness of her despair, there seemed to be a voice whispering an answer which she could not hear over the screams in her mind. In the predawn darkness, she feared for her sanity and contemplated how she could end her pain.

Her husband, John, stirred and mumbled, "Is it morning already?"

Elizabeth remained silent, hoping he would slip back into a restful sleep. She was envious of John's deep rhythmic breathing which told her that he was residing in a place where she could not go. Though only inches apart on the thick down mattress, it felt like a chasm she could not cross. Why, her mind screamed, can't I have peace?

Elizabeth admired John's ability to remain calm in the midst of chaos, but it also aggravated her because she sometimes felt he was distant. In sheer frustration, she slammed her fist against the bed.

Jarred from his sleep, John shouted, "I'm coming!"

Elizabeth was caught; she could not escape. She decided to take advantage of the moment and invite John to hike to the pinnacle—a journey she was unwilling to make alone in the predawn darkness.

Leaning over and giving him a kiss, she whispered, "It's time to get up."

She hoped the high ridge above the encampment would give her peace this morning. She often went there. The pinnacle was a place of solitude, peace and beauty. Perhaps the cool wind blowing across its peak would soothe the fiery emotions of her heart.

Elizabeth explored the cold floor with her feet in search of her slippers. Her infantry of toes failed to locate their goal and she wondered if PolkaDot or InkSpot, their two dalmatians, had commandeered her slippers again. She fumbled for some matches to light the lantern by the bed. The warm glow of the lantern revealed a room filled with mementos of a life that seemed so long ago.

She nudged John who had drifted back asleep and had started to snore.

He stirred and grumbled, "What time is it?"

"Five thirty," she whispered.

"Five thirty!" he scolded. "I have another hour yet. Ugh! And I have wood detail. Let me sleep!"

"I wish I could," she whispered.

John reached out and rubbed her back slowly. "More nightmares?" he asked.

Elizabeth nodded in response. "I'm going to the pinnacle. I feel I must."

"Now? Before dawn? That's too dangerous."

"At first I thought I could find some peace there, but there's something more."

"What is it?" John questioned.

"I don't know but somehow there's an answer there." Silently, in her mind, she added, "Or an end." She remembered the times she had stood on the precipice, imagining that when they found her, they would have thought she had slipped. She shook her head to clear her thoughts. She was never one to run from a challenge or, in this case, leap from one.

"Your dreams are that bad?" John questioned.

"Worse," she responded. "Now, I'm hearing voices."

John's eyebrows raised. "Voices? Whose are they?" He added tentatively, "And what are they saying?"

"I don't quite know. They sound kind and they're calling to me, but I don't know how to find them—yet I want to. I think the voices have an answer and I feel I'll be closer to that answer if we go to the pinnacle."

"Well, I always wanted to get up on a cold winter morning, climb a mountain and watch the sunrise," John jested as he grabbed his pants off the chair by the side of the bed.

Elizabeth knew this was John's way of acknowledging her insight and vision. John had often suggested to Elizabeth that the reason she experienced human suffering so intensely was because of her intuitiveness. He more than once had told her if anyone could find light at the end of a tunnel, it would be her.

A flash went through Elizabeth's mind: her thoughts momentarily transported her to an afternoon years earlier when she, John and their friend, Christopher, had sat in the darkness of the pit in the pyramid at Giza and she had led them up through the darkness to the light of the King's Chamber. This memory reminded her there could be a "way out." A rush of anticipation warmed her as her fears shattered like icicles falling from the eaves of her mind.

Elizabeth jumped up and began throwing on her clothes. "We don't want to miss the dawn," she urged John. "Let's invite Christopher, too." She knew their longtime friend and associate had come to tolerate her spontaneity and even appreciate her intuition. She hoped he would surrender his logic to her impulsiveness this morning.

"Oh, I'm sure Christopher will be really pleased," John said dryly, wiping the sleep from his eyes.

A few minutes later, Elizabeth and John stepped out of the warmth of their home onto the large wraparound porch. Immediately assaulted by the cold autumn wind, John pulled the collar of his coat tightly around his ears as Elizabeth slipped on her leather gloves. Only the dull flicker of a lantern in the dining hall betrayed that anyone else was awake. The encampment was eerily quiet as they walked through the darkness, guided only by the faint light escaping from the windows of the dining hall. Elizabeth found it amazing how the hundred fifty sleeping people barely made a sound.

As they reached the dining hall, she glanced at Christopher's darkened house across the stream. Giving John a hug, she whispered, "Good luck. I'll have the tea ready."

The scent of smoke and the fragrance of freshly brewed tea greeted her as she entered the dining hall. Ruby and Peter, longtime friends from New York, gave silent waves while Elizabeth whispered, "Good morning." No need to wake the sixty-some refugees who were asleep in the dormitory at the far end of the room.

Ruby, handing Elizabeth a steaming cup of tea, softly commented, "You're up early."

"Yeah, I had difficulty sleeping," Elizabeth responded.

"Troubling dreams again?"

Elizabeth nodded, as she sat down and silently sipped her tea.

Ten minutes later, John entered, startling Ruby. "Looks like we're going to have a party," Ruby said in surprise.

"No," John retorted sleepily, "just a hike."

A quizzical expression crossed Ruby's face. "Are you going to the pinnacle now? In the dark? Before dawn?"

"Yeah," Elizabeth acknowledged. "Don't ask me why, I just feel we need to go."

"We," John added sarcastically, "is the operative word here."

Christopher opened the dining hall door and peered inside. "Are we ready?" he asked.

Elizabeth smiled appreciatively at his appearance.

"This must be an event," Ruby declared.

"I hope so," Elizabeth agreed, waving goodbye. "Hold the

fort, we'll be back in awhile," she said as she closed the door behind her.

As Elizabeth, John and Christopher trudged up the steep path leading to the pinnacle, Elizabeth was concerned the weather was far too cold for an early November morning. Her anxiety increased as she noticed the edges of the stream, from which their community received its water, had begun to freeze. In the dim predawn light, she strained to see just how thick the ice was, as if in some magical way she could predict the severity of the coming winter.

Elizabeth absentmindedly stumbled over a fallen limb. She brushed her long auburn hair from her face as she quickly turned to let John know she was okay. He smiled and nodded as she continued up the steep grade. She did not think of herself as a leader, yet she led the way, doing what she always did, determined, focused and persistent in the pursuit of her goals and truth. Clearing the path by kicking a branch here, a stone there, seemed to reflect how she lived her life—a pioneer often taking the brunt to make the way easier for others. She was, as usual, sharing her light, but this morning it came from the oil lantern she carried.

The sound of John's footsteps behind her was the only thing that warmed her heart on this cold morning. John—her husband, her soulmate and her friend of more than twenty years—followed close behind her up the steep grade. Elizabeth pushed a low-hanging bough out of the way as her thoughts wandered to an earlier time which seemed more promising, a time when they had bought this property. She and John had always wanted a place in the Smoky Mountains as a place of refuge from the hectic day-to-day pace of New York. They had saved every penny they could from John's salary as a university sociology professor and from the sale of her artwork.

She thought of Christopher, their friend of many years,

whose small frame followed them up the steep slope. A shadow of a grin crossed her flushed face as she wondered if Christopher had known what he was getting into when he left the university to join them in the mountains. Her smile turned to a grimace when she thought, Heck! I didn't know what I was getting myself into! How could they have known, she reflected, that this very trail they walked, once used by hikers for enjoyment and recreation, would become a highway of refugees, a modern day Trail of Tears. Their hideaway for rejuvenation and creativity had become a sanctuary in the midst of a vastly changing world.

Pulling her hand out of her pocket, she tucked her scarf more closely around her neck to protect her from the onslaught of cold wind blowing across her back. She noted faint fingers of light beginning to move out across the eastern sky. She picked up her pace in anticipation of the awakening sun's glow, hoping it would warm her on the pinnacle.

Elizabeth faltered in her steps as she remembered a sky which was once robin's egg blue. In her paintings and drawings rendered in her hideaway, she had unwittingly recorded nature's gradual changes in response to humanity's chaos. She had seen the sky gradually lose its blueness and the sun its brilliance, while the moon had become cloaked in a crimson shroud. No longer did crisp shadows journey across the landscape; the earth and sky had become dull and muted, as if reflecting humanity's years of worry, struggle and dissipating hope. She shuddered at the thought of the turmoil which existed outside their makeshift sanctuary nestled within the arms of these ancient mountains.

A gentle wind blew, tousling her hair as if she had been lovingly stroked by some unseen hand. She was reminded of why she was going to the pinnacle this morning. She hoped to find a remedy to her despair—possibly a reason to go on or a forgotten promise that would give meaning to their plight. Her misery reached beyond physical desperation into the depths of her soul, questioning the meaning of her life and the purpose of existence at all.

The three scaled the last rocky grade and entered the clearing. The pinnacle was a simple clearing created by an outcropping of rock on the mountainside, not much larger than the average living room. It was walled on three sides by a thick forest of pines and hemlocks whose rich fragrance filled the cool morning air and whose needles created a luxurious rug on which to walk. The open side faced the rising sun. Two fallen hemlocks provided convenient and comfortable seating for those who came to savor the panoramic view. The tranquil green of the pine forest spread through the rolling valley below and over the next mountain ridge toward the distant horizon. The rolling hills in the predawn light made the terrain look like a deep blue-green sea, each summit the crest of a great wave about to crash at the foot of the mountain below.

Hunching against the cold, Elizabeth watched the crimson sky take on a blush of deep violet as the light of the sun sought to penetrate the film of atmospheric debris. The light of the coming dawn made the lantern in her hand unnecessary. She reached to extinguish it in order to save its precious oil but inexplicably set it on a boulder near the edge of the precipice, where it glowed like a lighthouse guiding some unseen ship through the mist covering the forest below.

She welcomed the balm which the pinnacle placed on her emotional wounds. It was her hideaway, her refuge against the onslaught of human suffering she encountered daily and her frustration at being unable to alleviate it. She and John did the best they could to provide food and shelter, yet it seemed so little against wounds so deep—and now she feared they would be unable to provide even that.

It was not her own pain, but the pain she witnessed which

drove her to the edge. Ironically, the pinnacle offered two solutions to her dilemma: refuge in its quietness and beauty; or release in the precipice which coaxed her to take one more step and be free of her burdens.

She turned toward the precipice and the expansive vista spread before her. Her complexion flushed by the cold wind against her face, she again pulled her scarf around her cheeks before returning her hands to her pockets. She thought about the first time she had climbed to this clearing and how winded she had been. She could feel the muscles twitch in her legs as they began to relax from the steep climb. She knew she had become strong physically, but questioned if her daily struggles had made her emotionally stronger. John said she was stronger, but she wondered if that was true—self doubt was her nemesis. Whatever her strength, she knew it came from a deep inner conviction of what was right and fair. Always for the underdog, she was dedicated to justice, her personality being that of an activist spiced with just a dab of rebel.

John, on the other hand, was a man who sought the status quo. Change was not his easiest ally. He had the same conviction for justice as Elizabeth but his study of history had convinced him the world was not always fair and justice did not always win. He was more practical in his approach, more the scholar than the activist, seeking to create the least disturbance in the status quo through well thought-out social changes.

Elizabeth took a deep breath, aware of how painful the toppling world had been for John. Whenever she saw him unconsciously fingering his short graying beard, an indicator of his frustration and worry, she reminded him that order would ultimately be victorious. He was always seeking to pigeonhole events and circumstances in his life and the world around him. The encampment and its ever-changing flow of people, concerns and problems turned John's world into a jumble—one he could never quite get in order. She knew his nemesis was his need for balance. It was both a curse and a blessing: providing ample reason for worry yet also a "solid rock" for the community to lean on. His willingness to listen and work things out provided the security and hope the community needed in reaction to a changing world. As Elizabeth admired him for his strength, John admired her for hers. As any good archway, both halves needed each other to stand firm.

Elizabeth glanced over at Christopher who was staring at the dead trees which soiled the higher elevations of the mountains in ever-increasing numbers. The trees on the mountain peaks were more vulnerable to the atmospheric pollutants than those in the valleys and these deep brown splotches of death were stains on the velvet green carpet of nature. She wondered if the earth wept at the wounds inflicted by her children. She wondered if the children knew enough to weep. "What have we done?" she grumbled aloud.

She admired Christopher for being willing not only to climb this mountain, but to share the burdens of responsibility which fell heavily upon their shoulders. He was a slim man with a stern countenance which often hid his big heart. During the last few months, she had noticed that his guard had begun to falter; his steely appearance and cynical attitude—his armor—had begun to show chinks. His thin face and straight jaw, which always seemed unemotional and detached, had begun to show the lines of stress and concern. His brown eyes had begun to show a depth of emotion and a window to a gentle soul hidden in a gruff exterior. She realized Christopher's worry was heartfelt and from deep within his soul, yet she knew neither the answer nor the way to console her friend—or herself.

John and Christopher had taken seats on the hemlock benches and were now discussing the encampment's overcrowding and food shortages. Elizabeth ignored their conversation, mildly annoyed they had brought their ongoing concerns of the encampment into her sanctuary. Her thoughts drifted to why she had come to the pinnacle this morning. Driven by some unknown force, she felt it was important for all three of them to witness this new dawn—and they weren't even paying attention!

Nervously pacing, she glanced over the valley for some sign which would give her hope. Watching the crimson sky, an old mariner rhyme crossed her mind: "Red sky at night, sailors' delight. Red sky at morning, sailors take warning." Mockingly, she whispered, "We're warned."

Cognizant of the stress they endured from a world which no longer felt safe or secure, Elizabeth could not imagine what it was like for those who did not have the relative security of the encampment. Most of the refugees had arrived hungry, dazed and confused by the absolute collapse of what they perceived their world to be. Each brought with them tales of fear and confusion. The government was faltering, financial institutions were weakened and churches no longer held the hope people desperately needed. There had been reports of tremendous earthquakes, volcanic eruptions and even nuclear detonations. Each time new refugees arrived, the scene was always the same—they would be besieged by those hungry and desperate for information about family or friends, and for news from a world which seemed to teeter perilously close to the brink of total collapse.

The sun was beginning to rise above the far mountains to the east. The deep hues of purple and gray had faded into a warm pink as the sun filtered through the crimson haze. The morning winds carried the sounds of the waking community up the mountainside as the increasing activity below became audible. Recognizing the various voices of those who had come into their care, Elizabeth felt the burden of her responsibility deep within her heart. Never! never! never did we think there would be so many needing our quiet place of retreat as a refuge, she thought.

The same breezes which carried the noises of the encampment also carried the aroma of wood smoke which heralded warmth, friendship and fresh tea. These fragrances reminded Elizabeth of what she and John had hoped their mountain retreat would be. She wondered what her life would have been like if she hadn't met John. Her thoughts drifted back through the years to a spring day in 1992. Her first sight of John was as a blur rushing by her, late for the first meeting of his newest project, a cutting-edge research group formed to study and document the holographic nature of humanity as expressed through ancient mythological beliefs and cultures. Elizabeth had been invited by Christopher, an associate of John's, to do the photographic and artistic compilation of the project.

"No records, no tangible evidence," John had quickly begun the organizational meeting for the project, "only legends. It's difficult enough to explore the remnants of the past," he said pensively, "but what if our only evidence is phantoms? Our job is to either prove the as-yet unprovable, or admit these cultures are figments of our imaginations."

Christopher chuckled, "So you've convinced the university to join you in this wild 'ghost' chase?"

John retorted, "I guess not only the university," as he looked around the room at the eager faces. "Doesn't it make you think? Wouldn't you like to know?" Elizabeth and the others nodded their heads in agreement.

"Thinking is exactly why I'm here," Christopher responded dryly. "How can you study what a culture does without understanding why it does it?" John and Christopher had a playful running battle about whether psychology, Christopher's expertise, or sociology, John's bailiwick, had the leg up in understanding humanity.

John continued, "We can't deny the facts that these cultures have had a profound impact on the beliefs and philosophies—and even the theology—of civilization."

Elizabeth was intrigued by the project because she firmly believed art was the unconscious expression of a society. If you really want to understand a culture, she thought, look at its art and architecture. The myths of so many cultures referred to magical societies unfettered by the bonds of physical existence that the possibility could not be overlooked. Beliefs, philosophies and theologies echoed a time when humanity's knowledge, both technological and intuitive, was greater. The thought that these societies could have existed intrigued her, and an unexplained affinity to them compelled her to proceed.

She knew the rumbles of the coming millennium were being felt as philosophers and theologians alike evaluated where humanity had been and where it might be going. These questions had spurred the university to accept John's proposal and generously fund the research project. They felt it was appropriate and timely to ride the crest of this intellectual wave. The idea of fulfilling her dream of visiting and studying such ancient sites as Stonehenge, Machu Pichu, the Acropolis, the Roman Forum, the Giza Pyramids and Easter Island fascinated Elizabeth. Not only was her dream being fulfilled but someone else was paying for it!

Elizabeth awoke momentarily from her reminiscing to the reality of the mountain. She realized what bound John and her together was their search for truth. She smiled as she wondered if John had realized what he was getting himself into. She chuckled to herself, "He certainly got more than he expected."

She recalled their life in New York prior to their move, with John's professorship at the university and her studio in Tribeca. She thought fondly of the hours spent in Central Park painting and drawing with her closest friend, Ruby. Elizabeth enjoyed watching people and expressing their essence on paper. Over the years she had witnessed children grow and noted that certain elderly people who used to stroll by Bethesda Fountain were absent. She savored the changing seasons in the great park, recording the ebb and flow of nature. She preferred watercolors to catch the spontaneity and feeling of the moment. With their translucent nature, she felt watercolors demonstrated that if one looked closely enough they might find something not seen before. She delighted in every picture, comparing the unique colorations of the trees and flowers. For years she had observed these changes, and it seemed to her that each fall came a little earlier and each spring, a little later. Elizabeth was an observer, always looking beyond the details to the deeper meaning of life. Her unique perspective sharpened her view of humanity and nature, allowing her to observe and record the messages declared by both. Indeed, she was an artist at heart and, unwittingly, a historian by spirit.

Her thoughts darkened for a moment as she wondered how her friends and associates were faring in New York. "But for the grace of God..." she prayerfully whispered in thanksgiving.

For some time, John and Elizabeth had discussed relocating in the North Carolina mountains to escape the fast paced technology driven world. The death of their infant daughter had been the catalyst which began their quest for new meaning in their lives and greater understanding of their existence. They believed the serenity and beauty which nature provided was the perfect backdrop for self-exploration and discovery. Their hope that others would join them in this exploration was realized over the years as their little valley became speckled with numerous homes inhabited by friends and associates.

A faint smile crossed Elizabeth's face as she wondered if they had accomplished what they had intended—just not in the way they had expected. Over the last few years, they had surrendered their private haven as it became a sanctuary for those who had been caught in the swirl of a changing world. They had opened their hearts and homes to all who found their way to the valley. Their seeds of kindness blossomed into a place of nurturing and healing where those who came for refuge became those who were able to give refuge—and in that transformation was their strength.

As Elizabeth stood on her perch high above the rolling valley, she strained to remember a distant past when the sky was blue and the air sparkled with hope and promise. She had come to trust her intuition, and this place seemed to enhance her sense of knowing. "Knowing what?" she questioned, as if seeking to dredge up some long-lost memory. This scene felt vaguely familiar and she wondered if she had dreamt about this.

Elizabeth had always had the gift of intuition, even as a young child, but never before had it left her so unsettled. Her mind was a kaleidoscope of images as she remembered bits and pieces of recent dreams: a grain of sand, a pink granite boulder, dancing with dolphins and soaring with birds. Even stranger, she recalled a great domed hall, filled with glowing beings of golden light discussing a great event which was about to occur. Puzzled, she wondered how these pieces fit with her recurring dream of standing on this mountain with John and the others, looking far into the future. What others? Who were they? She couldn't remember.

These vivid and recurring images occupied her thoughts this morning. She kept her eyes to the eastern sky, hoping to discover something which would validate her thoughts. She heard John and Christopher speaking of needed supplies for the winter ahead. Elizabeth looked up silently, pleading to an unknown benefactor. She could not be sure if the chill which ran up her spine was from the cold breeze which blew across her face, or the fear of what the upcoming winter would bring.

The sun began to rise above the distant horizon, immersing the three friends in a sea of pink. It heralded a new beginning, a new dawn full of possibilities. Somewhere in the drudgery and dreariness of what human existence had become, she now held a flicker of hope that—if she but looked—her faith would be renewed and her fears washed away.

∞

Far to the east of the pinnacle and hidden in the glow of the rising sun, the great Ship of Song hovered as a silent sentinel to a forgotten promise and a witness to a new dawn. The *Ohm,* the song of the universe, resonated from the great engines of this floating city and gently flowed unheard through the atmosphere to the planet below.

The "others," as Elizabeth referred to them in her forgetfulness, looked lovingly upon her and her friends. The twelve thousand aboard the ship had been on this mission for hundreds of thousands of what those on Earth called years. They would have been seen by humans as beings of light because they dwelt in conscious awareness and communication with All That Is—a reality humanity had long ago come from and forgotten.

Michael was well aware of the chaos below and the stress it had created in the minds of humanity. He had not missed Elizabeth's silent plea. In fact, it was he who had called her to the mountaintop in her mind. The grand adventure Elizabeth vaguely remembered was about to take an extraordinary turn.

Michael and his wife, Miriam, smiled at Elizabeth's unconscious response to their message to "be the light" when she kept the lantern burning as a beacon. The captain of this living ship of conscious thought, Michael rested his hand on his pilot's shoulder. "Hold steady. It's not quite time." Turning, he closed his eyes and took a deep breath. As always, his thoughts were in harmony and communication with the entirety of the ship, but he wanted to be sure he was listening to the collective consciousness of all on board.

Looking upward, a gesture he often used to create a sense of connection, he sent a subconscious message to his friends throughout the planet below. "Remember, please remember! Honor All That Is—to not remember is to deny yourself."

Hearing his thoughts, Miriam came up behind him and slid her arms around his waist, adding to his communiqué, "Remember, the pathway is love."

Michael and the captains of the other great ships hovered expectantly around the planet in labor, awaiting the birth of a new awareness. Each hoped for a little more time—that just one more of their friends would remember. He knew, as did all on the ship, that once the evacuation had begun, the great experiment was complete. The planet would not be able to support life much longer and the critical moment of choice was rapidly approaching when they would have to act quickly to evacuate their friends from the planet below. Ancient writings and religious theology promised an Eternal Dawn of enlightenment—a never-ending day bathed in the light of awareness when the creator and the creation would walk, again as one, in paradise. Those on Earth who chose to honor and recognize the creative source in all things would soon see the fulfillment of this promise.

This evacuation process was a highly complex maneuver. When the ship's vibrations were lowered into the third dimension, it and its occupants became susceptible to the physical laws of the planet. Gravity and atmospheric pressure had to be taken into account, and the ship and its crew knew it would have to respond accordingly. Michael knew it could be disconcerting for beings who could travel galaxies in the blink of an eye to move about in the planet's atmosphere, which seemed denser than stone. The crew was well-trained and had rehearsed many times for this complicated task, sometimes inadvertently being seen by the inhabitants below. Michael often reminded the crew, "Remember, in the process of rescuing someone from a storm, you have to enter the storm yourself."

On the ship, preparation was well underway to welcome the weary travelers home and gently awaken them from their slumber of forgetfulness. The new arrivals would be assisted in gently adjusting their physical bodies and thoughts to the higher vibrations of the fourth dimensional, spiritual realms. Freed from all vestiges of ego consciousness, they would once more be able to participate fully in the consciousness of All That Is.

"The evacuees will be in excellent hands as they awaken to their true selves," Michael mused to himself. Miriam nodded in agreement.

For a great armada of love, led by this mother ship, had gathered to be of assistance.

Walsh

Haluka

Chapter Two

The Ship

On the pinnacle, the burning red sun now appeared in the eastern sky, looking more like a sunset than a sunrise, offering little warmth against the cold mountain air. This clearing had always been a magical place for Elizabeth. No matter how worried, burdened or tired she might be, the gift the pinnacle always unselfishlessly gave her was a sense of renewal, well-being and hope.

But not so, today. She was jarred from her memories into the reality of their plight. John and Christopher's conversation had subliminally entered her mind, twisting her stomach into a knot. She turned to reprimand them for shattering the peace of this place but the strained expressions on their faces hushed her wrath. She knew that feeding the ever-increasing community was becoming a juggling act. The numbing reality was that there were not enough provisions to make it through another winter. The saturated ground from the wet summer had yielded little return on the precious seeds they had invested in the earth and the lack of sun had stolen yet half again. The unprecedented weather patterns had drowned their hopes and harvest, saturating not only the land, but their emotions, to overflowing. In response, John had organized regular hunting parties to search for food, but both ammunition and game were in short supply.

"Do we cut back on the use of eggs?" Elizabeth overheard John's query to Christopher.

"I think chickens in the pot will serve us better than eggs on the plate," Christopher responded. "We're going to need as much protein as possible this winter and the chickens are the quickest to replenish."

"I agree," John said, "especially now that we're without electricity—they won't need to be refrigerated like beef."

"Anyway, we can't afford to slaughter any of the cattle we have left. We need them for breeding," Christopher advised.

"There goes the milk. They'll have to go dry to conceive."

"The children have to have milk!" Elizabeth blurted, startled by her own intensity.

"We have to breed them, dear," John spoke softly. "We'll still milk some, but we'll have to cut back."

Almost inaudibly, Christopher whispered, "We might need to slaughter some just because we can't feed them." John's deep breath betrayed his frustration at the puzzle he could no longer put together.

A chill of fear rose up Elizabeth's spine. John and Christopher had always managed to come up with solutions to the innumerable difficulties they had encountered over the past few years. The thought that they may have run out of answers terrified her. The harsh reality that there were no more alternatives and, therefore, no security for those who huddled against the world in these mountains, sent Elizabeth into the depths of despair. She felt as if she had fallen from the precipice on which she stood.

In stark contrast to the fear, she could hear the laughter of children echoing off the mountains from the encampment below. "Oh, my God, the children! What will we do?" She thought of Stephen, the small boy she had found lost and alone in the forest. In the year and a half he had been with them, she and John had "adopted" him as their son and he had adopted them as his parents. She recalled her promise to him: "You are safe now." She was not going to break that promise to him, nor to the children or the adults to whom they had offered sanctuary!

But she felt like a tired sentry at a gate from which she could no longer hold back the intruders. The cancerous chaos of the world had finally crept into their sanctuary. She could not bear the thoughts of what the winter could bring. "If there is a God," she silently cursed the sky, "he would not bring such pain upon his children!" She questioned where her voices of hope had gone; she knew it was their reassurance which held her back from the temptation of ending it all on the valley floor below.

Her thoughts were interrupted by the sound of John's muffled voice conversing with Christopher. No matter what her pain, she could not inflict her death upon John, nor, she realized, upon those in the encampment who had come to depend on her and see her as a tower of strength. Her interaction with those in her care was often like a mother who hid her own fears to protect her children.

Though her hopes were dashed on the valley floor below, she decided not to join them. To have taken that step would have meant that everything she had ever believed in and to which she had ever committed herself was untrue. That thought was more chilling than starvation in the mountains. Somewhere, deep within her, she realized she had come to the point, "the dark night of the soul," where there is no hope or evidence of God. All one can do is reach heavenward, like the first man on the ceiling of the Sistine Chapel, and trust there is a greater hand reaching out to lift them up.

Elizabeth literally stood on the brink, her vision blurred by the tears in her eyes. The pressure in the top of her head from the strain of worry made her ears ring. At first she thought the low resonant tone she heard was coming from her own mind. Questioning, she considered that the children were singing in the encampment yet the melodious strains were beginning to crescendo as they echoed off the mountains. For an instant, fear gripped her as she heard what she perceived as a great wind approaching. What is nature or man inflicting on us now! her mind screamed.

As quickly as her fear had risen, a peacefulness descended upon her. Not knowing what to do or say, nor how to interpret this phenomenon, she turned to John and Christopher, who were also speechless and engrossed in the symphony which now filled the air. Elizabeth thought she heard wind whistling through the trees, yet not a branch was moving. Could it be music, and if it was, where was it coming from? She strained to determine the direction from which it was emanating, as she stood immersed in the rose-colored glow of a new dawn.

Unaware of the beams of spiraling light descending toward them and before she could utter a word—they were encompassed in light.

∞

Elizabeth's surroundings began to fade as if she were awakening from a dream. Her only guide was the resonant sound of the *Ohm* leading her very essence through a spiraling column of light. So immersed in the experience, she was unable to wonder what was occurring, nor did she care. Her only conscious thoughts were if she had slipped off the pinnacle and if she were on her way to heaven. Even that thought no longer frightened her. Her journey could have been a moment or hours, she had no conception. But when she arrived, wherever she was, it was as if someone had turned on a bright light in her mind. If it were possible for one to squint their mind against the light of awareness, as one might against a light bulb turned on in a dark room, she was doing it. Through the blurred images in her mind, she could see everything, everywhere, at once.

She heard a voice. "Elizabeth, awaken, it's Michael." She struggled to follow the voice through the caliphony of sounds and kaleidoscope of images which flooded her mind. "Follow my voice. Here, take my hand," the gentle voice lovingly directed.

Elizabeth timidly inquired, "Am I dead? Are you God?" She began to see a glowing, smiling face before her and a dim recognition crossed her mind.

"No, no," the voice said, almost chuckling. "I called you in the night of your forgetting and you are awakening. Rest, let your mind clear and your thoughts become still. Do not depend on what you think, but rather on what you know and all will become clear."

As she relaxed her thoughts and allowed the questions to flow through her mind unanswered, it was as if someone were focusing the lens of a camera. John and Christopher were beside her in an immense domed room with Michael and a woman standing before them in glowing radiance.

"If this isn't heaven, where is it? It feels like heaven. It looks like heaven. Are you angels?" Forgetting not to think and just to know, her vision began to blur again. "This is going to take some practice," Elizabeth thought. She looked at John and Christopher, who were shaking their heads in agreement without her having uttered a word.

She realized this was where her dreams came from. A collage of images filled her mind, encompassing the eternity of her existence. In an instant of remembering, she exclaimed, "Oh, Michael, Miriam, I've missed you!"

The Council Chamber of the great ship came into focus and she could see the glowing sphere of Earth wrapped in the blue velvet of the universe below. She was remembering what she had forgotten: where she and humanity had come from and where they were going, and that paradise existed in the realms of consciousness.

She mused, "Now I know where the singing's coming from," as she listened to the engines of the great ship. She was intrigued that the great ship was ancient beyond the understanding of most, yet it remained as new, light and fresh as at the very first thought of its creation. She noted the subtle differences created by individual consciousnesses coming and going from the ship, which changed its mass and structure to respond to the collective consciousness from which it was formed. Gently placing her hand upon the wall of the ship, Elizabeth sent acknowledgment and love to all who had assisted her and the world on this journey. Every individual aboard sensed her touch and experienced an exhilarating rush of love.

She would not be missed on the planet, as a journey to the ship and its return could occur in the blink of an eye. Though few remembered, most of humanity journeyed to the ship at one time or another for learning and rest. This process had been so arranged for good reason—in order not to create fear or confusion—for those upon the great ships wanted their presence to be an assistance, not a distraction. Humanity was welcome to run up the ladder of awareness as quickly as it chose, but without skipping any rungs. Subconsciously, these visits left an energetic trail which guided humanity through its journey of remembering. Therefore, out of the masses who had journeyed to the ships, only a few had a vague remembrance of the wonderment they experienced.

Five hundred feet above her, in the center of the domed Council Chamber, rested the light of conscious awareness, a glowing orb of the collective consciousness and focus of all upon the ship. Its light permeated every compartment, every hallway, every level of the ship. There was no darkness, no corner unlit, because consciousness is its own light, unfettered and unable to be diminished by something as simple as a bulkhead. Though a thousand feet in diameter and half that distance tall, the Council Chamber emanated a feeling of intimacy, comfort and love which belied its vastness. Here individuals gathered to converse, meditate and communicate with the center of conscious awareness.

An immense round table fashioned from a single piece of crystal stood in the very center of the room below the orb of consciousness. It rested in perfect balance on a unique pedestal which was pyramid shaped, one meter square at its base, moving to a single point a mere centimeter in size. The table symbolized the merging of thought and beingness with the twenty-two energies of creation. It reminded all who sat at this table that when thought is joined in balance and harmony, all things are possible. Twenty-two high backed chairs, each the color of a clear blue sky, were equally positioned around the table in alignment with the twenty-two hallways which led throughout the ship. All decisions of importance were made here since it was a reflection of the universe. Those called here to serve knew sitting at this table was an honor and a privilege.

From the perimeter of the Council Chamber, soaring to the center point, twenty-two arches supported the dome and pulsed the colors of the rainbow, as if in a synchronized dance of light and color. It was this very rotation of light revolving around the orb of consciousness which had been seen by the prophets of old and created the illusion of the "wheel within the wheel." This very ship was the fiery chariot which had lifted Elijah into the realms. These vaulting arches were a reminder that the universe supports all of its creation and that all creation is united in the consciousness of All That Is.

Elizabeth bathed herself in the light created from this consciousness of oneness and love. She felt a wave of energy flow from her feet to her head as her awareness of All That Is came into focus—a recognition which took her breath away. She stood motionless with her arms outstretched and her hands turned upward to more fully absorb the rays of light.

She surveyed the truth of the universe and acknowledged what could not be fully comprehended in its entirety from the planet below. The universe was not a place, but a living being; it was beingness expressed in physical form—consciousness made manifest. It was a dance of love between the creator and the creation, the creator and the creation being one.

The ship in form and function was a microcosm of the universe. Elizabeth knew that everthing in the universe revolved around and emanated from one central consciousness—that consciousness being the source from which All That Is emanated and to which it returned. Even the smallest atom on the planet below reflected this cosmic signature.

Enveloped by the crystalline blue-white walls created from pure thought, the friends continued in quiet conversation in the Council Chamber. The glow of the orb was reflected by the highly polished, opaline floor, casting its light throughout the chamber and warming the hearts of those gathered. These star travelers and warriors of light were deeply moved by the grand experiment initiated so many eons ago. The seed of consciousness of All That Is was awakening in the third dimension through the minds of humanity.

"It all seems so clear," Elizabeth whispered.

John nodded a silent acknowledgment.

Feeling an excitement in the air, she wondered what was occurring and turned to Michael for an answer. "In due time, my friend, in due time," he softly responded. "First, we'll take a walk through thought and all of your questions will be answered."

From the Council Chamber, she observed the ships which had surrounded the planet for centuries. Inspired by the awareness of this grand adventure, Elizabeth was honored and humbled to be a participant. What filled her heart with awe was the commitment and love for humanity she felt from her fellow star travelers.

The illusion of death melted from her mind in the realization that existence was eternal and assistance to one another was the lifeblood of the universe. She acknowledged that lifetimes were simply chapters in one great book of becoming. The assistant and the assisted were one and the same. The unseen hand and unheard voice which guided humanity was its own, for between lifetimes all of humanity was in service to those remaining on the planet. This cycle of assistance, created out of the search for self-awareness and union, was the seed from which love was born.

It was in this dance of self-recognition and self-acceptance that the universe sang the song of oneness, the *Ohm*, which resonated throughout eternity.

Eternity

Chapter Three

Creation

In a dimension where there is no time, one can relive anything they ever have or ever will experience. Settling into her chair, as if preparing to reread a favorite book, Elizabeth began to relive the journey which had brought her to the pinnacle on the mountaintop below. Her mind began to swirl with a collage of images as she prepared to thought-walk. Creation exploded in her mind. The universe which drifted before her in the immenseness of space was herself. She recalled the grand adventure of consciousness exploring the universe, and its de-evolution into physical form. Wincing, she recalled the moment of forgetting, when the "gods" in their chariots of fire forgot from "whence they came." Knowledge turned to corruption, expressed in greed, control and manipulation, with the promised land of Atlantis collapsing into its own destruction. She remembered the few who had escaped and had struggled to remember. She recalled the promise she had made eons before—that she would return to assist her friends. She was now fulfilling that promise.

Elizabeth thought-walked to the center of the universe, where all consciousness had sprung forth from a single point of self-awareness and self-acceptance—the only point which existed at creation. She experienced her awareness of All That Is dividing into a billion times a billion individual perceptions. As the universe expanded, she witnessed each aspect becoming more distant and more distinct. The exploration to find themselves and to again become consciously aware of All That Is had begun. The goal was for consciousness to be awakened in physicality, creating beingness—a state in which the creator and the creation are one. Every prayer ever whispered, every thought ever conceived, every tear ever shed, every sparrow that ever flew and every life ever lived sprang forth from the only mind that ever was or ever would be—consciousness. To the physical eye it would have been a fiery, globular mass beyond measure, exploding forth from a single point of light. To the conscious mind of the universe, however, it was the creation of a grand cathedral which would house the most sacred of all things—beingness.

The swirling fragments of fire and gas which held the seeds of possibility had slowed in their race to the ends of creation. Order had begun to replace the chaos of creation, and the fire had now become the firmament of the universe—fertile ground for life. Galaxies, solar systems and worlds emerged from the impetus of gravity, a reflection that all things are one. The universe had become an image of the very mind which had created it. Creation was fresh and new as the dawn of a spring day, as conscious awareness went forth to explore itself. In the vastness of all possible possibilities, it was now a millisecond after creation and the great clockwork of creation had begun to tick toward a distant date when the universe would again know that it was one.

Elizabeth observed the emerging universe before her, its beauty and magnificence reflecting the consciousness which had created it. She knew their challenge would be to understand that individual expression of All That Is was not a matter of separation, but expansion. The universe exploding before her was herself, as it was every individual expression of consciousness.

As all these individualized expressions—what humanity would later refer to as souls—continued to scatter throughout the universe, those of like consciousness began to gather. It was to one such grouping Elizabeth was drawn.

On the day of creation, Michael had no aspirations for leadership but his light attracted many to his presence. In a universe where consciousness was expressed as light, Michael's light had shown brightly in the heavens. So it could not have been otherwise that the more than twelve thousand individuals who gathered around him were in harmony. None was greater than the other—all were equal. Michael, the representative of this collective consciousness, would be responsible for leading them to the goals they had chosen. Those who gathered around him had chosen a path of exploration and service. Responding to the invitation that creation explore itself, each brought their own unique task and talents in service to the adventure. The garden had been readied and each prepared to go forth as ambassadors of All That Is to bring their unique expression into physical form. So it was in the beginning, as physical matter exploded into the universe, that consciousness began its journey into awareness.

Michael humbly took the reins of command and the responsibilities of service. Elizabeth and the others who had encircled him began to focus their thoughts upon a single point. This unified consciousness was to become the collective task and path of those who participated. The choices made that day were daring and bold—to experience all of creation. They were aware they would need to become one physically, as well as spiritually, with all they encountered. They realized the dangers inherent in the denser dimensions where the light of awareness could be dimmed in the intensity of physical sensations. Their goal was that in the process of exploring creation, they would more fully come to know themselves and, as a result, become one with All That Is.

Observing that other groupings had begun their exploration, Michael motioned to those gathered that it was now time to take their first steps into the universe. Those who had encircled him began to resonate in vibrational harmony. The union of their thoughts sang forth in the gentle melody of consciousness, the *Ohm*. This dance of thought created a harmonious chorus and their thoughts began to swirl into reality. They were enveloped in a glowing light, which would become the orb of conscious awareness upon the great ship. Their very thoughts and intents were creating the physical vehicle which would be their "chariot of fire." It was from this collective consciousness that the great Ship of Song emerged, a living, conscious being created by their willingness and intent.

Being a highly energetic concentration of thought, the great ship manifested as a perfectly designed immense radiant disk. It was approximately a mile and a half in height at its center axis and a half mile high at its outer perimeter. It varied between twelve and fifteen miles in diameter, depending upon the number of souls it contained. Since the ship was a living expression of those on board, it adjusted accordingly to accommodate their needs, desires and states of consciousness. It had all the attributes and components everyone desired: each heard their own melody of consciousness; each saw the colors which were pleasing to them; and each had their own compartment for personal rest and relaxation, created exactly as they wished.

Elizabeth observed Michael holding Miriam closely and was moved by how much he loved her. They were born of the same thought and had been together since the moment of creation. They were perfect expressions of harmony and oneness, spiraling energies of light and love. Known for her tenderness, Miriam was a good balance for Michael and magically drew out his gentleness; in turn, she was empowered by his strength. Elizabeth admired the perfect alignment of their energies, as she did John's and her own. They, too, were a perfect match: Elizabeth's creativity, spontaneity and desire to explore counterbalanced John's mathematical approach to the universe. She was inspired by creation's unexpected turns and twists; he, by its predictable order. Both were magnificent expressions of the universe—order and chaos, the cosmic dichotomy of creation.

John, knowing her thoughts, threw her a kiss. In the time it took his kiss to drift to Elizabeth, a billion years had passed in the universe. The gardens of creation had been prepared and were awaiting inhabitants. In what would have seemed but a few moments in earthly terms, the great ship traveled across the vastness of the galaxies.

The plan was to go to the furthest possible edge of creation to explore the denser physical vibrations forming on its outer rim. Though the advancing edge of the universe was only milliseconds older than the center of creation, vast differences were already occurring in its density and vibration. New dimensions of existence were being formed and those on the ship were anxious to explore what had become the third dimension, a dimension so dense even the light of conscious awareness was dimmed. In order to become physical, they would need to lower their vibrations to the threshold of forgetting their oneness with All That Is. In this pursuit, they would face their greatest challenge—forgetfulness, and their greatest promise—beingness.

It was their desire to experience all things which propelled them to a galaxy in a far corner of the universe. This galaxy, filled with pristine orbs, offered abundant opportunities for discovery. Vibrant hues never before seen splashed across their conscious minds. Cool breezes never before felt whispered in their ears. Fiery suns filled the void with a veil of light which would later become known as the Milky Way. It seemed to Elizabeth that consciousness had chosen this place to express the extremes of light, color, texture and temperature, as if the primordial energies of creation—fire, wind, water and earth—had decided to see just how inventive they could be. She marvelled at how variation and difference enhanced the awareness of oneness. She now fully understood that the reason All That Is had divided into so many consciousnesses was to more completely comprehend itself.

Like children in a candy shop, they viewed each world and the delicacies offered. One planet seemed to shimmer more brightly in the glow of its yellow sun. To their delight, as they approached this jewel called Earth, they found it to be an uncut gem, full of potential and hope.

On the evening of their discovery, all on board the ship celebrated the treasure they had found and the adventure which was about to begin. In the Council Chamber, Michael stood in silent prayer and spoke to his brothers and sisters throughout the universe. "We have come to a place that is beyond my ability to describe. It awaits us with open arms full of both promise and, I fear, perils. Take note of our location in case we forget who we are." Immediately an immense awareness of an infinite presence filled the chamber as the engines of the great Ship of Song sang a melody in harmony with the chorus of voices which now resounded throughout the ship. The dance of the creator and the creation was about to begin.

So it was in the beginning, the young planet was full of possibilities and potential. Like the young of many species, she exuded energy, spontaneity and unpredictability. Earth was experiencing her growing pains, trembling under the internal shifts and pangs of maturing. Funnels of smoke evidenced her internal transformation.

Ten million years passed on the planet as the great ship kept its vigil. As a midwife assisting a mother in labor, they sent cool breezes to refresh her brow, rains to moisten her parched lips and a gentle blanket of clouds to protect her from the violent rays of an adolescent sun struggling to become the gentle parent of life throughout the solar system. In the clockworks of the universe, it was but an hour past creation.

Now released from its seething internal transformation, Earth's barren landscape had become lush and living, waiting to be explored. The planet had shed its youthful rebellion and had matured. Its aqua oceans, emerald mountains and turquoise skies teemed with all forms of living creatures, each a unique expression of All That Is. The palace had been prepared; the kingdoms had been born. Earth shined as a unique gem against the blue velvet vastness of space. All living things had become interwoven into a single tapestry of life—the butterfly fluttering erratically over the wild flowers on the mountaintop and the great whale singing melodiously in the depths of the ocean. Those who had learned to work together had survived Earth's adolescence. As a result, Earth had become a garden existing in perfect harmony and balance. All inhabitants of the planet, from the eagle who sat in the redwood's branches to the ant who burrowed at its base, innately understood that they were interdependent upon each other for existence.

All on board were entranced by Earth's textures, colors and fragrances. These beings, who existed in the light of conscious awareness and were not blinded by its radiance, could barely comprehend the beauty which consciousness had created. Earth was like a mother waiting her fullness in time to give birth to a new existence fathered by these travelers from the stars. The moment of conception was at hand when the creation—physicalness, and the creator—consciousness, would conceive beingness.

Elizabeth viewed the deep blues of the oceans and the vivid

contrast of the lush white clouds which now collected the life-giving water which nourished all life on the planet. She marvelled at the perfect partnership between the plant and animal kingdoms which graced this masterpiece with life. Earth had become a perfect expression of the mind of the creator—a living being filled with diversity, yet intricately connected in a web of oneness.

The garden had been prepared and it was time to venture forth into this new dimension. Michael reminded all who were about to walk in Earth's gardens to honor and be non-disruptive of its delicate balance. Elizabeth and John nodded their agreement as they prepared to descend to the planet below. Like leaves falling from a tree, they drifted slowly and effortlessly from the ship to the fertile ground awaiting them. Unaffected by physical limitations, they gently glided and floated across the varying terrain, sometimes a hundred, sometimes a few hundred feet above the surface. One moment they dove deep into the cool blue-green water of the oceans, at another they hovered in the heat of an erupting volcano. Unable to experience the physical sensations Earth offered, they tried to imagine what it would be like to feel heat or cold, and longed for the time they could.

Elizabeth giggled as she attempted to stand on the surface—one moment, a foot above the earth and the next, half submerged in the ground. It'll take some practice, she thought. Her laughter was joined by the chorus of others who had arrived floating softly, and were now leaping, flipping, twirling and playing. Earth rejoiced at the sound of their laughter.

As Elizabeth sought to gain her equilibrium and balance, John's antics caught her eye. She laughed as she saw him attempting to kick a pebble, only to have it pass through his foot. Watching John trying to stand on the planet's surface and swing his leg at the same time amused her. If he could have fallen, he would have, but instead he merely floated away when he lost his balance.

Drifting away, she turned to him and exclaimed, "Isn't this a wonderful place? I can almost feel sensations pressing against my consciousness!"

Peter and Ruby, who had joined them on the planet, took to the air—soaring on their backs, flipping, turning and diving with the birds. Their physical forms were so light they literally passed through the bodies of a flock of doves. This was the first time the consciousness of beingness had entered another living creature in this dimension. In honor of this occasion, the dove would later become the symbol of the spirit of humanity.

John and Elizabeth took to the seas, gliding thousands of feet down to its very depths. Immersed in the great weight of ten thousand feet of water, they were overwhelmed by the complete exhilaration of their beings.

Elizabeth wondered, "Isn't it curious, not one of the animals even notices our presence?"

Knowing her thoughts, John chided, "My love, our presence doesn't even stir the water!"

"Oh," she thought with disappointment, "I hope we can truly embrace this wonderful new world." A school of dolphins swam by and a mischievous grin came over her face as she eyed John. "Now wouldn't it be fun…"

John grimaced, afraid to hear what she would think next.

"…to be a dolphin."

"Well," he responded hesitantly, "I don't know."

"We'll ask their permission!" she chirped in response. "Oh, we won't harm them."

Almost immediately, the lead dolphin made an about-face and swam within an inch of Elizabeth's nose, staring straight into her eyes. It so startled her that she wondered if it could see her. With a dolphin smile, she knew she had permission. They melded their consciousness with the bodies of the dolphins, embracing and entwining themselves in gentle exploration of each other. They rode the waters of the third dimensional reality which they now shared. Immersed in sensations, Elizabeth became dizzied by the movement of water flowing over her body. Her host soared from the depths in one great leap and danced upon the waves, singing as it splashed back-first into the water.

"That's it. I've had enough," Elizabeth gasped as she stumbled out of the dolphin.

Having had a more gentle ride, John smirked, "I told you so!"

Regaining her equilibrium, she smiled wryly at him. "Watch it, smarty! Your day'll come!"

Laughing, they glided away as two lovebirds in exploration of more tame adventure.

"John," Elizabeth inquired, "do you feel different?"

"Kind of strange. I can't quite put my finger on it," he responded.

"And did you notice," she continued, "the dolphin seemed different?"

"Yeah, it was as if…" he paused, reaching for the right words, "our consciousness rubbed off on them."

"Hmm," Elizabeth teasingly responded, "maybe they rubbed off on us."

"Curious," John retorted.

"Curious, indeed," Elizabeth laughed as they drifted away.

∞

Curious was not the thought on Michael's mind as he observed his friends at play on the planet below. Caution, like flashes of lightning, pervaded his thoughts and he knew his concern must show on his face.

With a puzzled look, Miriam asked, "What is it, dear? What's wrong?"

"I don't know," he whispered.

His response sent a chill up her back. Miriam had never heard these words uttered before. The threshold of the edges of consciousness had been reached. The future was yet to be known. The expansion of consciousness had begun.

"Michael?" Miriam implored him for an answer.

Before he could respond, Joshua, who was in charge of the away parties on the planet, hurriedly entered the Council Chamber. Michael raised his hand and uttered, "I know."

"Know what?" Miriam asked with alarm.

Michael leaned back in his chair and focused on the orb of consciousness hovering overhead. "Something has occurred we didn't expect," he began, "and I'm not sure what it means. Yet my mind warns me to be cautious and concerned." Looking at Miriam, he said, "You know, we're walking on the brink of consciousness and we don't want to fall off."

"What do you mean?" she pleaded. "How could that possibly happen?"

"Remember when we began this journey, we discussed that we were about to step into a dimension so dense that it dimmed conscious awareness of All That Is?"

Miriam nodded solemnly.

"Well, I was aware the vibrational density around us could distract us. I never thought that we, ourselves, could become dense," Michael said with frustration.

"What are you saying?"

"Were you aware of John and Elizabeth's romp with the dolphins?"

"Oh, yes," she responded delightedly, "it was wonderful! How could such an experience be cause for concern?"

"I suspected it before, but the dolphins confirmed it," he continued. "Our friends' interaction with the planet is causing their vibrations and, therefore, their consciousness to change."

"Can we become one with this dimension," Joshua interjected, "without losing our awareness?"

Michael responded, "That's the question at hand."

"What should we do?" Miriam asked hesitantly.

"We can do nothing," Michael answered. "We cannot interfere with our friends' choices. They'll become aware of what we suspect."

"We must be able to do something." Miriam beseeched.

"We can do what we are," Joshua offered. "We are the light, as they are the light. And if the dusk of the night of forgetfulness descends upon our friends, we can be a candle in the darkness to show them the way home."

Chapter Four

Paradise

Having retired to his private quarters, Michael was alone with his thoughts. His mind was troubled by his concerns for those who were descending to the planet. Joshua's words had rung true, yet he feared that once his friends were enveloped in forgetfulness, they would neither recognize the light nor desire it. His hope, and on a deeper level his belief, was that love—the source of light—could not be dimmed by its own creation.

Most of the ship's complement were in the Council Chamber where there was a spirit of anticipation and celebration for the new adventure which lay ahead. Reports of delicious new sensations, tantalizing aromas and vibrant sounds were drifting into their awareness. In reality, only about half of the twelve thousand on board would physically journey to the planet, but since all thoughts were known upon the great ship, those remaining on board were able to experience Earth through their friends' adventures.

From the inner chambers of his own mind, Michael observed the festivities in the Council Chamber. He was now certain those who had ventured to the planet were leaving a trail of energy affecting all they came in contact with on the planet. But more importantly, everything they were coming in contact with was leaving an energetic residue on their consciousness, resulting in a lowering of their vibrations and a solidification of their physical beings.

Michael understood the desire to experience creation fully and the inner call to merge with All That Is. Leaning back in his chair and folding his hands in a prayerful position, he reviewed the reports he had received from the planet that day. He merged into what his friends had experienced on their visit to the planet. His heart beat faster and exhilaration flowed through his being as he saw himself through the eyes of his friends gliding just a few feet above the surface of the deep blue-green ocean. His whole being surged with the undulation of the tides as he dove into the depths of the sea. He felt as if he were experiencing the very heartbeat of the planet pressing against his chest. He felt the great vents of steam and fire on the ocean's floor, a gift from Mother Earth to her children, so they might not grow cold in the night. The sensations were indescribable. The weight of millions of tons of water above him, pressing down and through his being, was the densest, most physical sensation he had ever experienced, a level unknown upon the ship—in fact, unknown in all the universes.

Emerging from the depths, he captured the sunlight dancing on the surface of the water like a million stars twinkling in the depths of a deep blue universe. He was humbled as he experienced the life force of the gentle doves which Peter and Ruby had inadvertently passed through, aware it was the same life force which pulsed through his veins. He experienced John and Elizabeth's wish to dance upon the sea, and the moment when a school of dolphins had appeared in response to their desires. He was grateful that in their enthusiasm they had not forgotten to ask permission—after all, they were guests of Earth. He smiled, aware their union with these gentle inhabitants of the sea had created an indelible bond which would last for eternity. In a distant future, the dolphins would vainly attempt to remind humanity of what they had remembered from this encounter—but humanity had forgotten.

As Michael awakened from his thoughts, he was filled with wonderment and awe at the awareness that all he had experienced was just one fraction of all that exists. He now had a deeper awareness and understanding of not only the desire, but the need to explore this new world—to not explore it would be denying a part of themselves. He realized it was not becoming denser which was the problem but the effect of density on consciousness. It was not difficult to love in a reality where you were aware that all was one. Love was the cement which unified all creation and, as a result, this ability to choose to love or not intensified the gift of free will.

As they became denser in physical form, a point of critical mass would be reached when forgetfulness, the state of unawareness, could become possible. This forgetfulness would create the illusion of separateness. In a world where things are seen outside oneself, there is a greater possibility of forgetting the bond which unites all things in oneness. The danger was that in denying the existence of oneness, one denied their own existence. The reality was that whatever one does to any of creation, be it a flower, a tree or a fellow being, one does to oneself. He quivered at the realization that it was possible for an individual consciousness to so deny the oneness of All That Is and, as a result, deny itself and cease to exist.

Michael assured himself that if the night of forgetfulness settled upon the garden, there would be a light which would shine greater than the darkness. That light was as real as the gravity his friends were now experiencing on the planet below and a force far greater—the inner desire and call given at the moment of creation that all become one. If night were to fall in the garden, Michael vowed, the great ship would remain as a bright star in the heavens to remind their friends of the truth. They would remain until their friends experienced the Eternal Dawn of awareness that all is one.

Michael felt the mood of excitement increase as the last of the travelers prepared for their extended stay on the planet's surface. He sensed the great ship adjust in size and shape with each departure. As the ship's collective consciousness adjusted, the private compartments of those traveling to the surface disappeared, reflecting that their consciousness had moved to their new home, Earth.

∞

On the surface, Elizabeth was exploring her new playground. Barely able to hold her childlike excitement, she waited patiently for John to catch up with her. They had agreed to explore the five major islands which graced one of the planet's oceans. Atlantis, as it later would be called, was an excellent base for planetary exploration. Soaring high above the terrain, her patience was rewarded with the arrival of John swooping like an eagle after its prey.

"Gotcha!" he yelled.

"Okay, smarty! We'll see who's mastered flying! The first one to the big island wins!"

They soared and then dove toward the island. "Oh, by the way, to win you must land perfectly on the surface," Elizabeth challenged.

She knew this would be difficult since their physical mass was so ethereal their bodies would easily pass through solid objects. It was more a challenge of accuracy than the ability to stand on the surface. Their physical bodies were not much more than ghostly distortions of light, much like the heat waves rising from the beach they were about to land on.

With the challenge accepted, they both laughed and giggled like children as they descended just a little too fast toward the surface. Both ended knee deep in the warm sands which encircled the island.

"Oh, well," John laughed, "maybe next time."

They floated through the white billowing clouds of mist which hovered over the lush green of the Atlantian mountains. Elizabeth observed the blue sea rhythmically lapping against the white beaches. She marveled at the unique and curious variations in climate and terrain which were refreshingly different yet barely noticeable on her high vibrational body. She was delighted to be on the planet, for it already felt like home. She could sense her friends throughout the planet and knew that in the twinkling of an eye she could visit them.

Everything was so new and fresh, she wanted to explore it all at once, to touch, to feel, to taste, to become one with her new environment. She longed for her physical body to become more dense, as a child awaits maturity, and with about as much impatience. She knew it would take centuries upon centuries for her body to be able to fully experience this physical world. For now, she had to be content with knowing that each time she merged or became one with the creations of Earth, her goal became just a little closer.

The seasons were as hours and the years as days as she and the others experienced this new concept of time. Time had little meaning for them in their newfound playground, as they romped and rejoiced like children experiencing a magical land. Already a few centuries had passed, and Elizabeth had become more skilled at touching physical surfaces. She would giggle when her hand passed through a tree or rock if she was not concentrating.

One warm, sun-filled day a millennium after her arrival, she decided to test herself and experience what it would be like to merge her consciousness with a rock. She glided over the landscape in search of the ideal formation for her experiment. She drifted along the white beaches, looking at each potential rock as one might observe the delicacies on a table set for a great feast. She knew it was one thing to pass through an object—it was another thing to touch it and, even greater yet, to become one with it. So this was not only a challenge to her physical senses, but a challenge to her conscious awareness.

From the moment Elizabeth arrived on the planet, she had realized she could not fully comprehend the third dimension without becoming one with it. The question which gnawed at her soul was, Are we here as guests or family? The question perplexed her and the answers swimming through her mind confused her. She wondered, Are we in it or of it? She hoped to soon find out.

Elizabeth had chosen a rock because it was the densest and most foreign to the concept of consciousness. She was aware John had merged with a tree. Determined to choose an even greater challenge, she smiled at the ongoing yet friendly competition between them. Allowing her foot to dip into the waves as she effortlessly glided along the ocean's edge, she thought she could feel the press of the wind against her body ever so slightly. Noting that her foot left no wake, she longed for the day when the wind would toss her hair and her touch would ripple the waters.

She focused her attention on Atlantiana, the largest island of Atlantis, whose vast northern white beaches were scattered with various rocks and boulders, many jutting into the ocean. She found them all fascinating, some but a few hundred pounds and others hundreds of tons. She saw each of them as unique, pink crystals sparkling in the spray of the sea. Each had been torn loose from the granite bedrock beneath the island during its formation. Elizabeth was humbled by their beauty and the creative power they represented.

Gliding among these natural sculptures, Elizabeth passed through a cluster of smaller formations. As she rounded the last one, she found what she was looking for. Jutting out from the water's edge was a magnificent boulder fifteen feet high. She floated admiringly around it. It delighted her. She could see the waves crashing against its massive body, spray dashing across its surface, promising a multitude of sensations. Its form was a symphony of textures and shapes smoothed by the ocean's touch, but jagged and cracked where the waves were unable to reach.

This sparkling pink monument called out to her soul. And then beyond her fondest hopes—she saw it! There, in the loving bosom of this wonderful creation, was a pool of water. So overcome with the grandeur and beauty of this gift from the earth, an unexpected sigh passed her lips. With the thrill of anticipation she thought, In merging with this great rock, I'll be able to hold the ocean before my time. She smiled as she watched the waves lap unhindered through her bare feet as she stood ankle deep in the crystal clear water. Though her senses were still muted, she trembled as she reached out to gently touch the cool stone. Focusing all her concentration, she stroked this magnificent being, gently touching its surface as a mother might lovingly touch her child's cheek. Her fingers sought to feel the coolness of the rock, as one touches the cold of winter through a pane of glass.

Even though she could pass her hand through the rock without a thought, it was far more difficult to maintain her touch on its surface. Stopping at an object's physical edge took extreme concentration and sensitivity to energy. A grin flashed across her face as she thought of the years ahead when the opposite would be true—when she would have no difficulty touching physicality but would have great difficulty getting through it.

No matter how physically limiting the third dimensional experience would become, she was like an adolescent waiting to grow up. Far in the back of her mind, though, she knew the day would come that as an "adult" she would wish to be a child again. Briefly it entered her mind to question what the effects might be to lower her vibrations to such a level, but the thought was quickly dismissed by her youthful enthusiasm to merge with this glorious creation. As a young maiden awaiting the passionate embrace of her lover for the very first time, she knew there was no turning back.

Spring, summer and fall had come and gone on the island of Atlantiana and her hand had moved but an inch upon the stone. She allowed her fingers to lightly flow over the curves and ridges, seeking to sense the most minute changes in its direction and form. She savored each variation as a sweet morsel of delicate sensations. Over the following year, she became quite adept at allowing her fingers to journey across the mountains and valleys of its surface. A decade passed while Elizabeth kept her vigil. Exploring this object of her affection, she examined every ridge and curve, both above and below the ground. She knew it and loved it as she knew her own body and, just as her body was changing through the years, she became aware of the minute changes in the rock's form and shape caused by the ocean's unceasing onslaught.

Undistracted by the need for food, water or sleep, she dedicated all of her energies to her quest. When she needed rest, she simply quieted her mind into a meditative state. During one of these rest times, she remembered the time when, in her enthusiasm to touch a scurrying rabbit, she had put her hand right through the small creature, nearly scaring it to death. Smiling, she recalled her penance, a large patch of sweet clover created by her thoughts. Her gift was readily accepted, forgiveness given and they each went on their own way.

She recalled on a particularly warm, moonlit night having seen the great ship in the heavens. Speaking to Michael, she had invited him to experience this precious rock through her thoughts. He readily accepted, as her hand caressed a particularly textured formation in the rock. Now adept at touch, her contact with the cool, moist surface was particularly strong. Sending a resounding *Ohm* throughout the heavens, Michael acknowledged and gave thanks to his friend.

Elizabeth was ready. The time had come for her to become one with the earth through this rock. She had been a good student and had learned her lessons well. She had only come upon this great work of art forty years ago. "Quite expedient." She smiled to herself. "I'm a quick study." She had learned a lesson that would later be forgotten by humanity and would take eons to remember—to become one with something, you must first observe it fully, know it completely, honor it unceasingly and respect it totally.

The moment had arrived. Her yearning to become one with this creation was to become a reality. She was aware of the rock's willingness to participate in her adventure, and with gratitude, she stepped into it. For years she had studied the exact place within the rock where she perceived she would experience the most delight. Now totally encompassed in pure pink granite, she sat cross-legged, cupping her hands around the water-filled bowl created by the waves. For twenty-eight years, moment by moment, hour by hour, day by day, month by month, year by year, the creator and the creation became one as she sat in the bosom of the rock in quiet stillness. It was impossible to distinguish a separation between herself and the object of her love, for their consciousnesses had joined. She knew the thoughts of the rock, its yearning to become one with the sands of the beach— its brothers and sisters. To her amazement and delight, in this union she had become one with each grain of sand. In becoming one with the rock, she had become one with the tree, the bird, the sea, the earth itself. Upon her hard stony face, she could feel the spray of the ocean imperceptibly tearing her down. She could feel the very heartbeat of the Mother, resonating through the rock firmly implanted thirty feet below the surface. She could feel the pool of water in her hands, refilled by the waves over-flowing from the sea, as a gift and an offering to her. She thanked the rock, the earth, the sea and the wind for what she had learned—the oneness of all creation. Never before had she felt so complete, so whole and so at one with herself, this world and the universe.

Each year their union became stronger. She learned how to honor change and adjust accordingly. She came to understand the cycles of existence in this garden and willingly gave up mor-sels of her body to be devoured by the sea, knowing that noth-ing was lost. It amazed her that some of her was now a thousand miles away, drawn by the tides and the currents to grace other beaches. She had come to understand that nothing was ever lost, only changed. Physicality was a vibrant, moving exploration of itself in which the ingredients would have the opportunity to experience everything in creation. She realized that a single drop of water would become part of the sea, would pulse through the veins of a tiger, or fall as a raindrop, or a tear. What a wonderful adventure this world was and, indeed, it was good.

About a century and a half after her union with the rock, a great storm arose. As the waves submerged her being, she could feel tiny particles of sand being thrown against her body like needles. As a matter of fact, some of the particles were from herself.

The winds calmed and the skies cleared as the dark, threat-ening gray clouds turned into white puffs of cotton in the sky. She had experienced and lived as the earth. She had felt the but-terfly land on a twig on the far side of the globe. She had held the little crabs, laughing and giggling as they climbed over her body, their tiny feet tickling her as they rejoiced in the pool of water she held for them to play in. That same pool of water became a dinner plate for a seagull as it devoured her little friends, the crabs. She had experienced an entrapped fish die of starvation in her hands and she felt that same life return ten thousand miles away in an inland cove. As energy cycled through her body, so did the seasons and the return of life upon this great planet.

She remained one with the rock for a thousand years, and it was now time for her to depart. She had experienced what she had desired to learn, and she bid farewell to her host. Thanking Earth and kissing the rock with her consciousness, she stepped out.

As she did, she heard a little splash and turned just in time to see a slight ripple in the water by her feet. She moved her foot again but no ripple was seen. Was it her imagination?

She didn't think so, and the rock agreed.

Chapter Five

The Sleep

Elizabeth was thrilled by the rock's concurrence that her foot had actually disturbed the waters. She stretched as if awakening from a deep sound sleep. She could feel her energies adjust as she freed herself from the vibrational density of the rock. It seemed as if it had been a dream—yet no matter how wonderful the dream, there was pleasure in awakening.

Now energetically awake and excited to share her experience with John, she scanned her consciousness to locate him. Her enthusiasm blinded her from the realization that, for the first time, she was unaware of him and the others. After searching her awareness, Elizabeth found him with Peter and Ruby on an adjacent Atlantian island one hundred fifty miles away. She was relieved to locate them; for a moment, she had felt something she had never experienced before—loneliness.

She hurriedly thought herself into their presence so as to escape her uneasiness, yet she did note her energies seemed sluggish. "Maybe I'm not fully awake yet," she thought, assuring herself everything was okay. To her surprise, her journey took seconds rather than an instant. It was not as big as the surprise she experienced when she landed with a "thud" rather than the gracefulness to which she had been accustomed. Curious that her friends had been unaware of her arrival, but relieved they had missed her clumsiness, she ran to meet them.

"Hey!" she called as she approached.

All three jumped in surprise.

John, Peter and Ruby had been exploring the mountain-side, which was covered with spring flowers. "It's beautiful, isn't it, Elizabeth?" John declared. "By the way, where have you been? We've missed you."

She looked quizzically at him, wondering why he would not know where she had been. She figured her forgetfulness had been due to her years merged with the rock. What was his excuse? She wondered, Could it be contagious? That's a silly idea, she chided herself—yet the thought of it haunted her. Not knowing how to respond to his odd inquiry, she stammered, "It's…it is beautiful up here."

Now distracted from his question, John agreed and asked her to follow him. As they glided carefully over the landscape, they shared their experiences of this new world. John had become quite adept at merging with the great cypress trees which blanketed the far side of the mountain. He shared with her his fondness for uniting with animals, their energies being far more varied, vibrant and stimulating than inanimate objects.

"I have even heard," John hesitantly shared, "some from the ship have taken up permanent residency in some of the animals."

"Why?" Elizabeth asked incredulously.

"This physical world can be quite intoxicating," John responded, "an opiate to the consciousness when not understood and respected."

"Hmm," she murmured, remembering the millennium she had spent united with the rock. "I understand."

"There's more, and it gets worse," he continued solemnly. Elizabeth cringed as she awaited his words. "Though I haven't seen it myself, there are rumors that some of our shipmates have found if they consume plants or animals when they're tired, it replenishes their strength."

"What!" Elizabeth recoiled. "That's cannibalism! Why don't they nourish themselves from the light of conscious awareness?"

Peter, who with Ruby had caught up with them, added, "The light seems to be a bit dim down here."

"How is that possible?" Elizabeth quizzed them.

Peter answered. "Our density is increasing our sense of individuality and separateness."

"Oh, Michael," she cried, "we're drowning in this dimension!" Straining to hear the *Ohm* of the great ship, Elizabeth listened vainly in the silence. A pall of abandonment fell over her as she turned pale. Weighted in fear, she fell like a rock to the ground.

"Are you okay?" John yelled as he bent over her.

"Yeah," she winced, realizing not all sensations in this garden were pleasurable. Regaining her composure and sitting in a bed of pink and white flowers, she took comfort in the beauty of this place. Surrounded by her friends, she rested on the steep hillside facing the sea, its azure color dotted with white caps from the strong easterly wind. She deeply breathed in the cool air blowing off the sea, aware it seemed to soothe her troubled mind and aching body.

Too tired to continue up the steep grade to the pinnacle of the mountain, they decided to remain there for the night. As dusk settled on the mountain and the crimson of the setting sun turned into the deep violet of the night sky, Elizabeth saw the stars overhead—a reminder of a fading memory. She stretched out on the carpet of grass and ran her fingers lightly over its soft blades. Feeling them move under the pressure of her touch, she wondered if the prize of experiencing this world was worth the price.

The mountaintop, with its proximity to the stars overhead, gave these explorers a sense of familiarity and connectedness with the universe. Consoled by the promise that the dawn always follows the night, they drifted off to sleep for the very first time. These great travelers of the universe, whose consciousness had witnessed creation, were progressively less aware they had come to explore themselves. Their experiences were as the brush in the master's hand painting a portrait of themselves. They had found creation to be exquisitely perfect, whether in the delicacy of a petal or the grandeur of a granite stone. They had now become as fragile as the grass on which they lay. The creator— one with its creation—walked in the garden.

As they slept undisturbed, a gentle wind carried a soft melody, as if someone were singing in the distance. And high above, a great star drifted slowly across the heavens, hovering momentarily above the sleeping explorers.

∞

Those upon the great Ship of Song enfolded their friends on the mountaintop, and around the planet, in love.

Holding Miriam close, Michael softly stated, "They will sleep well tonight, and I promise, my dear, we will speak to them in their dreams until the end of time."

They were aware the reports from the planet had become less and less frequent over the centuries. Miriam wept as a mother whose children no longer heard her call. "How," she pleaded, "are we going to speak with them?"

"In their hearts," Michael whispered. "Love is the link."

Free will was an intrinsic gift given to all consciousness, and it was about to experience its greatest challenge and promise.

Never before had free will and unawareness of All That Is re-sided in the same mind. Michael knew the sun had set on the night of humanity's forgetting.

"Miriam," Michael promised, "we will call to them in the night of their forgetting until we have brought them home."

Miriam smiled upon her friends and whispered in their minds, "The dawn is coming."

∞

The sun was beginning to peer above the eastern horizon, its warmth slowly burning off the haze in the valley below. Elizabeth stirred from her sleep as the first rays of light touched the hillside and tickled her nose. She knew she had dreamt, but could not remember its content or meaning, only that it gave her a sense of well-being. She turned to her still-sleeping companions and wondered if they had been dreaming, too. Sitting upright on her bed of grass, delighted yet confused, aware yet forgetting, she attempted to pull her thoughts together. Refreshed by her physical rest and rejuvenated by her dreams, she sat in the glow of a new day near the summit of an island in the middle of a blue sea on a speck of creation in the farthest corner of the universe, and remembered.

For an instant, Elizabeth knew, and looked up and whispered, "I will not forget."

∞

Michael and Miriam smiled from the great Council Chamber. A chorus of voices from across the universe could be heard as one, echoing the song of oneness, the *Ohm*, to the inhabitants of a blue-green gem in a far corner of the universe, on a planet called Earth.

Michael whispered to Miriam, already nodding in acknowledgment, that help was on the way.

∞

Ten thousand years had passed on the planet below. Nations were born and science and technology flourished. Civilization had developed in an attempt to capture a sense of order and balance, while religion sought to give meaning to human existence. It had been millenniums since Elizabeth and her companions had fallen asleep for the first time. Unknown even to them, they had become enmeshed in a dream from which they could not awaken.

Hidden behind a dark blanket of clouds, the sun was beginning to rise in the east. Elizabeth, John, Ruby and Peter slept peacefully on the very mountain which they had played on so long ago, leisurely drifting up its steep incline. The white and pink flowers still remained but their floating had disappeared long ago.

Over the years their physical bodies had become dense, needing nourishment as well as rest in order to function properly. Now deeply embedded in physical existence, they were no longer able to fully utilize the energy which emanated from the conscious awareness of All That Is—they were dependent upon the elements of the planet for their physical existence.

Sleep had become a normal part of their daily routine and they had become susceptible to the elements, as they would be reminded this morning. The previous evening, Elizabeth, John, Peter and Ruby had hiked to the mountaintop to view the stars. Their conversation had turned into a debate on the political situation in Atlantiana, the capital of Atlantis. As they sat on the mountain slope, they reminisced about a time when the world seemed more sane. Their memories had melded into their dreams, as they had unwittingly fallen asleep under heaven's canopy rather than in their warm beds in their homes nearby.

But now the morning sky was filled with fierce-looking rain clouds which threatened to drop their heavy burden indiscriminately. The first drop was not even detected as it fell upon Elizabeth's hair, and even the gentle mist did not awaken her. But the second drop, as if aimed by the hand of an unseen marksman, splashed strategically on her forehead. Startled, she awoke, wiping the offending drop away with the back of her arm, as a clap of thunder jarred the heavens as if to make sure she was awake. Sitting up to reduce the target for the increasing onslaught, Elizabeth pulled the blanket she had been lying upon over her head like an umbrella. Sitting under her makeshift tent, she remembered a time when she could have simply said, "Cease," and the rain would have stopped and the clouds would have parted. Now, more often than not, she would have to leave and seek shelter.

Deciding she was not going to be aggravated by this rude awakening, Elizabeth threw off the blanket and leaned her head back to welcome the rain upon her body. Ruby, John and Peter, now awake, and far less enamored by the rain, sought protection and headed down toward the house. Elizabeth watched them grumble as she stood to embrace the cool liquid which splashed in puddles by her feet. Spinning around, she raised her hands to the sky in a gesture of welcome as droplets of water, propelled by centrifugal force, spun off her long hair.

Running over, she grabbed Ruby's arm pleading, "Come, let's dance!"

Obligingly, Ruby agreed.

As the two swung each other around like young girls, Ruby's glumness, like the water on Elizabeth's hair, was flung off.

Elizabeth trembled as a cool breeze blew across her drenched body. "I think it's time to head home."

Already turning toward the house, Ruby nodded in agreement.

Elizabeth welcomed the warmth of the fire crackling in the fireplace and was thankful John and Peter had gone ahead. She pulled a dry blanket around herself and snuggled close to the fire. The sound of the rain falling upon the roof lulled her as she savored the safety and security of their home. She smiled as she contemplated how, without their need for shelter, she would have missed this opportunity to be warmed by the glow of the fire and the companionship created by the bond of their common need.

"You know," John spoke tentatively, "what we need to do..."

Elizabeth scowled at him for interrupting her pleasant reverie.

"Peter and I..." John continued.

"Yeah, Peter and you think we should go back to Atlantiana!" Elizabeth accused him.

Startled, John inquired, "How did you know?"

"It's obvious! I don't want to go back! We left there to get away from Mica's watchful eye." Elizabeth continued, "You know, John, and you, too, Peter, that Mica sees us as obstacles on his path to power."

"I'm no coward," John defended.

"It has nothing to do with cowardice—it has to do with common sense," Elizabeth explained.

"Yeah, that's what's lacking—common sense," John declared. "I can't believe we've forgotten our right to be individuals, free from the oppression of others."

"I wonder," Peter suggested. "Sometimes we consider it easier to be powerless than powerful."

"Well," John surmised, "we certainly seem to have made our choice."

"What do you mean?" Elizabeth shot back.

"It looks to me," John answered, "that being powerless is easier—for us, at least."

"What do you want us to do?" Elizabeth shrieked defensively. "We've tried for years to convince the Atlantian Council to serve, rather than be served. Did they listen? No! Will they listen now? Definitely not!"

"But, we don't go to convince the Council," John countered.

Elizabeth hesitated, staring quizzically at him.

"We go," John declared solemnly, "for those who are willing to listen."

Elizabeth recalled distant memories of when this chasm of perception which now separated them from each other did not exist. The "one" had come to mean the individual rather than the All. The result was fear, insecurity, powerlessness and abandonment.

Elizabeth's thoughts wandered to Atlantiana, the capital and the largest city of Atlantis which had flourished into a center for education, trade and science. Within its crystalline edifices, some of the greatest minds on the planet sought to study this new world. Atlantiana held the promise for paradise on earth. Nothing would ever be built which would compare with this city of wonderment. Its buildings vaulted thousands of feet into the sky; its architecture and engineering, so perfectly merged, could have soared thousands of feet higher if the builders had chosen. Every curve, every corner, every wall, every street was designed to be in perfect balance and to be a conduit of the energy of the universe. Atlantiana had harnessed the power of creation which emanated from the source of All That Is. It was the crown jewel of the star travelers' creations upon the planet and would become either their destiny or their destruction—the choice was inevitably theirs to make.

Many had flocked to this great city for the opportunities, comfort and abundance it promised. Anyone who wished to control Atlantis needed to control Atlantiana, with its centers of scientific understanding and philosophy. Mica, once a trusted friend and associate of Elizabeth and John, had accomplished just this through promises of power and prestige to those who were the guardians of technology and thought. As a result, Atlantiana had become a den of thieves, rather than a cradle of civilization. A city once dedicated to exploration and self-discovery had prostituted itself to power and greed.

Elizabeth's thoughts were interrupted as her friends, Christopher and Stephen, suddenly appeared in the doorway. Soaked from their own excursion in the cool morning rain, they shook their coats off and hung them on a chair near the fire to dry. They stopped short, seeing the serious expressions on everyone's faces.

"So you've been keeping up with current events," Christopher surmised.

"That sure is a foul wind blowing in from the west," Stephen added, apparently attempting to make light of it. "Can you believe Mica overthrew the Council—and the people supported it!"

"What?!" John cried.

"Oh!" Stephen gasped, his eyes widening and his hand coming to his mouth in a feigned attempt to halt his words. "I thought you knew!"

"Stephen! How about a little tact? Must you always be the first with news?" Christopher accused.

"We would've found out sooner or later," John replied, defending Stephen. "But why? How did Mica get the support of the people?"

"He promised them more land, greater wealth and..." Stephen said slowly, "can you believe it—a better climate?"

Elizabeth's eyebrows raised in disbelief.

"And guess what the people gave Mica in return for his 'generosity?'" Christopher added, scowling at Stephen. "The ultimate say for what's best for Atlantis—and the governmental power to implement it!"

"No more Council?" John jumped to his feet. "The people have given their power to Mica!" he screamed in disbelief.

"No," Christopher answered solemnly, "there's a Council, but they're just Mica's puppets."

"Like sheep to the slaughter," Elizabeth whispered.

"And what's this about a 'better climate'?" John asked incredulously. "Does Mica now think he's a god?"

"Not only," Stephen said, reveling in the absurdity, "a better climate, a perrr-fect one."

"How?" John asked dumbfoundedly.

Christopher explained. "Mica has commissioned a scientific task force to study the means to modify and change our weather patterns using crystals. There are banners already going up announcing 'Atlantiana—the Gateway to Paradise!'"

"And," Stephen interjected, "there's a movement by the new government to collect all crystals and gold for the project."

The group was speechless. Finally, Elizabeth muttered the only response she could muster. "Don't they realize what's happening?" With a panicked look on her face, she continued. "We don't fully understand the power of the crystalline deposits found under the city. We only know they're conduits of energy—misuse could be catastrophic."

"We know it. They know it—but no one seems to care," Christopher responded sardonically.

"We do," John reminded them.

Elizabeth swung her arm to encompass the group, as she stared intently at each of them. "The six of us against a city? No...A continent!"

"There are many in the city who believe as we do. They just need to be organized," Christopher answered.

Elizabeth stared blankly into the dancing flames which lapped across the freshly placed log in the fireplace. She wondered how they had come this far. She questioned how their paradise had become a purgatory, a non-ending maze of confusion, strewn between two worlds. She no longer felt she belonged to the world from which she came nor at home in the one in which she now dwelled. The limbo of her existence was agonizing. The only hope, even if it meant her life, was to take a stand. Retreat was not an option. To do nothing would be to not exist at all. To forget why she had come in the first place would have made this journey a travesty.

Elizabeth knew John was right. What would she want someone to do if the roles were reversed? To reject her friends in Atlantiana in their hour of need was to reject herself and diminish her own worth. She made a commitment at that moment—one which would be fulfilled on a mountaintop in a country not yet conceived and millenniums in the future—that she would remain to assist, until the last of her friends remembered again.

Needing to refocus, Elizabeth remembered her rock, which had remained a place of solace and sanctuary for her throughout the centuries. The rain had stopped and blue sky was appearing. The sun, now able to penetrate the diminishing clouds, warmed her body as she set off for the rock. No longer could she glide effortlessly in thought over the rough terrain—each step down the rocky slope to the white beach had to be carefully executed.

Over ten thousand years had passed since Elizabeth had bonded with the beautiful pink granite sculpture. It was a holy place to her, reminding her of a time when she was fully aware of who she was. As any holy place, it served as a bridge between the known and the unknown. Having stood the winds of change and the onslaught of time, the rock's endurance spoke to her and gave her hope.

The warm white sand squeezed through her toes as she approached her friend, the rock. Today she would hold in her hands the water from the same pool which she once held as the stone. She could no longer merge with her friend, for the very surface she once desired to touch had now become a barrier. She and her friend had become separated by a chasm and this awareness only added to her sadness today. She sat cross-legged, watching the ripples created by her hand in the pool of water. She grimaced as she remembered anxiously longing for this day. Shaking her head, she once again whispered to herself, "I hope the reward is worth the price."

She watched the sea foam dance around her feet as the warm water lapped against the shore. The only sounds were the rhythm of the waves and the distant cry of a sea gull calling to its friends. Though not a word was spoken, the eternalness of the ocean seemed to whisper, "All is well." As the waves sang, Elizabeth, for the first time in ten thousand years, felt one with her friend, the rock. For a moment, while lightly touching the water in the small pool in the rock, she thought her fingers had passed through the water without making a ripple. "It might be my imagination," she thought, "but I don't think so."

And the rock agreed.

∞

Upon the great Ship of Song, throwing Elizabeth a kiss, Miriam whispered, "I also agree."

"Miriam," Michael called, "the Council's about to convene."

Distressed by the news of horrific tales of injustices, environmental destruction and total social collapse, Michael had called the Council. He opened the meeting with a report on the ever-increasing disintegration of consciousness throughout the planet. Atlantis and her capital city, Atlantiana, were just one cauldron of corruption simmering on the planet below.

Joshua discussed his concerns. "We have a dilemma. Our messages are seldom, if ever, heard by their consciousnesses anymore. There are small numbers throughout the planet who are hearing our communiques, but not fully understanding them. Some are aware of our presence, yet do not understand who or what we are."

Michael interjected, "They don't really even know who they are anymore."

Joshua nodded in agreement and continued. "The deeper dilemma is that we cannot interfere with their choices, we can only assist—but how can we assist when they don't even know we exist?"

"The situation is far more grave than we first imagined," Michael stated. "A chasm has formed between our friends and us, creating separateness. The inhabitants of the planet can no longer sustain their consciousness in our realm. Having become so individualized in consciousness, they no longer can fully participate in All That Is. How do we help our friends and ourselves? For without them, we are incomplete."

"And there's more," Joshua continued. "Their dysfunction has driven them to the point of destroying each other and the planet. We now shelter in the great bosom of this ship alone, over ten thousand souls whose physical lives were terminated either by natural events or, the unthinkable, by the hand of their fellow companions. We know consciousness cannot be destroyed, yet their physical bodies have become so dense they are vulnerable and can die. The dilemma is that they can no longer exist physically in this dimension or survive in the third dimensional world of Earth." Joshua paused purposefully, allowing everyone to fully comprehend his words. "Earth's inhabitants are heading for a collision course with themselves. Their creation, both in consciousness and in physicalness, will soon snuff out their lives. As a result, we'll be faced with countless souls with no place to go, no place to call home and no place to express physically."

Utter silence filled the great Council Chamber. Even the orb of conscious awareness hovering above them seemed dim. Only the never ending *Ohm* resonating from the ship's engines seemed unaffected by this seemingly unavoidable catastrophe. Aware a tragedy was about to occur, the Council vowed to sit in deliberation until an answer was found. For what was an evening for those on the ship and ten years on the planet below, the Council searched their consciousness for an answer.

Finally, Michael addressed the assembly. "What we need is an opportunity, not a solution. Those who are less enmeshed in the dimension and willing to listen, we will evacuate physically to the ship. For those unwilling to hear, upon their death, they will be brought unaware into this realm, since they will be unable to comprehend it or us. Some will be able to adjust and reintegrate completely, while others," he hesitated, "must return to the planet."

"But that dimension is unawakened in its awareness of All That Is," Miriam commented.

"Those friends," Michael said solemnly, "now belong to the third dimension. To awaken them, we must awaken the realm in which they dwell."

The Council agreed. The plan was set. The call went out to those who would listen to prepare for the evacuation. Beyond that, they could only wait to bring their friends home.

With the Council adjourned, Michael directed the great engines of the ship to send throughout the universe the first distress call of consciousness. "Our friends have forgotten."

And in response, a million times a million voices were heard resounding in harmony throughout the universe, "We are on our way."

Chapter Six

The Plan

It had been ten years since Elizabeth and John had left their mountain hideaway to return to the din and debauchery of Atlantiana. They now stood tentatively outside the doors of the Atlantian Hall of Justice waiting to be summoned by Mica and the Atlantian Council. Elizabeth could hear angry voices coming from inside the hall and grimaced at the peril of their situation. She, John, and a handful of others had sought to incite the people to reclaim their power from the Council and exercise their birthright of individual thought and expression. They had been seen by many as dissidents and the few who had joined them were now in hiding.

Elizabeth had instructed those sympathetic to their cause to meet the next day at a rendezvous point far outside the city. It was time to flee. She hoped that she and John would be alive tomorrow to meet them. Thinking aloud, she mumbled, "Like sheep to the slaughter."

"You mean us?" John asked nervously.

The great brass doors portraying images of Atlantian history swung open, revealing a large crescent-shaped table at which Mica sat scowling. Taking a deep breath, Elizabeth grasped John's arm as they entered the cavernous chamber. They had rehearsed their strategy for one last plea. No one welcomed them nor introduced them, so Elizabeth started to begin.

"Silence!" Mica commanded before she could utter a word. "You have nothing to say here. Your words are like poison to the people. You have sought to undermine the government and destroy the grand technological future of Atlantis." Mica stood, shaking his finger at Elizabeth and John. "I will not allow you to stand in my way!" he screamed, his voice echoing off the walls. "You have a choice to make—either join me, or die! Be careful how you answer. I'd already have disposed of you if you weren't of value to me."

"What value are we to you?" John questioned.

"You're a scholar, and you, Elizabeth, an artist. Our history has been misinterpreted," Mica explained wryly. "We need a new interpretation, and the two of you and your reputations could be an asset to me."

"Never!" Elizabeth exclaimed.

"Don't be too hasty, little one," Mica warned with a menacing glance. "Impulsiveness has always been your downfall. Out of my graciousness, I will give you until tomorrow to reconsider. Return here at sunset."

Realizing it was pointless to argue, Elizabeth and John stood for a moment, hand-in-hand, in the center of the Hall of Justice. Elizabeth looked intently around the chamber, knowing she would never return and wishing to indelibly imprint it on her mind. It had been built centuries before and it was rumored to have been styled after the Council Chamber of the gods in the sky. It was a perfect domed structure designed to focus energy upon those who governed there. Unfortunately, it functioned as intended and gave those who now sat in the chamber an edge over the people. Now devoid of wisdom and integrity, it had become a dungeon of darkness rather than a cathedral of enlightenment.

Elizabeth was about to speak, but John squeezed her hand and whispered, "Let's go." The two turned and flinched from the jeers flung at them as they started to leave.

Mica screamed a reminder, "Beware! There is no greater power on Earth than Atlantis! And there is no greater power in Atlantis than I!"

Elizabeth could not resist. She tearfully turned back and spoke just above a whisper, yet her voice reverberated loudly in the acoustically perfect hall. "You're right, Mica," she stated slowly and deliberately, "there is no power on Earth greater than Atlantis." Her words caught him off guard. Before he could regroup, she stared him straight in the eye and vowed, "I'll be back."

Mica paled as he realized deep in his soul that her words were not a threat rising out of anger, but a promise out of love.

Elizabeth's eyes met John's and with a gentle nod of her head they left, arriving home as night fell over the city. The sky filled with threatening clouds and howling winds soon began to viciously slam against their home.

John peered out the window onto the deserted street. "Let's control the weather," he mocked. "It'll be paradise. Springtime all year round. They're fools," he said angrily, "to have thought they could do it better than nature!"

The door rattled, straining against the onslaught of wind. "Move away from the window, John," Elizabeth pleaded, fearful it would shatter.

"See!" he declared as he moved toward her. "Even the earth is rebelling against us!"

She raised her voice over the wind. "I hope this ends by morning or we'll never make the rendezvous."

The gusts subsided slightly. John put his arm around her and led them to chairs in the center of the room, away from the exterior walls. Still recovering from the humiliation they had experienced at the hand of Mica that evening, John looked at her questioningly. "How could we have been so foolish? We thought he'd hear us out."

Elizabeth sat quietly for a long time. She wanted her answer to be honest and helpful. Finally, she offered, "What is foolishness? Is it in the attempt, or the failure to try?"

John abruptly stood and began pacing anxiously. Slowing down a few minutes later, he finally came to a stop as he turned and faced her. "You're probably right," he conceded, "but they're still blind fools dancing their way to destruction!"

"Let's just hope we're not the fools—that our intuition is correct about leaving tomorrow," Elizabeth confessed.

"If it's not, then there are lots of us who are wrong," John responded. "In any case, I think we'd be fools to stay."

Seventy-two people had agreed it was imperative to leave Atlantiana at that time. Elizabeth did not fully understand the intensity of her desire to return to the mountains, or her lack of concern about leaving the city without permission. It was as if she were being called. By whom or for what purpose she did not know, yet she must go. In some ironic way, she felt she had no choice.

As the wind began to slacken, Elizabeth mercifully slipped into a deep sleep, filled with the sweetness of dreams. Memories long forgotten were awakened in her mind. A kaleidoscope of sensations and images filled her thoughts. Even in her sleep she could feel her heart pounding as her ethereal dream body floated gracefully over lush green mountains and deep blue seas. The planet was fresh and new. Her heart rejoiced as she watched her friends playing like children in a strange yet magical land. Some studied the petals of flowers, others danced with dolphins. Overwhelmed, Elizabeth experienced herself merge with the rock again; she and her friend were now one. She relived the playfulness and the promise of her first adventures on Earth. She winced as she recalled the pain and purgatory that she and her friends had created.

A soft, father-like voice was heard throughout her being. "Hush, be still. Rest, my dear."

"Michael," she mumbled, in her sleep.

"All is well, nothing is lost. I'll awaken you in the dawn."

The next morning Elizabeth awoke knowing she had dreamt. Unable to remember any images, she found it curious the only thought she remembered was the phrase, "I'll awaken you in the dawn."

In the early morning light, John and Elizabeth left their home. Their mood was melancholic as they hurried through the streets of the awakening city. They feared being detected, yet knew the crowds were their best place to hide. They moved quickly while attempting to blend in with the people, stopping and speaking to familiar faces only when necessary. As if some unseen hand blocked the guard's view of their presence, they passed through the city gates unnoticed. Safe and out of sight of the city, they hastened their pace. The road, being smooth and meticulously constructed, was easy to travel. They hurried, aware it was still more than two hours to the rendezvous point. Reaching the top of the mountain ridge overlooking the city, they surveyed Atlantiana, drinking in her beauty and grandeur one last time. She shimmered in the sunlight as her magnificent crystal edifices reflected the morning sun.

They had agreed to meet the others at Peter and Ruby's home on the far side of the mountain ridge which skirted Atlantiana. Others had already arrived and were quietly talking among themselves when Elizabeth and John entered. They joined the conversation, attempting to untangle the web of events which brought them to this place. Some whispered to themselves, some cried, a few laughed; hope was sparse and fear was great. What would happen if nothing happened? The dye had been cast, the risks taken—their fate lay in the hands of something or someone who had called to them in their minds.

The sun, now high overhead, beat upon the landscape. Sitting in concentric circles around the room, they shared meager provisions for a noon meal. Elizabeth wondered why nothing was moving—why the curtains on the open windows and the leaves on the trees were still, while she was sure she could hear the wind. She thought she could hear someone singing in the distance. No one was eating. All seemed to be transfixed by the gentle strains of music being carried on the wind. The air had become electrical and the hair on her arms stood up. She started to speak yet, before she could utter a word, she saw what looked like tongues of fire above her friends' heads.

And in an instant, in a brilliant spiral of light, they were gone.

∞

In the twinkling of an eye, after thousands of years, Elizabeth, John and their friends had returned home to the great Ship of Song.

∞

It was but a flash, an instant of knowing, not detectable by the conscious mind. There was neither a groan, nor a sigh, nor a prick of pain, but in less than a millisecond over ten thousand years of civilization were gone. In the next millisecond, the earth quivered and the very foundations of Atlantis collapsed. The highly conductive crystalline structures disintegrated, virtually evaporated by the implosion. Great tidal waves crashed across the island of Atlantiana, plunging it to the bottom of the sea.

All that remained of Atlantis were some stones scattered in the darkness at the bottom of the ocean.

Atlantiana was no more.

Over the centuries, the inhabitants of the planet had lost much of the knowledge of their former selves, yet some of their intuitive abilities had remained. Atlantis' destruction was the result of a misformed and misshapened philosophy—the pure thought of creation malignant with the pursuit of power and greed. The Atlantian Council, which had been created to serve the people, had ultimately sought to be served by the people.

Mica, through his ignorance, had created a deadly formula. He had skillfully devised a plan to obtain all the crystals held by the inhabitants. The ploy had been that these crystals would be used to control the weather and generate energy. Unwittingly, he had instead created an amplifier which intensified the negative energy of the Council and the inhabitants of Atlantis.

The results were disastrous on a planetary scale. A critical point had been reached when the negative charges of the amplifier became greater than the collective consciousness of those on the planet, causing consciousness to implode. Any living creature within a thousand-mile radius of Atlantiana was destroyed and the very islands of Atlantis disappeared into the sea. Beyond that perimeter, the original inhabitants—the plants and animals—survived, but the star travelers became a dying species on a planet which no longer welcomed them. Once they were gone, the Earth began the laborious task of removing the effects of their ignorance and the evidence of their existence.

The delicate fabric of consciousness had been torn, creating a veil hiding the truth from those who tore it. It could only be mended by those who had abused it—by healing themselves. In awakening themselves to the awareness of All That Is, the veil would be mended and transformed, thereby returning it to the tapestry of existence.

∞

The garden had been violated and, though the physical wounds might heal, an indelible mark remained on Earth's consciousness. The planet was pure and pristine again, but it was no longer paradise. The energetic link which had fed all of creation had been damaged and could no longer adequately feed its dependents; out of fear rather than need, the animals of the planet now violently destroyed each other.

The great ship became a beacon until all the star travelers on the planet had died and returned to her care. She cradled them like a mother, lulled them to sleep with the hymns of the universe and whispered in their ears, "You are safe now."

Those, like Elizabeth and John, who had been rescued from around the planet and had physically ascended to the ship needed centuries of rehabilitation and reintegration. Assisted by the tutors assigned to them, they gradually readjusted as their comprehension of who they were returned. For them, the centuries were like a long, slow awakening from a dream in which pieces of the puzzle need to be put together to fully understand the picture.

They completed their rehabilitation and returned to full conscious awareness. The nightmarish details of their experiences faded in the light of understanding what had occurred and were replaced with renewed hope for the future. What they had seen as tragedy on the planet had now been transformed by the light of awareness.

Mica and the others not physically evacuated had lowered their consciousness to such a point they were no longer able to fully reside in the fourth dimension. They slept, not as a punishment, but because of their inability to comprehend the spiritual realm. Now only a shadow portion of their true selves, it was much like being trapped in a two-dimensional picture. Though the picture reflected the world they knew, it was only a symbol of what truly existed. The tragedy was not that they were unaware they were trapped, but that they did not remember from which they came. Unless returned to the planet, they would remain in the eternal limbo of nonexistence. In order to awaken them again to the awareness of All That Is, the planet's vibratory field would need to be raised to the frequency of the fourth dimension. The issue was that not only would they need to be integrated into the planet, but that their existence would need to contain elements of both the third and fourth dimensions. They would have to be physically of the planet and spiritually of the fourth dimension if they were to become whole again. Thus began the epic journey of lifting a planet and its soon-to-be inhabitants into the conscious awareness of All That Is.

Millenniums had passed on the planet below. Michael convened the Council, inviting representatives from the armada, which now encircled the planet, and individuals who had been evacuated from the planet prior to the collapse of Atlantis. The Council Chamber was filled with the greatest concentration of consciousness since the moment of creation. Its purpose was to devise a strategy to awaken their "sleeping" friends from their night of forgetting. The means to assist their friends in that process was the question at hand. First, a suitable physical form would need to be found or developed for reinhabitation. Second, a plan must be devised which would guide them to their own self-awareness, without infringing upon their free will. The risk was that with free choice and unawareness of All That Is, their friends could choose not to return.

The Council and its guests met through the cosmic night. In a place where there was no time, their meeting was equivalent to twelve hundred years on the planet which passed slowly beneath them on its perpetual rotation. The reverberating effects throughout the planet of the implosion caused by the inhabitants of Atlantis had ceased. Pristine and new once more, Earth again called out to the travelers above. As a mother, she called to her prodigal children asleep on the ship, now one with her in consciousness.

Michael began. "Nothing is lost. Nothing ever can be." His words echoed in the deep recesses of Elizabeth's mind. "The only failure would have been not to try. This situation is neither right nor wrong, good nor bad. It's simply choices made by those who are equal to ourselves."

These words consoled Elizabeth as she thought of Mica and the others who were unable to consciously awaken on the ship. They existed in a limbo between two worlds—citizens of both, yet at home in neither. Deep in her thoughts, she remembered the rock on the white beach of Atlantiana. She remembered how profoundly she had felt one with the planet yet one with All That Is. "That's it!" she exclaimed aloud, without thinking.

Heads turned. Michael nodded knowingly and questioned, "Yes?"

"We went about this backwards," she declared. "We wanted to experience this new world without becoming one with it. Ironically, my friends," Elizabeth continued, "our error pointed us in the direction we needed to go in the first place. It was a leap in consciousness we were unwilling to take before—now it's a leap we must take."

The profoundness of her words reverberated throughout the chamber. Raising third dimensional consciousness to the awareness of All That Is was not their penance—but their destiny.

In one grand gesture, Elizabeth reached down to Earth hundreds of miles below and gently touched her granite friend, now resting at the bottom of the ocean. She picked up a fragment of the pink crystalline stone and brought it to the ship. It glowed in the perfection which resulted from the creation and the creator being one again.

"This stone," she said, as she placed it deliberately in the center of the great table, "will remain as a symbol of why we have come here and as a bond between heaven and earth while our friends inhabit the planet below. On the day of their conscious return to the ships, we will return this stone to Earth as a token of our thanks and appreciation for caring for our friends in their time of need."

Elizabeth stood prayerfully with her arms raised. "And with these words, I dedicate this stone and our destiny. Come join with us. Become the grain of sand that we might know the desert, the drop of water that we might know the sea, the star that we might know the universe. To know the All," she concluded, "is to know the One. To know the One is to know the All. They are one and the same."

Her words echoed across the universe to all consciousness, to all the worlds which were exploring what it was to be One—the individual—and All—the universe—at the same time.

As the Council retired, the ship sweetly sang a lullaby of hope and promise to her children waiting to be born from the womb of consciousness, conceived of the earth and the stars.

The stars shown brightly that night in the skies above Earth, wrapping the mother in a warm blanket of love as she awaited the birth of her children.

Chapter Seven

The Encounter

Tens of thousands of years had passed since that night in the great Council Chamber. The fragment of Elizabeth's granite friend glowed iridescently in the center of the council table. The new species—humanity—was thriving throughout the planet. The souls of Mica and those who had become enmeshed in the third dimension had now returned to the planet in this new species.

Humanity was a perfect design for physical existence on Earth. Those on the ship had genetically enhanced the human body. They had given the body a larger brain, greater dexterity and expanded vocal cords. Michael was pleased to see that these changes, created to accommodate his friends and enhance their abilities, had been successful. Their friends had quickly adapted to their new bodies and the evolutionary process was forging forward. Civilizations had sprung up throughout the planet like gardens by water, the cultures varied and distinctly unique.

But humanity had come to a critical transition in its development. They began wondering what was beyond their understanding. What were the powers which controlled their destiny? They worshipped and sacrificed to anything they perceived greater than themselves, in the hopes these "gods" would look kindly upon them. In fact, numerous crew members had visited the planet to offer guidance and assistance, and in so doing they had been mistaken for gods. Michael had hoped that seeing their light bodies would jar humanity's remembrance of their true identity but it only alienated them further from the truth. A new approach had been needed.

Joshua had agreed to be one of the pivotal characters in this deepening plot to awaken humanity. He had visited the planet many times before and this time he had chosen the name Abram.

∞

It was a moonless night and the haze did not allow the stars to be seen. Abram had braved the darkness beyond the safety of the camp and stood on a rise which overlooked all he knew and all that was important to him. Below him in the flickering light of campfires, the many tents holding his family and servants stood out against the blackness of the desert. The night air was sprinkled with the sounds of laughter, singing, and even arguing, from the camp. He could hear the bleating of the sheep as they huddled together against the cold desert air. He was mesmerized by the shadows which danced on the sands from the numerous fires.

Warmed by the sight and sounds of home, he acknowledged what he had been given and looked up gratefully into the mist to give thanks to a God he did not know by name. He had come to recognize that when he gave thanks to this unnamed power his flocks and family flourished. In the simplicity of his faith, he believed there was a shepherd, like himself, who tended and cared for the flocks of humanity. He felt an affinity to this unknown benefactor who, just like him, was standing on a higher mountain watching over all he loved. He glanced toward the main tent where his wives and children were sleeping and, thinking how blessed he was, gave thanks to this unknown shepherd of the skies. Standing on this small rise, this loving father viewed the camp below, secure there was another who loved him.

Abram often left the protection of the camp to venture into the wilderness to pray. He was not only known for his great wealth but for his great devotion. It was rumored that he would go into the desert in the dark of the night and God would speak to him. Sarah, his first wife, seeing him as less mysterious, figured these escapades were a means to get away from the din of the encampment, leaving her to deal with the commotion. It was common for him not to return to camp until the following morning, so he was not missed. Sarah often mused, "Ah, my dreamer is out catching dreams again."

Huddled in the darkness against the cold, Abram could hear the braying of wild donkeys and the howl of jackals in the distance. More tired than fearful, he pulled his cloak around him and leaned against the smooth surface of a large boulder. Adjusting himself to find a more comfortable position, he pulled down his robe to cover his feet, now vulnerable to the cold wind which blew across the darkened desert.

He was born in the desert, he had lived all his life in the desert, and he knew he would die in the desert. The desert was his home and he was most at home resting under the night sky. The rocks were his pillow and the howls in the night were the melodies which lulled him to sleep. As a man who had become one with the land, he listened to the winds and heard the messages from the raven which led him to the most fertile grazing and the purest wells. He was able to thrive in what to others would have been a desert wasteland.

Tonight, though, his rest was fitful. The pressures of leadership lay heavily on him. A parting of the ways was imminent. He and all his family would usually soon leave for winter pasturing but the tribe had become so large that some had decided to go to the lowlands near the cities instead. This dissension had sparked heated arguments regarding the equitable division of the herds and flocks. Abram was known as a fair and righteous man, one who could bring justice and equity into any conflict. Today, his patience, tolerance and skills had been tested—tested to the limit. "Family," he mumbled as he turned over in his sleep.

The night had become still and was wrapped in that darkness which comes before the dawn. Every soul was fast asleep, every animal hushed in the stillness of the predawn quiet. The haze had dissipated, leaving the sky clear and the stars bright. The sheep and goats stirred as they heard a sound in the distance which was calming and comforting, like the melodies sometimes played for them by shepherd boys.

Since Abram often chose to be out of the camp area, he had trained himself to awaken at any unusual sound in the night. The strains of song broke into his fitful rest, songs like those Sarah and the other women sang while making bread or spinning yarn. It neither startled nor frightened him but made him wonder if someone in the camp had awakened early. He remained as he was, quietly listening to the song, more pure and melodious than any he had ever heard. It seemed to come from all directions, as if the wind itself were singing. Watching the stars twinkling above him in rhythm with the melody, he felt one with the music now resounding deep within his entire being. The hypnotic melody lulled him into what he perceived as a welcome deep sleep.

Startled by what he thought was glare from the sun, he sat up quickly, thinking he had overslept and groaning that the night had seemed too short. Stumbling to his feet with a loud yawn, he stretched and turned to welcome the morning sun. Instead, he was greeted by a great light moving toward him from the east. An enormous circle within a circle of brilliant light illuminated the sky. As the apparition continued toward him, light flowed from it and cascaded over the earth in a spectacular display of sparkling color.

In terror, Abram fell to the ground, twisting his hip. He clenched the earth in hopes that he would not be carried away. He ignored his pain and waited for something terrible to happen. Nothing did, and nothing would, as a sense of safety and security enveloped him. Now showered with light, he cautiously opened his tightly closed eyes. He gazed awestruck at a world now transformed. The very ground to which he clung was alive with color. Every object glowed from within and kept beat with the melody resonating from the ship. To this humble shepherd it seemed creation itself was singing. "This," he thought to himself, "must be what paradise is like."

Regaining his senses, he could hear what sounded like a shepherd's song echoing from the great light. He smiled to himself. "Even God sings to his flocks." He thought he heard his name called but did not dare to look up, thinking to himself, "I cannot look upon the face of God."

Abram remembered nothing else of his encounter with the "great shepherd" or his journey to the great ship where he visited with Michael and Elizabeth deep into the night. They reviewed the plan which would unfold over the centuries ahead, hoping humanity would not again misunderstand the message that the shepherd and the sheep are one.

∞

That evening on the planet, a pathway had been created through the underbrush which had sprung up in the overgrown garden of human consciousness. Abram neither fully understood the message nor was he aware that he would plant seeds which would bear abundant fruit in human awareness. Yet he was comforted by what he had experienced and confident in the fact a good shepherd tended the garden and cared for its flocks.

Holding Abram in their hearts, the Council remained in the great domed chamber surrounded by the crystalline blue-white walls created from pure thought. These star travelers and warriors of light were deeply moved by their encounter with their friend.

As if to awaken Joshua from his forgetfulness, Elizabeth whispered, "Joshua, Joshua."

∞

Hearing someone call his name, Abram assumed it was time to return to the camp. He was sure it was Sarah worrying that something had happened to him or, worse yet, that she thought he was shirking his responsibilities. He shook the sleep from his body and rubbed his eyes, wondering if he had been dreaming—until he winced from the pain in his hip. He picked up his cloak and started to limp back to camp.

As his curiosity surrendered to his logic, he dismissed it all as a fitful sleep on a hard, cold ground. "I must be getting old," he muttered.

∞

Through the millenniums, Michael had observed the species, now called humanity, during its gradual ascent into sentient beings. Those upon the ships had gently nudged and coaxed their now human friends throughout the years. A hint of a smile crossed Michael's face as he recalled Abram's response to their not so gentle nudge, yet the message had been given. Before Abram's celestial encounter, he believed there was a "shepherd in the skies" who watched over them. Now he knew there was.

Sprinkled throughout the planet, similar encounters were occurring to assist humanity into a new age of awareness. Increasing numbers from the ships were incarnating on the planet to aid and experience this new species. The numbers were now in the millions and were increasing daily. Humanity's influence on the planet was increasing and Michael knew that foresight was important. The potential for disaster increased as humanity became more technologically inclined. Changing consciousness, though, was a slow and arduous process. Michael was aware that the Eternal Dawn of awareness was commencing and there were only a few millenniums until Earth reached a critical point in which it could no longer sustain life that was not in alignment with All That Is.

Elizabeth had reminded Michael of her promise to Mica and the others that she would return to help. Michael had hesitantly agreed while reminding her that he had hoped she would stay and assist him with the cultures developing on the planet. He had particularly wished to utilize her expertise in symbolic markings and sacred geometry to trigger humanity's subconscious memories.

"I will," she assured him, "just from the other side of the mirror." Michael had smiled in acknowledgment.

It was now the eve of Elizabeth's, John's and Christopher's first return to the planet since their evacuation from Atlantis. They were about to venture into humanness. Elizabeth's mind was an unsettled mix of anticipation and excitement, creating something akin to the rush of adrenaline one experiences before jumping out of a plane, trusting their parachute will open. This "jump" was more daring, however, and there wasn't any parachute.

In an attempt to relieve Michael's concerns, she assured him that she would pay attention. Michael was not only her captain, but her friend. She admired his warrior-like strength which had been transformed over the eons into the strength of a loving father. His concern for her moved her deeply. She longed for the day that the notion one could be separate from another would disappear.

She moved to one of the crystalline windows and surveyed the planet which would be her home for the next thousands of years. She felt John's hand touch her shoulder as he joined her. She realized that she and John would need to be very attuned and perceptive to find each other as they delved into physical creation. They both knew the love they now so deeply shared would be dulled by the glare of human existence. They would have to listen with their souls if they were to find each other on the planet. Elizabeth squeezed him tightly, offering him a gentle yet lingering kiss, hoping that he would remember her touch. She turned back toward the planet glistening against the deep blue sea of the universe in a feeble attempt to hide her emotions.

John wrapped her in his embrace, kissed her neck and whispered, "I won't forget."

They were about to explore the eternal mystery of oneness in a way they had never experienced before. Soon to be separated by a wall of individuality, the two, as those before and after, would be called upon to search through the muck and mire created by loneliness and alienation when souls forget that it is impossible to be alone.

Her thoughts drifted to her friend, Joshua, and the life he had created for himself as Abram. "I hope I make choices as wise and honorable as he has."

Continuing to read her thoughts, John spoke softly, "How could it be otherwise?"

Her eyes moistened as she stood on the threshold between

two worlds she loved so much. The burning desire for these two worlds to become one inspired her to leave the paradise she knew and the people she loved to plunge into the murky waters of consciousness which swirled about the planet below. She, John and Christopher were taking their places in the great march of assistance with those who had gone before them and who would go after them until the Eternal Dawn of enlightenment shone upon the planet. As a parent hears the cry of their child in the night and responds to their call, so did these warriors of light respond to the call of their friends.

From this plateau of conscious awareness, Elizabeth viewed a collage of images and thoughts, her mind filled with what had been, what was and what might be in the future. She promised herself that she would remember the vision of what she had seen here this day. The images of prophets and pyramids, temples and tombstones, caravans and crucifixions, rest and resurrection enveloped her mind. Most precious in the album of images yet to be created was one of a mountaintop in the distant future where the great ship would again appear. With that vision embedded deeply in the recesses of her mind, she turned and walked hand-in-hand with John to join Christopher, Miriam and Michael.

"It's time," Christopher said.

They nodded in agreement.

Elizabeth glanced at the fragment of her granite friend glowing in the center of the council table.

Observing her, Michael promised, "I'll be returning that to you shortly."

She smiled in appreciation. "I'll be waiting."

"So will we," Miriam softly added.

And with a gentle gesture of Michael's hand, Elizabeth, John and Christopher spiraled down in shimmering light to join humanity's march to consciousness.

∞

A few thousand years had passed before these three friends again met on the banks of a muddy river. Midwinter along the Jordan could be cold and this day was no exception. The numerous clouds, the threat of rain and the briskness in the air had not deterred the crowds from gathering along the reed-filled bank to hear the prophet speak. If not for his bellowing voice echoing off the ridges and the fervor with which he spoke, John would have been deemed almost comical, a wild man whose uncut reddish-brown hair and beard looked like a mane. By many he was seen as the lion in the desert calling out in the wilderness; his prey were those who had deceived the people in the name of the law. Loved by the common people, he was ridiculed by "respectable" society whose scorn did not bother this man with a mission. He railed against government and religion alike. It was a dangerous occupation. There was little allowance for dissent and no tolerance for speaking out against either secular or religious authorities. This prophet had angered conquerors, kings and priests alike. Many thought he remained in the wilderness for his own safety. Rather, he was a man called to the wilderness to escape the distractions of the world. Educated by the Essenes, he chose the life of a hermit over that of a missionary. It was the wilderness which inspired him and solitude which comforted his soul, yet his words were the light of hope in the darkness of despair.

It was rumored a traveling caravan had been the first to trespass on the "lion's" lair. So impressed were the merchants from the east that they spread John's fame throughout Jerusalem. The more he tried to hide, the more people sought him out. Surrendering to the onslaught of humanity entering his sanctuary, he decided his "guests" would have to listen to him.

Thus, the reluctant prophet ministered to the people. He spoke to them of the error of their ways and the need for renewal of their lives. He promised them hope and better days ahead— and one who would lead them to the truth. The fire in his eyes and his rage at the world softened when he spoke of the one to come after him.

∞

From the great Ship of Song, Michael and Miriam looked down upon their friend. "Quite the theatrics," Michael quipped as he watched John standing waist deep in the Jordan River and looking as if he were drowning the penitents rather than baptizing them.

"Nothing compared to what you've planned," Miriam teased.

"Well," Michael smiled sheepishly, "where do you think he got his love for theatrics?"

Today the ship would be visible to those on the planet. Not since the time John, as Elijah, had been whisked away in the "fiery chariot" had this occurred. It would be a significant event and, hopefully, a pivotal point in the human awareness of their celestial origins. None who huddled around the water's edge to hear the prophet's words would fully comprehend the significance of the event. Even Peter, Ruby and Elizabeth, who stood in the middle of the crowd, and Christopher, who stood at a distance in case the authorities arrived, were blinded by human forgetfulness. Only John, the prophet, and Joshua, the one to come after him, had a glimmer of the importance of this event. For them it was the passing of the torch in humanity's evolution toward truth. For those upon the ship it was an opportunity to reveal themselves to a group of people most likely to respond and remember.

∞

Peter and Ruby, with their nine-year-old Elizabeth, squeezed forward into the unusually dense crowd which had gathered at the river's edge to hear the prophet. They had come here many times before because Peter felt drawn to this strange man. He was surprised and even a little annoyed at how many people had traveled the distance from the city on such a threatening day. Huddling closer to Peter, Ruby decided the crowd pressing to hear the prophet's words was actually a blessing against the cold wind.

Without taking his eyes from the strange man standing nearly naked in the river, Peter whispered to his wife, "There's something about him. He reminds me of someone." Scratching his head as if he might uncover a buried memory, he continued, "I feel I know him but I've never met him." He paused. "His words touch my heart like those spoken by a friend."

"He's a rabble-rouser!" Ruby exclaimed, fearful Peter might want to become a follower. "If you ask me, he's going to end up in some dark hole without his head if he doesn't watch it."

Focused on the prophet's words, Peter ignored her warning and absentmindedly responded, "Shhh, listen to what he's saying."

"All I hear is sedition and treason," Ruby snapped. "The authorities won't tolerate that for long. Last week he even spoke directly against the king's family—that'll not set well with them!"

"I've heard that story but have you noticed—it doesn't seem to matter to him?" Peter asked, admiring the prophet's courage.

"If he's willing to march down the road to his own destruction—that's his problem!" Ruby retorted.

Secretly, Peter wished he had half the prophet's spirit and courage to confront their oppressors. Startled by what he thought was a tap on his shoulder, Peter caught a glimpse of a stranger now brushing past him. The sunlight on the man's white tunic seemed to cast a glow around him, piquing Peter's curiosity. The stranger's unusually fair complexion and tall stature gave him a regal appearance. Peter thought admiringly, "He must be of royal descent, yet he seems at home with the poor who have gathered here on the water's edge."

Intrigued, Peter grabbed the arms of Ruby and Elizabeth and began to worm his way through the crowd, following the stranger walking toward the shore. He wanted to keep his eye on this man so as not to miss anything. Soon he found himself pushed tightly against the back of the stranger as they stood ankle deep in the cool, muddy water of the river. With no place to go, Peter felt awkward and hoped the stranger was unaware of his pursuit.

"Oh, no! What a shame," Ruby thought, looking down at the muddy water lapping against the hem of the stranger's tunic. "To show such lack of care for such a beautiful garment! It'll take his wife a week to return it to half its brightness!"

The stranger turned and looked at her. Fearing she had spoken her thoughts and was about to be reprimanded, she avoided his glance. A gentle smile crossed his face as he noticed her obvious discomfort. His eyes fell upon Peter, who was afraid he had been pushed too tightly against him by the crowd and was embarrassed. But the stranger's eyes betrayed a gentleness and a depth that deeply moved Peter. "This man must be a rabbi or a prophet," Peter thought, now filled with a sense of welcome, familiarity and family. The stranger nodded an acknowledgment to Peter and turned to listen to the prophet.

John's voice could be heard over the din of the crowd as they watched the wild-looking man standing waist deep in the river. He was so intent on his message that he forgot he was holding a young man under the water. Bordering between comic and tragic, the crowd watched the young man struggle in an attempt to free himself. Finally, as the young man pushed his head above the water gulping for air, an audible gasp of relief reverberated through the crowd. The prophet smiled absent-mindedly in response.

Without a word, the stranger began wading into deeper water.

"Ugh! I can see the robe now," Ruby lamented. "His wife's going to kill him tonight. She must have sun bleached that fabric for weeks to get it so white!"

Peter wondered if he would need the prophet's absolution, too. If this man, so obviously filled with peace, needed cleansing, he must also. Peter's mind quieted as he intently watched this regal stranger walk into the muddy waters, easily balancing on unseen rocks below the surface.

While reassuring the young man who he had almost drowned, the prophet did not notice the stranger's approach. Sensing a presence, John turned and, seeing Joshua, embraced him. Those on shore were amazed at the prophet's welcome. They watched the two men talking and acting as if they'd known each other for years. Peter strained to hear what they were saying but their distance from the shore made that impossible.

Playing into Peter's interest, Ruby whispered, "How could such a fine man know this strange prophet?"

Peter nodded, oblivious to her words, as he watched them sharing secrets he wished to know.

There was a tug on Ruby's dress and turning she saw little Elizabeth looking up at her. She was beaming with the answer. "They're cousins, you know."

"How do you know that, little one?" Ruby inquired.

"My friend, Stephen, is a friend of his. Stephen's mother knows his mother."

That information seemed to put Ruby at ease. She could not imagine this fine young man knowing the likes of this wild man. She nodded to herself, aware that she had a few relatives herself that she would rather ignore. "But such a public display of affection and camaraderie? Doesn't he realize he could lose his own head?" Ruby thought, wishing to protect him. "In fact, we all could!" she reminded herself. Suddenly she felt it was time to go and she tugged at Peter's robe saying, "We must leave now. This is no place for Elizabeth!"

"No, she's just fine. I'm staying awhile longer." Peter said just as firmly, causing Ruby to release his robe.

The crowd's attention was riveted on the two men standing in the water. They watched in silence as the prophet's friend knelt deep in the river's flow. The forerunner gently lifted what seemed to be a precious handful of water and lightly poured it over Joshua's head. Those on shore wondered why this stranger had been spared since so many of them had been so vigorously plunged beneath the water's surface by the wild-haired prophet.

A sense of serenity was evident in John and Joshua's encounter and it enveloped all those present. The messenger and the message had been presented, yet neither man had spoken to the crowd. The people stood in silence, not fully understanding what was occurring but sensing it was important. Nature itself seemed to acknowledge the two as they stood waist deep in the river. The wind had become still, the birds hushed and the river itself seemed to flow more quietly.

This tranquil scene was shattered by the clap of what some thought was thunder. "What was that?" Ruby jumped, looking into the sky. "Is it going to rain?" Becoming aggravated, she complained, "It's one thing to be dragged out to the ends of the earth to see this crazy man and it's another thing to get wet!" Her anger broke as she chuckled at herself. "Well, I guess to be around this man is to get wet one way or the other."

She searched the sky for the offending thunderhead. To her surprise the sky had cleared except for one gigantic round cloud directly overhead. Her anxiety softened as she wistfully remembered studying clouds as a child and seeing what objects they formed. Visions of camels, birds, houses and even people floated through her mind. She barely had to stare at this cloud to realize that it looked like a fine silver tray, one you might find in the palace of the king.

At the same moment, Peter looked around and questioned, "Who said that?"

"What do you mean, who said that?" Ruby inquired. "It was thunder."

"No, I heard a voice," he retorted.

"It was thunder!"

"A voice!"

Christopher, now standing next to them, declared in an attempt to end the volley, "It was thunder."

To his frustration a woman standing behind him countered, "No, it was a voice!"

Soon the whole crowd was arguing over what they had heard.

"I know! I know!" Little Elizabeth beamed as she again tugged on her mother's robe. "It was a voice," she said triumphantly. "It was Michael!"

"Who's Michael?" Ruby asked dismissingly.

"You know! My friend," Elizabeth declared, unable to believe her mother didn't remember him, "Michael!"

"There's no Michael here! Anyway he's imaginary." Ruby snapped, turning away from the now exasperated Elizabeth.

"No, he's not! I just heard him," Elizabeth pouted.

John and Joshua, undistracted by the clamor of the crowd, smiled at each other. Little did the onlookers understand what these rather odd looking men were doing—they were passing the torch. Each saw the ship clearly and wondered if any in the crowd could comprehend the vision overhead.

To the men standing in the river, the experience was "otherworldly." The voices of the crowd became faded and distant as everything seemed to be in slow motion, even the current of the river. Spiraling above them like a pinwheel, the ship hovered in the cloud above.

To those on shore, the world had taken on the quiet that comes before a storm. The sharp shadows of the noonday sun had faded into a mediocre grayness. Ruby was sure it was going to storm, feeling the electrical charge against her skin.

With the flutter of a dove's wings above the two men, nature again became alive and the earth was abundant with sound and movement. On the shore, those who had been watching saw the two friends embracing. To those who were very perceptive, they would have known it was not the embrace of a simple goodbye. It was the embrace one gives a loved one they will not see for a long, long time—an embrace that needs to last a lifetime.

Joshua had tears in his eyes as he draped his arms over John's shoulders and rested his head against John's cheek. Joshua was not sure if he was weeping for what lay ahead for his friend or what lay ahead for himself. Whatever the case, the appearance of the ship confirmed for both these men that the dreams and visions they had been having were, indeed, true.

John heard no words from Joshua's lips but could feel his body gently heaving with quiet sobs. John said not a word but in that silent embrace gave his friend Joshua a double portion of his spirit. Regaining his composure, Joshua stood straight, his regal appearance now returned. The two faced each other and looked deeply into each other's soul. It was an act of recommitment and reconfirmation of the vision they shared. These two childhood friends and eternal companions embraced once more, promising they would meet again.

Peter, Ruby, Elizabeth, and Christopher could not explain why these two men interrupted their embrace and looked directly at them. Whatever its meaning, they were greatly moved that they were included in such a personal moment of farewell.

Standing waist deep in the river, Joshua turned from his friend and walked east toward the crowd and his destiny. John turned west, away from the shore, so they could not see him weep. As if in celebration, two doves danced above their heads, one flying toward the east, the other toward the west, each to meet again at another time and in another place.

Again the solemnity of the moment was shattered by a roll of thunder across the sky. This time no one questioned what it was but all were awed since the sky was cloudless. Those gathered at the water's edge knew there would be no more to see or hear that day, yet many remained for some time in silence, reluctant to leave the aura of this unexplained event. It was not until the sky had turned a deep pink and lavender that the last of the pilgrims returned to their homes.

With the crowds now dispersed and Joshua gone, John trudged up the embankment toward the opening in the great cliff wall he called "home." A few of his intimate friends and followers accompanied him to his cave. They knew they would no longer see him standing waist deep in the river or hear his voice echo off the mountains. They were there to wait on him, in honor and respect.

John sat apart from the others in silence and prayer that night. He knew his time had come and was heartened by the vision of the great Ship of Song which uplifted his soul. He knew he would be with Joshua again in the heavens but first they would meet on a mountaintop in the not-too-distant future.

The prophet sat cross-legged, a little too far from the fire's warmth to feel its comfort, and with his finger drew in the sand an image of a wheel within a wheel—as Elijah had before him.

This time, though, his return home would not be a flash of spiraling energy lifting him from the surface of Earth in what would be remembered as a "fiery chariot." This time his departure would be quieter and in more humble circumstances.

After seventeen months locked in seclusion in the depths of the Palace of the King, barely fed and ill, the prophet would be sent home by a flash of steel.

His only visitor was a king who wanted his head rather than his truth.

∞

Upon the great Ship of Song, they welcomed their friend John home.

Chapter Eight

The Messenger

It had been two years since Elizabeth and her parents had first seen Joshua by the river. The pain shot through her frail frame as she struggled not to scream. Peter and Ruby knew this illness was more than their daughter's young body could bear and Ruby prayed the end was mercifully near. The fever wrenched Elizabeth's body and in her delirium she was barely aware of her mother attending her needs.

Ruby looked helplessly at Peter, tears in her eyes. "Our little one, she can't endure much more."

Unwilling to surrender, Peter desperately declared, "I'll go find the teacher." Peter hurried out of the room and through the courtyard past the mourners gathered for the deathwatch. They were puzzled why a father would leave his daughter's side in what was surely the hour of her death. Shaking their heads, they murmured that she would certainly take her last breath before his return.

Alone with her daughter, Ruby struggled to hold back her tears while fetching the last blanket in the house in an attempt to keep Elizabeth warm. As she placed the wool blanket from her own bed around Elizabeth's shivering body, she hoped against hope that if the master could be found he could be of assistance. She herself had seen the miracles Joshua performed on those near death—but death itself, she feared, was a chasm that could not be crossed. It was a race for time. She hoped Peter's feet would carry him quickly to the master and she prayed her care would keep Elizabeth alive until he arrived.

Even with the additional blanket, Elizabeth could not get warm. Shielded from her agony in her delirious state, she spoke of deceased relatives, angels and beings of light. She whispered of dancing with dolphins and floating majestically above the mountains. She murmured words of which Ruby could make no sense—of a beautiful pink granite rock on the white sands of a blue ocean. Ruby dismissed her ramblings as coming from one too ill to make sense yet wondered how she spoke so clearly of the ocean and its creatures which Elizabeth had never seen.

In a moment of seeming coherence, Elizabeth declared that the teacher was coming. Thinking that Elizabeth had overheard Peter's departing words, Ruby whispered reassuringly, "Yes, my little one. Yes, he's coming." Inwardly, she doubted the master would be found in time.

Since that day along the river two years ago, Joshua and Elizabeth's family had become close. Often he and his followers had enjoyed their hospitality and the feast which Ruby always prepared in their honor. Elizabeth had endeared herself to the master. His face, weary from his long journeys, always brightened as Elizabeth bounded toward him, greeting him with an enthusiastic hug.

Ruby cried softly in despair, "Why can't you be here? Why aren't you here when she needs you most? You must know!"

Elizabeth lay drifting in and out of consciousness, seeing her mother through blurry, unfocused eyes as Ruby put another cool cloth on her forehead or tucked the blankets more tightly around her. At other times, she was surrounded by a group of friends whom she knew loved her very much, but she wondered why she could not quite remember their names. They stood in a beautiful domed room which she thought must be a palace. She had never seen a room so beautiful. There were twenty-two doorways leading out of the great hall and at the very peak of the dome was a light too bright to look at. She heard a man and woman surrounded in golden light speaking to her of things she could not comprehend. Away from the pain of her physical body, she thought this must be heaven.

Peter had spent many hours searching for his friend, the teacher, and had just about given up hope. He had begun his search at high noon and the sun would now soon be setting. He feared he would be too late to save his daughter. In the desperateness of his plight, he had searched everywhere he thought the master might be. Driven by love for his little Elizabeth, he now reaffirmed he would not stop until he found him. He had seen the teacher heal the greatest of illnesses and knew he could help his daughter.

A tragic thought pierced Peter's heart, an irony beyond comprehension—that he, who had brought so many to the teacher to be healed, might lose what he loved most in the world. A flash of anger shot through his mind—that his own inability to locate the master would seal his daughter's fate. It was a burden more than he could bear. He stumbled to the ground, burdened by his own guilt. His heart weighed heavily as he sank to his knees, exhausted, hungry and thirsty. In the twilight of the night descending upon the desert, Peter cried out in despair, "Show me where to go! I don't know where to find him!" The deserted street echoed his plea, for there was no one to hear his call. The utter silence in response crushed him as he sat in a crumpled heap weeping.

"Dear sir, why do you cry?"

Peter looked up, startled by this unexpected voice, and saw a girl with long flowing hair about the same age as his beloved Elizabeth. Leaning over with food in her hands, she consoled him. "You must be very hungry and tired, dear sir."

"She must think I'm a beggar," Peter thought while gratefully accepting the bread and dried fish she held out for him. Her gift was bittersweet, though. It reminded him of how his Elizabeth had proudly brought him his plate when she was barely old enough to walk. Yet his despair was lightened by her kindness and he quickly ate in order to continue his search.

As he prepared to stand, the child put her arms around his neck and whispered in his ear as she pointed to a fisherman's house by the lakeside. "Dear sir, you will find the teacher there." Before he could respond, she scampered off into the darkness which was settling over the countryside.

Without questioning, he leapt to his feet and ran toward the fisherman's house. Panting, he raised his arm to knock on the door but, to his bewilderment, the teacher himself opened the door as if expecting him. Outer garment already in hand, the master stepped out into the cool night air, closed the door behind him and smiled, as if to assure Peter all was well. Peter thought the teacher must have seen the urgency in his face since not a word had been spoken by them but obviously communication had succeeded. Although exhausted, Peter hurried up the embankment and the teacher followed closely behind.

It took a few minutes for those remaining in the house to realize the teacher was not returning. They wondered if he had been called upon to preach or to heal at such an hour—or had Peter come to warn Joshua that he was about to be arrested for treason? Whatever the case, they figured this was not the place to be and wherever the teacher was going was better than where they were.

Never letting up their pace, it still took nearly an hour to reach the village. As they approached Peter's street, they could hear the weeping and wailing of the mourners, yet Peter's pace did not waiver.

Having turned onto the street which led to his home, Peter scurried toward the glow in the courtyard and the shadows which danced on the sandstone walls. In a surreal impression, he saw the frantic dance of the mourners and finally heard the wailing coming from his own house. For a moment his steps faltered as he glanced back toward the master as if to say, "You needn't hurry any longer," and he ran on ahead.

Joshua slowed his pace, not out of defeat but out of respect for his friend, giving him a private moment of grief with Ruby. Joshua loved all the children, yet eleven-year-old Elizabeth held a special place in his heart. She often sang and danced for him as he ate and she often begged her father to let her wash Joshua's feet. As he trudged toward the grief-ridden scene, Joshua looked down at his dirty feet and watched the small puffs of dust explode around his sandals with each step on the desert sand.

Those who had followed Joshua from the fisherman's house also slowed their pace, resigned to the fact the master was too late this time. "His timing doesn't seem too good," Christopher whispered to Stephen, hoping against hope he was wrong. Christopher had recently joined the teacher's followers. Afraid the master might be just another false prophet, he often spoke cynically so as not to be disappointed when the perceived inevitable occurred. He continued, "The master couldn't save John, his own cousin. Why would he be able to save this child? It seems even he can't overcome the sting of death."

"But he does do a good job at cheating it," Stephen responded defensively. "He's saved many from the brink of death."

As he entered the courtyard, Joshua became overwhelmed with grief at the sight of the mourners. Tears muddied his dusty cheeks as he thought of the pain his friends were experiencing.

Stephen tentatively approached Joshua and noticed his tear-stained cheeks. He had seldom seen the master cry and it touched him deeply. Attempting to console him, Stephen said, "It's always sad for one so young to die."

Joshua wiped a tear from his cheek as he turned and whispered, "You don't understand." As Joshua stood in the flickering light of the fires built against the cold in the courtyard, he responded, "I do not weep for the child. She only sleeps."

Fearful the master was denying the obvious, Stephen started to speak but held his tongue, seeing the pain on Joshua's face.

Joshua, aware Stephen wished to respond, clarified his thoughts. "I weep for humanity because they believe in death."

The wailing of the mourners made further conversation impossible. In an attempt to avoid the pandemonium, Joshua moved to a quiet corner of the courtyard and sat silently by himself. In an instant, he knew what he must do for himself, for humanity and for little Elizabeth. Drying his tears, he stood and brushed off his dusty robe as he walked toward the room where the child lay.

Elizabeth, lying lifeless on her bed, dreamt of being in what must have been the palace of a king. Its domed ceiling glittered with sparkling lights and its grand columns vaulted to the sky. "Angels" floated effortlessly throughout this great room and, to her wonderment, they all seemed to know her.

Joshua entered the dimly lit room and knelt beside the grieving parents. Ruby continued to tuck the blankets tightly around her child, as if hoping to keep her warm against the chill of death. No longer able to contain himself, Joshua wept openly, his tears lightly sprinkling the wool blanket which now served as a funeral shroud.

With an arm around each of his grief stricken friends, Joshua whispered, "Elizabeth, wake up. Elizabeth, Elizabeth." Ruby sobbed and Peter looked up to console his friend, interpreting Joshua's words as a sign of despair.

Now floating effortlessly through the vast hall of "angels," Elizabeth, in her childlike innocence, knew she was in heaven. In the deep recesses of her soul she could hear the master's voice, "Elizabeth, wake up."

"Oh!" She exclaimed to herself. "Must I go?"

"Elizabeth, Elizabeth," she heard in response.

"I hear you," she said as she started to stretch. Opening her eyes and looking up, she was warmed by Joshua's smiling face. Seeing her parents weeping by her cot, she realized they were unaware she had awakened. "Mother! Father! I had such a wonderful dream. It was beautiful!"

Startled and overcome, unable to respond, Peter and Ruby wept uncontrollably.

Elizabeth lay still for a moment wondering why they continued to cry. Finally, she pushed off the heavy burden of blankets, sat up and declared, "I'm hungry."

Hearing her child's request, Ruby's sobs turned to laughter. "I'll gladly get you something to eat, my love." She gently kissed her daughter's forehead, as if to assure herself she was not dreaming, and dashed out of the room.

Peter enveloped his daughter in a hug so tight Joshua smiled, secretly wondering if he would squeeze the very life out of her again. When Peter finally turned to give his hearty thanks to the teacher, he was gone.

Joshua walked unseen, even by his followers, through the courtyard and out the heavy wooden gate. The night was cool and the stars shimmered in the sky. As the clamor of conversation from the courtyard faded behind him, the night became silent. Following the road out of town and far away from the possibility of questions, he propped himself up on an outcropping of rocks and silently gave thanks.

Those in the courtyard perceived they had been misinformed about the child's death, thinking she had either experienced a miraculous recovery or was not as ill as the parents had thought. Few had noticed Joshua's arrival or his quiet departure. Ruby and Peter never spoke of the events which occurred in their child's room. Only Stephen and Christopher had an inkling of what had transpired but not enough understanding to comprehend it and, therefore, speak of it.

In his solitude, Joshua looked into the heavens from which he had come and smiled as he saw a distant bright star rising in the east. In the depths of his soul, he heard a voice float gently through his being.

It was Michael. "She's been home, my friend. She's been home and she will never forget."

It had been several months since that night at Peter's home and Joshua's notoriety had increased dramatically. In order to escape the crowds, he and a few of his followers had left the relative cool and shelter of the city and headed into the heat of the desert. A hot wind blew through the lowlands as the small grouping sought comfort in the shade of an oasis. The small cluster of trees offered little relief from the sweltering heat of the midday sun. Some questioned the master's wisdom in venturing out on a day like this. Certainly he would not be bothered this afternoon, as the heat would keep people away. Peter thought longingly of the cool of his home and imagined Ruby and Elizabeth resting during the heat of the day. He assured Christopher and Stephen that the master would not venture further, for it would be foolhardy—possibly fatal.

Too tired to move and too hot to talk, Christopher, Peter and the handful of others who had ventured forth with the master lay sprawled in various positions on the ground. Only the master seemed not to mind the heat. Their fears were real-

ized when the master stood up and looked toward the far hill-
top, saying, "Let's go on." He glanced around at the weary
group and started out toward the high ridge in the east without looking back.

Dismayed, Christopher and Peter stared at each other in
disbelief. Slowly Peter rose to his feet and surveyed the exhausted
men. Only Christopher and Stephen reluctantly stood to follow. Some avoided Peter's glance, embarrassed by their unwill-
ingness to continue, while others just shook their heads and
waved them on. They simply had no energy left, even if the
master was going to the mountaintop to pray or teach.

Christopher grumbled as he stumbled forward, "Why
doesn't he simply command the wind as he did the sea?" The
three men gazed in the direction of the Sea of Galilee, an ap-
pealing image for their overheated bodies. Peter could hear
the crackle of the hot sand under their sandals. Stephen pulled
the hood of his robe over his mouth and nose to keep the razor
sharp sand from his lungs.

Joshua glanced behind him to see who had accepted his
invitation and continued toward the steep grade ahead. He had
been with his little band of followers for well over two years and
was aware his mission would soon be coming to an end. Without faltering, Joshua began the climb up the worn path as he
fought back fears that there was not enough time left to accom-
plish what he had hoped. The steep mountainside, riddled with
boulders, offered a surrealistic setting reflective of the obstacles
he had encountered. He hoped what he was about to do would
answer all their questions and awaken them to the reality of
their existence.

As they reached the steep grade, Peter reached down and
patted his water skin to assure himself he had brought enough
for the journey. He questioned the master's wisdom in venturing so deep into the desert and wondered if they should have

brought more water. The hot container told him the precious liquid was safe and warm. He wiped away the sweat pouring from his brow and faithfully followed Joshua, whom he trusted.

Christopher, on the other hand, wondered if the prophet was going to be the death of him yet.

At that moment, Joshua turned and looked directly at them, "Friends, why are you following me?"

The three abruptly halted. Fearful the master had somehow heard his thoughts, Christopher stammered, "Why do you ask? You...you invited us."

Joshua smiled at the flustered Christopher and again asked, "Why are you following me?"

"You give me hope the world's better than I perceive," Christopher sincerely stated.

"And how's that possible?" Joshua questioned.

"You know something I want to know," Christopher blurted out. "To have your understanding."

"I promise you, you'll understand," Joshua paused for emphasis. "You will understand."

Turning, Joshua continued up the steep slope, offering no further explanation. As they scrambled to keep up with him, they noted how Joshua effortlessly ascended the ridge, using one hand to hold the hem of his robe and the other hand to balance himself. Christopher whispered to Peter, wondering if this was some test they needed to pass. Confused and a little nervous, they struggled to be as graceful as the master, even watching where he stepped so they could follow in his footsteps.

Finally reaching the top, the three men joined Joshua who was resting against a rock. Peter reached down and unlaced the water skin from his belt. He lifted the warm liquid to his lips and paused. Embarrassed, he gave it to the master who drank appreciatively. The tepid water pouring from the mouth of the hot skin refreshed their parched lips.

No one spoke as they rested from the climb. Finally, the silence was broken by Joshua's words, "What do you want from me?"

The men looked at each other, confused, afraid they had offended the master. Had they misinterpreted his invitation? Had he wished to go to the mountain alone? Peter thoughtfully answered, "To be near you."

Overwhelmed by the sincerity of his friend's words, Joshua whispered, "I'll always be near you, even when you don't see me."

The four sat in the bond of camaraderie created out of their search for truth. As they rested, each drifted into their own thoughts. The heat of the afternoon sun seemed much less harsh in this place. Peter wondered if the cool breeze he felt could be from the sea far below. He thought he could hear Christopher and Stephen snoring softly as they stretched out on the earth. His mind full of questions, he wondered if this time alone with Joshua was the moment to ask the most pressing of them. In preparation, Peter cleared his throat and sipped a small portion of water.

Joshua looked up. The dye was cast. Peter cleared his throat again and asked, "Why did you come?" his voice trembling more out of anticipation of the answer than fear of the question. "And where did you come from?"

"Why," Joshua repeated the question, "did I come?" His face lightened. "And where did I come from?"

To Peter's chagrin, Christopher and Stephen immediately sat upright. Rubbing their eyes against the bright sun, they eagerly awaited Joshua's answer to Peter.

Joshua inquired, "Why would you ask such questions?" Without waiting for an answer, he continued. "Do you think I'm different?"

Again Peter was afraid he had insulted the master, while Christopher and Stephen wished they had remained asleep. Awkwardly, Peter responded, "Ah, yes…no." Confused, he shook his head and blurted out, "Yes, you're different!"

Joshua disarmed Peter's fears with a laugh. "Let me answer you this way, my friends. Where did you come from? And why are you here?" The men sat silently. Peter now understood why be had hesitated to ask these questions before. Not waiting for a response, Joshua stood up, seeming to tower over the three men. His words came forth with a power and depth they had not heard before. "I am here for the same reason you are and I came from the same place you did." He turned and walked about fifty feet from them, stopped and looked toward the heavens.

Neither Peter, Christopher nor Stephen followed, for they were overwhelmed by what he had spoken and by its resonance within their souls. Humbled and in awe, they sat with their heads lowered and eyes closed in quiet prayer.

At first, Peter thought the melody carried on the wind was a far off shepherd boy singing. Its melody soft and low, in perfect pitch and harmony, it touched his very soul.

The wind grew stronger and the air became cool and electrical. Christopher wondered if it was about to storm. He remembered that as a child, when tending his uncle's flocks in the fields, lightning storms would be announced in this same way and he would know to take shelter. Yet this was different; there seemed to be no threat.

Stephen's mind focused on the song which filled his being. Now louder and clearer, it sounded like the low resonant chants of the priests in the temple, yet far more perfect than any he had ever heard. Its familiarity sent chills throughout his entire being.

The mountaintop was immersed in waves of music and the glare of the afternoon sun was dimmed by radiant light. Through their closed eyes, the men could see the brilliance and wondered how the sun could be so bright. Hesitantly, Peter opened his eyes and was surprised the glare did not hurt them. As he looked at the earth beneath him, the shadows were sharp and defined. Suddenly, in the rush that comes with awareness, he realized the shadows were falling in the wrong direction! Trembling, he turned his head toward the master and the direction from which the light came. Before him were three luminescent beings of light. He instinctively knew one was the master and the second was the master's cousin, the prophet, John. Though he had never met him, he realized the third figure was the master's father, Joseph, the carpenter.

In awe, Peter fell prostrate to the ground. Christopher sat wide-eyed, unable to move, while tears of joy ran down Stephen's cheeks. The three men were unaware they had also been transformed. For one precious moment on the mountaintop, they experienced the answer to Peter's questions.

Regaining his composure, Peter observed the phenomenon before him. It appeared as if the translucent beings standing on the mountaintop were prisms in the sun, their bodies surrounded with waves of rainbow colors as their countenance radiated with the fire of a thousand suns. Why he did not cower in fear, Peter did not know, as the white cloud overhead turned into what looked like a shining silver plate reflecting the sunlight, mountains and sea against its mirrorlike appearance. And in the twinkling of an eye, as quickly as the apparitions and the vision had appeared, they were gone. Joshua had answered their questions in the only way he knew how and the only way they would believe.

Peter, Christopher, Stephen and Joshua now stood alone in the light of the setting sun, their sandals worn from miles of journeying and outer garments bleached white by the sun. Disoriented and bewildered, Peter was unclear if it had been a dream or his imagination, reality or an illusion caused by the heat of the day. He could only respond by saying, "It is good to be here."

Joshua grinned. "Now you have the answer to your second question."

The teacher, reaching down and taking his friends' hands, helped them to their feet. As they prepared to begin their descent, Joshua knew they did not fully understand what they had experienced but they would never forget it.

And they would understand, as he had promised, when they returned to the stars.

∞

The great ship hovered above them, now unseen, as the four weary travelers descended the mountain. The ship's engines cooled their way by sending a breeze.

John, back from his visitation on the planet, entered the Council Chamber where Miriam and Michael had watched the occurrences.

Grinning, John came up to Michael and quipped, "I always like a good show."

"I know," Michael responded. "Why do you think I volunteered you for this job?"

"I think we've stirred the pot," John added.

"Give it a couple thousand years," Miriam interjected, "and it'll be soup."

John nodded his head in agreement. "Something wonderful's happening."

∞

Something wonderful was about to happen.

There was still a hint of coolness in the late spring Galilean air. The cold hearts of those who had brutally murdered the teacher seemed to overshadow the arrival of summer which was struggling to emerge in this desert land. The weary followers had gone to the mountaintop in an attempt to feel close to the master, who had become as elusive as the warmth of this summer.

Peter's inner pain and guilt tore at his soul. The cold morning and the hard rock on which he sat was little penance for his sin. He found it impossible to forgive himself for denying his master. His cowardice haunted him like a specter in the night, stealing his peace and joy. He looked up guiltily at the others, comforted by the dubious consolation that most of them had also abandoned the master in his hour of need. Each had their own regrets and felt a deep sense of remorse in having betrayed what they believed in. Coming here, as they often did since his death, gave them a sense of connection and a hope for absolution.

Peter felt a hand on his shoulder. He looked up from his squatting position into Christopher's deep brown eyes, hewed out by life's experiences and now softened by love.

"Christopher, why did it need to end this way?" Peter asked, holding back his emotion. "What are we to do? I feel so lost and alone." Peter suddenly stopped short, aware Christopher knew of his denial. Embarrassed, Peter began to apologize.

Christopher raised his finger to his lips as if to quiet Peter's guilt. Putting his arms around the neck of the great hulk of a fisherman, they both wept openly. Others seeing them could no longer hold back their own tears.

Only little Elizabeth was unaffected, because she knew where the master was. Her attention was on a large platter-shaped cloud appearing over the eastern horizon. Its luminescence reflected the hues of the morning sky, giving it the appearance of a pink and purple dish against the backdrop of the blue sky.

Peter shook his head as he remembered the last time he had seen the teacher. They had gathered in their usual hiding place, an upper room of Stephen's home, soon after their master had been put to death. There had been rumors instigated by some of the women of the group that he had risen from the dead, but many of the followers had not believed them.

"How could it be possible the master's alive?" Christopher had mumbled.

Overhearing him, Peter had reminded Christopher, "Anything's possible."

"Didn't I assist in preparing his broken body for burial?" Christopher had declared. "Didn't it take three strong men to roll the great rock into its rut? Even you, Peter, heard the hollow thud it made as it slammed the door on death. It's a cruel joke." Christopher wondered how many soldiers it had taken to roll the rock back. Or worse yet, how many of his friends?

Like Peter, Christopher wrestled with guilt, even though each had been forgiven by the master. Peter remembered the shame Christopher had felt when the master appeared. The locked doors and the windows shuttered out of fear had not hindered the master's entry, he had appeared mysteriously in their midst. His familiar smile eased their pain yet his countenance seemed different. He had assured his questioning followers he was now more of who he truly was.

Christopher and Peter discussed what would become of this small grouping now that the master was gone. They knew he had changed their lives and they would never forget—yet they were unclear what to do with the message they had received. For whatever their guilt, doubt or fear, they had all come to this mountaintop in an attempt to touch divinity again.

They did not know where else to go.

They did not know what else to do.

They did not understand.

Where was their master?

In the days since the women had seen him in the garden, Joshua's presence had become more elusive. He would mysteriously appear and then instantaneously disappear, as if to tease their emotions and pull at their heart strings. Some still thought it was their imagination. Yet they all came to this mountaintop again, where they had come so many times before, hoping to sit at his feet just one more time.

The mid-morning sun started to push away the coolness of the night as the friends continued reminiscing. How greatly they needed to forgive themselves. How they only wished to understand.

∞

Upon the great Ship of Song, Joshua was aware of the pain his friends were experiencing and was saddened over their sense of loss and confusion. "I must return for awhile," Joshua said thoughtfully, turning to Michael, Miriam and John, "to remind them—once more—and then I will say my goodbyes."

Michael nodded in agreement.

Joshua acknowledged his response and added, "My time's complete. This is their time."

John put his arm around his friend, mindful of how he and Joshua had said their goodbyes along the Jordan years before. He whispered to Joshua, "Goodbyes are painful for those who believe we can be separated."

Joshua nodded solemnly. After a pause, he brightened, "I have an idea! We can show them the mystery, invite them to view their own destiny by letting them witness my ascension."

Michael paused. "Ummm. Some of them might grasp the meaning. Such a spectacular sight can't be easily ignored!"

"Yes," Joshua eagerly agreed. "And it would answer their questions, helping them understand that one day they, too, will ascend."

"And such a fitting exit for you," John said teasingly to Joshua. "A fitting exit for a great prophet."

"Is the pot calling the kettle black?" Joshua retorted, remembering John's dramatic exit as Elijah.

John conceded. "Hopefully they'll understand it better this time."

"Let's begin," Michael interjected.

They all agreed.

∞

The sun was now high in the sky and the follower's stomachs began to grumble, mirroring their attitude. They had resigned themselves to the fact that it was time to leave and nothing extraordinary would occur. None of them openly expressed their disappointment but it was evident on their faces.

Peter, first to surrender, stood and said, "Let's go." As he turned to leave, he walked straight into Joshua. "Master!" he stammered. "We've been waiting!"

"I know," Joshua responded lovingly.

Seeing Joshua, Christopher exclaimed, "Where have you been?"

The others, now aware of his arrival, ran to greet him. Little Elizabeth squeezed through the crowd to be close to him again. Tears ran down his face as he whispered to her that it was time for him to go.

Overhearing him, Christopher blurted out, "Not again!" Peter sharply elbowed him.

Joshua smiled and motioned to his friends. "Sit down, let me speak to you one more time."

They formed a semicircle, as they had done so many times before, and listened to Joshua speak of things their hearts yearned to know. He told them the story of the origins, purpose and destiny of humanity. He reminded them that they were from the stars—and to the stars they would return. He invited them to look upon this world and its experiences as an adventure they had chosen years before. He spoke of how they were emissaries of the universe on a grand journey and he promised them that they would return to paradise.

"In these years I have spent with you," Joshua concluded, "I have sought to show you who you are. And you, my good friends and teachers, have taught me, as well, to remember who I am. What you see in me is in you. What you have witnessed is in yourself. I have but one thing left to do before my journey is complete."

Joshua walked a few paces away from the group, stopped and turned to them. "Remember," he said, "what you are about to witness is so that your understanding might be complete. I have shown you who you are. I now," as he raised his hands upward in prayer, "show you where you're from."

Elizabeth clearly heard the melody and knew it for what it was. Peter, Christopher and Stephen remembered what they had forgotten on a mountaintop months before. For the others, it sounded like the song of a shepherd boy carried on the breeze.

A great cloud, which had approached from the east and hovered above their heads, was now transformed into spinning wheels of light and color. The "fiery chariot" had reappeared. Blessing his friends, Joshua was transformed into a swirl of golden light and before their amazed eyes, the prophet, teacher, friend and brother ascended home.

There was a long silence as they watched the great ship disappear into a cloud again.

"Friends," Michael greeted, having descended to Earth. "What are you looking at?" His question startled those who had been staring into the sky. They did not know which was more marvelous to behold, the great cloud drifting away or the radiant being by their side.

Michael bowed in honor to his friends. "We'll meet again," he promised.

And in the twinkling of an eye, he, too, was gone.

Some weeks later, still seeking to comprehend what they had experienced, the group met again in the upper room of Stephen's home. As they discussed what they thought it had all meant, they were unaware the room had become filled with a gentle breeze. The only thing they would remember of this event was that for an instant, as they looked at each other, they saw what seemed to be flames of light above each other's heads.

What these brave journeyers would forget was that these flames were spirals of light which carried them to the great ship where they were reunited with their friends. They danced that night with Joshua in the great Council Chamber and this event, not remembered by their conscious minds, would inspire them for the rest of their lives.

Chapter Nine

The Millennium

Two thousand years passed and humanity was about to celebrate the new millennium. Elizabeth paced nervously outside Mica's office high above New York City's financial district. Wearing her most businesslike suit with her long hair pulled back, her high heels clicked on the hard marble floor. She could not remember the last time she had dressed this way. She hoped that her attire would, at least, present her as credible, if not professional, to Mica. Every few paces, she turned and looked at John who was calmly counting the rows of tiles on the floor. His relaxed and almost bored behavior annoyed her. She wondered how they had allowed Ruby and Peter to convince them to finance the property they planned to purchase in North Carolina through Mica. Staring at the ornate mahogany doors which led to the inner sanctums of Mica's suite of offices, Elizabeth had an ill feeling in her stomach, a vague recollection she could not identify of having stood outside his door before. She felt that either she was trapped or walking into a trap. She wondered if she was the proverbial fly being invited into the spider's web. Mica represented everything she detested: self-serving power and greed.

"What are we doing here?" Elizabeth abruptly asked John. He looked up from his daydream with a puzzled look. "You know what I mean!" she said. "We should have gone to the bank."

"Not a chance," John retorted. "Remember, I'm taking early retirement and we need additional money for construction which the bank would never give us."

"Maybe we should've waited."

"What's wrong, honey? I don't understand. We've discussed this," John responded patiently. "You know that on my retirement alone they'd never approve the mortgage. Remember, the sale of your artwork and royalties from my books aren't considered consistent enough income? Besides I trust Ruby and Peter's advice."

"I don't know. I feel like I'm selling my soul."

"Do you want…" He paused as the door abruptly swung open.

"Too late," Elizabeth whispered. Hand-in-hand, they walked into the cavernous complex of offices. Emerald leather high-backed chairs, looking as if they had never been sat in, appointed the reception area. Elizabeth wondered why they had not been invited to wait here. While being led down a long hallway to an austere conference room, she questioned if they had acted too hastily when they found the property in North Carolina. She deeply desired to move to the freedom and peace of the mountains—but at what cost? She did not like owing anyone or being dependent on credit and here she was in the lair of one of the most notorious "money changers" of the twentieth century. He was known for his ruthlessness and willingness to trample anyone underfoot. Ruby had assured her that because of their friendship with Mica he would treat them well. Elizabeth wondered how Ruby and Peter could have remained friends with him since college. She concluded it must be because of his wife, Helena.

The receptionist gave them a curt smile and asked if they would like coffee or tea. They both shook their heads. She informed them that Mica's assistant would be with them shortly and she closed the door behind her.

Elizabeth looked around the room, noting if there were any surveillance cameras. She turned to John and said, "He's not even going to give us the courtesy of attending the closing?"

"He's a busy man," John responded matter-of-factly.

"Are you sure we're doing the right thing?" she asked. "I don't know if I'm scared of him, or scared of this step. It's such a change in our lives."

"Elizabeth," John spoke softly yet directly, "we've discussed it. We felt it's important to buy the property now. I don't really understand it any more than you. I know we'd planned to save our money so we wouldn't have a mortgage. Listen here," he said, pointing to his heart, "not here," as he tapped his forehead.

Elizabeth's mind wandered to last summer. They had purposefully vacationed in Asheville, half hoping, half expecting to stumble across the "perfect" place. It would be a bold step yet John figured he could write his next book; Elizabeth felt her art would become more inspired and flourish; and, together, they would create a mountain retreat for themselves and others. They had spent two days enjoying the serenity and cool mountain breezes at the Grove Park Inn and had decided to take a day trip into the mountains. Heading west along the Blue Ridge Parkway, taking random turns and making spontaneous choices when Y's appeared in the road, they entered a long, narrow valley nestled within the ripples of two great mountains. A stream lazily meandered beside the dirt road on which their car bumped rhythmically over the potholes.

The road suddenly ended at an old wooden bridge which did not look safe enough to drive across. A bright red 'For Sale' sign was tacked on a nearby tree. Turning off the vehicle, John stepped out and Elizabeth followed. The sun was warm against their faces yet the air was cool. John eyed the old wooden barn. "I wonder who owns it," he mused.

Elizabeth's attention was drawn to a rambling two-story wood framed farmhouse with a wide wraparound porch nestled deep in the notch of the mountain ridge. "Hey," she exclaimed, "let's go look in the windows."

As she gingerly started across the rotting planks of the wooden bridge, John cautioned, "Let's be careful! Stay over the beams." Safely across, they started walking lazily arm-in-arm up the gentle slope toward the farmhouse.

Turning slowly around in a circle, Elizabeth surveyed the valley. "It feels like I'm home," she exclaimed. "I feel safe here. There's more than enough land to build my studio and work-shop space, with room for expansion."

They continued the remaining hundred yards to the stone steps of the old house. John declared hopefully, "It looks pretty solid."

Elizabeth peeked in the windows at large rooms with high ceilings. "It's wonderful!" she said gleefully, turning around and hugging John.

"It warms my heart to see you so happy," he whispered. "I haven't seen you so happy since…since Rebecca…" he said hesitantly.

"Was born—and died. It's okay to finally say it, John." She sat down on the top step and took a deep breath. "Rebecca would have liked it here."

"I think if it weren't for Rebecca—would we even be here?" he added, sitting beside her.

"She did so much for us, in such a short time, didn't she?" Elizabeth spoke softly.

"She brought us closer together," John said.

"She brought us here," Elizabeth emphasized. "This is Rebecca's place. Let's call it Rebecca's Place."

John nodded in agreement as he held her tightly.

The door to the conference room opened and Mica's assistant, armed with a folder full of papers, descended upon them. Elizabeth felt a peace and understanding as to why they were doing this—in some inexplicable way, she felt she would meet Rebecca again in those mountains.

The last papers now signed, they were assured the monies would be present at the closing the following week in Asheville.

The sun's warmth enveloped Elizabeth's body as she stood knee-deep in the cool waters of the stream which flowed through the valley of their new home. She watched the shadow of a solitary cloud ripple across the far mountain ridge. She could hear the workmen's saws whining through the lumber and the rhythmic thud of nails being driven deep into old wood. The farmhouse was becoming a home and the contractor had "promised" that it would be done before the holidays. Elizabeth wanted to start the new millennium with the house complete.

Suddenly she was sprayed with cold water. "Stop that!" she shrieked, giggling and threatening to splash John in return.

"I give," he said, quickly surrendering.

She hugged him and gave him a kiss. "I'm so glad we're here. I feel so relaxed," she paused, "and so much better."

"Nature has a way of healing," he observed.

She smiled ruefully. "I'll take a double dose of this medicine."

"They're going to be starting the foundation for your studio next week. Have you finished the plans?"

"I'll finish them over the weekend," she answered. "John, I've been thinking, though. I feel we should go ahead and start the workshop building."

"What?" he questioned.

"I know it's ahead of schedule but I feel it's important," she continued. "I know we agreed to wait a year or so, but look at what this place has done for us. There are so many who could benefit from what we have."

He nodded in agreement. "Maybe that's why Peter and Ruby are so anxious to get down here."

"I can't believe they've already picked the spot for their house—and from the photos we sent them, no less!"

"Yeah," he acknowledged, looking toward the wooded rise on the other side of the barn.

"It's funny, I couldn't wait to get down here and away from the crowds," she chuckled, "and now I can't wait to fill it with people."

Moving to sit on a rock along the stream, Elizabeth savored the moment. "It's been an interesting life we've led, my friend," motioning John to share her rock. "Who would've thought? You know, I do feel like Rebecca's here."

John smiled. "It's been a good life and it promises to get better. I wonder what the next century will bring?"

"I don't know," she responded, "but I couldn't think of a better place to begin it."

Ruby and Peter were dining with their old friends, Mica and Helena. "I can't wait to see the fireworks," Ruby said excitedly. "I've heard the city spent a fortune on 'em." Savoring her elegant surroundings, Ruby surveyed the streets of New York sixty floors below from their prime table for which Mica had heavily tipped the maitre'd. All seemed to be as it should be, a city in celebration.

It was Ruby's and Helena's friendship since their days as college roommates which maintained the connection between these two diverse couples. Mica looked absentmindedly around the room, wondering what contacts he was missing at the Governor's Ball. Helena had insisted on an intimate evening with friends. Peter and Ruby would not have been Mica's first choice. Mica chose his friends based on what they could offer him. He felt he gained nothing from a friendship with Peter, a social worker, and Ruby, an artist. Well, at least I don't have to watch my back around them, he consoled himself.

Mica was not in a festive mood; the promises of the new millennium did not seem hopeful to him. He had clawed his way to the top of the world monetary exchanges and his grip was slipping. The unrest in world economies threatened to collapse his house of cards. No matter what he feared, though, he would not be outdone, he thought, his hand swooping down to grab the check out of Peter's hand. Always in charge, Mica glanced at his watch and stood up—he was a much better leader than a follower. Leaving their unfinished coffee, the two couples stepped into an evening which was unusually warm for the last day of the year.

The last hours of a millennium begun in the distant, almost-forgotten past felt important, even awesome. For the last few years the media had focused on ancient events and future hopes. The media had inundated society with messages about how far humanity had come and predicting how far they would go in the next thousand years. It was a celebration of technology, science and industry. Corporation after corporation vied for media space to carry the very first ads of the new millennium, predicting where their companies and philosophies would propel them in the future. High hopes expressed and high dollars spent indicated they might even believe some of what they said. Mica knew he didn't.

On the surface it was a time of great anticipation and hope, spiced with some anxiety and uncertainty. The press had intentionally avoided emphasizing the many predictions of doom offered by both the famous and the infamous. There were those saying the world would end at a second after midnight, technology would collapse and economies would falter.

Some came out to see if that would happen, but most came out to celebrate a beginning rather than an end. It was a milestone—another year, another century, another millennium.

It was as it had always been, time marching on.

∞

Many lights shone that night in celebration but none truer than the one which seemed to be just a glow in the eastern sky, increasing in brilliance as it moved across the heavens—as it had done two thousand years ago, heralding once again truth and promise to humanity.

Upon the great Ship of Song, Michael instructed the illumination to be increased. "A little brighter now, a little brighter."

Miriam smiled. "Will wise men once again follow the star?"

∞

Something caught Peter's attention as they watched the fireworks. "Look there, Ruby!" he shouted over the crowd while pointing to the east. "I've never seen that star before, especially against the lights of the city."

Obviously annoyed at being distracted from the volley of light and color cascading over the river, Ruby ignored him. She was mesmerized by the reflections of light and the silhouettes of ships dancing upon the water in a surreal scene of fire and smoke.

He persisted as he poked her arm. "Ruby."

"What is it?" she demanded, aggravation in her voice.

"Look," he said emphatically, pointing to a now glowing star.

She gave a cursory glance to appease him. Her attention did

not return to the crescendo of fireworks lighting the city, as she now stared intently at the celestial display. She was inexplicably unaffected by the volley of rockets, the cheers of the crowd or the rumbling echoes of explosions reverberating off the canyons of glass and steel.

She squinted to see it more clearly. "What is that?" she questioned. "You know, it actually seems to be moving."

"I thought so, too." Peter paused and then laughed sarcastically. "Yeah, right. And it just might be that last glass of wine wanting to be heard from."

∞

Upon the great Ship of Song, Miriam and Michael smiled. The new millennium had begun.

∞

On that same evening, at that same moment in the mountains of North Carolina, other eyes were looking to the east. There were no fireworks, there was no great man-made celebration. John and Elizabeth sat huddled together, hand-in-hand, against the cold mountain breeze. The night was clear, the air was crisp and the stars glimmered as diamonds on a backdrop of deep blue velvet. Facing east from their pinnacle, they became enveloped in the beauty of the universe, their relationship and the life they had created.

"I'm so glad, Elizabeth, that we decided to stay here for New Year's," John said without moving his gaze from the stars.

She nodded in agreement. "Ruby's invitation sure was tempting. I bet the fireworks in New York are spectacular. But an evening with Mica is not my idea of a good time. I can't put my finger on it, there's just something about him I don't trust."

Cutting her thoughts short, Elizabeth looked down on the rolling valley illuminated by starlight and lifted her eyes toward a sky immersed in a million lights, representing a million worlds—the universe's perpetual celebration of itself.

Without another word, they pulled each other a little closer. Tucking the blanket around their feet, Elizabeth knew they had made the right choice and were participating in the greatest celebration of all.

She saw a strange new star in the east shining more brilliantly than even Venus. As she turned to ask John if he saw it, she felt a tingle and her mind filled with sparks of light. It felt as if the air had become electrified. A cool breeze rose up through her body and she became light-headed.

Had there been an observer, they would have told of a grand spiral of light flashing between the earth and the sky. One instant John and Elizabeth were there, and the next, they were not.

The new star in the sky, the great Ship of Song, welcomed its visitors and continued its journey around the world to connect with each new midnight of the new millennium.

$$\infty$$

It took a few moments for Elizabeth to become acclimated to her new environment and oriented to her new reality. The experience was like waking from a deep sleep in a strange place. Though unaware of where she was, all seemed vaguely familiar. First she realized she was no longer cold; second, that it was no longer dark; and third, that she was no longer on the pinnacle.

The appearance of Michael and Miriam and their welcoming smiles was the "Aha" which awakened her to the reality in which she now dwelled. Their radiant beings did not startle her and she looked down to acknowledge her own radiant light body.

"Welcome home," Miriam greeted. "Rest. We'll visit later."

John and Elizabeth strolled to their private compartment. Elizabeth's mind meandered over things she now understood more clearly. In oneness with All That Is, she avoided thoughts of returning to the planet and undergoing the process of forgetting again. The perfection experienced in this dimension of consciousness, the sense of love, peace and understanding, was impossible to bring back to the planet. It was not something that could simply be given but rather something needing to be born in the hearts and minds of humanity. This retreat to the great ship, like so many before, was a forgotten journey into awareness for the purpose of subconsciously reminding humanity of who they were and where they had come from. The ship, the beings of light which inhabited it, and the innumerable stars in the sky were all beacons to remind humanity that they were more than they perceived themselves to be.

In their quarters, Elizabeth surveyed the vastness and beauty of the universe through the crystal windows. She endeavored to make an indelible imprint of it upon her mind. She wanted to hold this image and the feelings it inspired so that it would be reflected in her art. The eastern coast of the United States and the glow of its great cities disappeared below her as the ship continued its revolution around the planet. She thought of Ruby, her friend and fellow artist, and smiled. "I'll remember," she thought confidently, "so I can share this with her."

The *Ohm* created by the engines of the great ship resonated throughout her being and lulled her into a deep state of rest and rejuvenation. Sleep was not needed on the great ship, or in this dimension, but all minds, all consciousnesses, no matter where they resided, needed a period to still the body and quiet the mind, to attune themselves with the consciousness of oneness, the All That Is.

Elizabeth's thoughts drifted to Ruby and Peter's upcoming visit to North Carolina. "Upcoming? Oops," she mused. "I forgot

where I am. Everything's happening now. Past and future are mean-
ingless." Time, or its absence, took on a whole new meaning in
this dimension. On the great Ship of Song, everything was eternal and everything was now.

In this swirl of time and place called eternity, Elizabeth's
thoughts wandered through her lifetimes with her friends. She
smiled. How blessed she was with so many good friends—Michael
and Miriam, Joshua, Peter and Ruby, Stephen, Christopher, and
of course John. From the perspective of eternity, all of her lifetimes were understood as chapters in one great story. Basking in
the realization that all was well and as it should be, she rested
deeply in the womb of conscious awareness upon the great ship.

As John and Elizabeth rested, they met in the paradise which
is born from knowing the truth and they relived their journey
together throughout the eons of time. They remembered how
the recognition of the perfect harmony between them was in-
stantaneous. They recalled how it had taken years on the planet
to discover what they had known in an instant in eternity. They
considered themselves blessed, for there were many who had that
perfect bond yet never found each other on the planet below.

In a spirit of celebration and thanksgiving for a love which
had grown strong through the years, the two entwined themselves and spiraled upward into a perfect union of consciousness and energetic harmony. In a dimension where there are no
limitations or barriers, the two truly became one.

∞

An instant after the spiral of light had disappeared from the
pinnacle, John and Elizabeth again sat overlooking the valley.

Elizabeth, with a quizzical expression, was staring blankly
into the sky. "What was that?" she questioned. "Did you see
something?"

"I…I…I don't know. I think so," John replied. "It looked like a flash."

"Yeah, but I don't know what it was. Oh, well," she sighed, relinquishing her thoughts and returning to the fullness of this reality. Sated with the beauty of this place and her love for John, she could not think of a more appropriate or sacred way to welcome the next thousand years.

Wrapped in a warm blanket and cocooned in John's arms, Elizabeth sought to remember what she had promised herself not to forget. As her thoughts roamed through her mind to discover what she had forgotten, it intrigued her that the answer seemed to be in the question.

Her attention was drawn to a bright star which seemed to reappear in the east. She could not explain why it filled her with hope and promise, nor why it seemed so familiar. The smile on her face and the glisten in her eyes were a hint of the inexpressible truth they had unconsciously witnessed. They had begun the new millennium on the great Ship of Song and would end this millennium together upon that same great ship.

Elizabeth, the artist, drinking in the beauty of the night sky, turned to John and said, "Remind me to tell Ruby how brilliant the stars are from up here—we should paint it." That thought felt vaguely familiar to her and she wondered if that could be what she had forgotten.

In New York, the four friends worked their way through the crowds of revellers dispersing from the New Year's celebration. Peter and Ruby laughed as they watched Mica and Helena snare a cab. In one synchronized motion, Mica jumped in front of an unsuspecting cab as Helena scurried into the back seat before anyone in the crowd could reach it. Peter and Ruby caught the kiss Helena threw them and they waved as the cab sped away.

Though having been squeezed in the press of humanity and

overly stimulated from all the excitement, Ruby somehow was left with a greater sense of well-being than she had expected. Why, she wasn't sure. The din of screaming celebrants had given her a headache and the smell of stale alcohol which permeated the crowd had soured her stomach. She was unable to comprehend what had occurred, since none of them had noticed the spiral of golden light which had plucked the four of them from the earth and returned them between the flashes of light in the sky.

As they continued their walk home, the crowds lessened and the night took on an eerie stillness. "It feels magical," Ruby commented, breaking the silence and pulling Peter closer. "Almost mystical."

As Ruby watched their shadows dance along the sidewalk, the streetlights seemed brighter than usual. Having just escaped from the throngs of people, this moment seemed almost surreal. If it hadn't been for the wisps of breath escaping from their mouths, Ruby might have thought it a dream.

She thought of Mica and Helena, and how their paths had diverged over the years since college. "Underneath it all, Mica's a good man," Ruby reflected, her words an odd mix of melancholy and excitement.

Peter nodded in acknowledgment. "Just distracted."

"Different choices."

"Never know, you might see him in North Carolina yet," he said hopefully.

"Yeah," she replied cautiously. "I hope it's not just to check on his investment."

"What?" Peter exclaimed.

"I hope, in hooking Elizabeth and John up with Mica, we helped them." Peter gave her a quizzical look. "Helena confided to me that Mica planned to make a surprise visit to North Carolina to approve the construction."

"Why would he bother?"

"Control, Peter. Control."

"Oh," Peter grimaced. "I bet that clause wasn't written into the mortgage."

In an attempt to change the subject, Ruby asked, "Who would've thought we'd head in such different directions? Remember college," she turned, looking pleadingly into Peter's eyes, "when we promised each other we'd change the world?"

"You say it like you think we aren't?"

"Sometimes I wonder."

"I think we each change the world in the way we see it. Who's to say we aren't doing exactly what we promised, each in our own way?"

"I hope you're right," she whispered, deep in thought.

Peter stopped and turned toward Ruby for emphasis. "What is it that you're really asking? I don't think," he said cautiously, "this has anything to do with their choices or ours. It has to do with being happy with whatever you choose."

Ruby's face lightened, "That's it! I don't think Mica and Helena are happy. I wish they were."

"I can't think of a better gift you could wish for a friend," he said lovingly.

They continued their walk home in an easy silence. Ruby reflected on her own life, savoring its richness and beauty. Not always easy choices, she thought, but her peace hinted they were the right ones. When you make the right choices, she observed, it's interesting how things just fit together when you least expect it.

One such synchronistic gift had been Elizabeth. Ruby remembered meeting her at an art show in the park and how they had clicked immediately. By the time they had finished sipping their cappuccinos, they felt as if they had known each other for years. Their ensuing friendship seemed to enhance their work and nurture their interest in nature and art. Their long discussions while painting in Central Park were very precious to Ruby, serving as an ever expanding source of ideas and creativity.

Of course, as synchronicity would have it, Peter and John became like brothers. Both philosophers at heart, they could spend hours contemplating how to make the world or the backyard a better place to live. The couples' friendship grew beyond mutual respect and common interest into a union which seemed to transcend the world in which they lived.

Ruby wondered, as she unlocked the door to their apartment, if the magic she felt this night was the promise the new millennium held for them. She smiled as she closed the door behind them and they entered the peace of the life they had created.

The world had not come to an end at the stroke of midnight as some had predicted—but rather it seemed like a new beginning. Ruby and Peter slept deeply, unaware that the significance of their choices would soon be revealed deep within the mountains of North Carolina.

Winter melted into spring as it had done for millenniums. In the fertile North Carolina valley, the brook now ran full and deep from the spring thaw. Elizabeth paced excitedly back and forth across the porch. "When will they get here? They should have been here by now."

"They just called an hour ago from the interstate. Give them some time," John assured her.

"I hope I gave them good directions," she questioned herself.

"They were perfect. Relax, let me get you a cup of coffee."

"Yeah, I'm sure that'll settle my nerves," Elizabeth laughed.

The wooden door swung closed behind John, aided by the cool breeze running through the valley. Elizabeth pulled her sweater around her neck and wondered if Ruby and Peter would get there before dark. The brilliant yellow sun was just beginning to spread a cloud of crimson and purple across the western sky. The pines rustled in the breeze and their rich, sweet fragrance floated heavily in the air, giving the arrival of their friends a festive quality.

From Elizabeth's vantage point, the valley stretched out before her. Her studio was finished and miniature stakes with orange plastic ribbons indicated the future home of the workshop building. The remnants of snow remained in the folds of the mountains and in the shade of their peaks, yet spring was upon them and the rhododendrons were preparing to bloom. Elizabeth's attention was caught by the sound of a vehicle still hidden by the barn. She jumped to her feet and ran to the far corner of the porch in an attempt to see who was coming. Almost immediately, she spied a white jeep bouncing up the dirt road.

"They're here!" she called and raced down the steps waving her arms wildly. As the vehicle clattered across the wooden bridge, she could see Ruby's and Peter's smiling faces. The jeep stopped short as the door flew open and Ruby jumped out. Elizabeth and Ruby hugged, swinging each other around like children.

"I'm so glad you're here! See," Elizabeth exclaimed as she pointed to the wooded knoll overlooking the barn, "we've saved your place for you."

Ruby giggled as she took in the site of her future home.

Holding a cup of coffee in each hand, John yelled from the porch. "Welcome! C'mon up!"

"What wonderful land!" Ruby declared. "The pictures only hinted at its beauty."

"We were lucky to find it and lucky to get it," Elizabeth agreed. "Thanks for the help with Mica."

"You're welcome," Ruby replied with an inaudible sigh of relief.

The sun had set, the dinner dishes had been put away and the dancing fire crackled in the stone fireplace. Elizabeth often wondered if these rocks had been collected when the fields were cleared for planting. The fireplace was a collection of rocks of various shapes, sizes and color woven into one intricate puzzle. She doubted if she would have had the patience to attempt such a feat. Whoever the unknown artisan, she thanked him.

She often found herself mesmerized when gazing into the fire or while studying the design, texture and hues of the fireplace stones. One particular rock always fascinated her: it was a large piece of what appeared to be pink granite. She wondered where it had come from since there was no similar rock anywhere on the property. If this was Rebecca's Place, this was Rebecca's rock. Every once in awhile, Elizabeth felt an irresistible urge to run her fingers across its cool, rough surface, savoring each sensation its texture offered.

"Wake up, Elizabeth," John whispered. "The fire's caught you in its trance again." He handed her a cup. "Here's your tea." She sipped the soothing liquid and watched the flames lap across the new logs John had placed in the fire.

"Yeah, Christopher will be building in the spring," John said, responding to Peter's inquiry.

"I wonder what it all means," Peter responded.

"What do you mean?" Ruby asked.

"Well, don't you wonder what it's about and where it'll lead?" Peter answered.

"I think it's about getting out of the city, interacting with nature and allowing our creative juices to flow," Ruby declared.

Peter retorted, "I think it's more than that."

Elizabeth sat up and put her cup on the table. "I agree. I know what we're doing and I understand why we think we're doing it—yet it feels like there's something else. That something else is what drives me to get the workshop building done, the barn repaired and the fields tilled."

"Self-sufficiency," John added, "seems to be the day's order."

"So you came down here to be farmers?" Peter laughed. "That's a switch."

"Yeah, ready for this? We're even thinking about getting some chickens," Elizabeth giggled, rolling her eyes.

The four friends laughed and the evening drifted in and out of speculation about what the future might hold.

∞

"They're listening, Michael!" Miriam declared.

"I know," he responded. "They're right. They don't know what they're doing. The important thing is they're doing it."

"If they'll listen, that still small voice inside them will never lead them astray," Miriam confirmed.

"I believe all the trips to this ship, though they were unaware, have served them well," Michael added.

"It was an excellent plan," Miriam acknowledged, "bringing individuals from the planet to the ship on a regular basis to instruct, guide and remind them of who they are and where they come from."

"The jump in technological development has been astounding," Michael declared, "but they're still missing the spiritual message entwined within the knowledge."

"The method without the meaning." Miriam paused. "The awareness without the insight. It could become a bumpy ride."

"Yes, but they're remembering."

In that instant on the ship, seven years passed on the planet.

∞

"Here you go," Christopher said proudly, handing Elizabeth a bowl of ice cream smothered in hot fudge and whipped cream. "And it's our cream."

"Nothing like being self-sufficient," John laughed.

"Chris' idea of self-sufficiency and mine are slightly different," Elizabeth snickered as she licked the whipped cream off her spoon.

"I'm reading here," Ruby interjected, flipping through a book on animal husbandry, "that getting some goats would be a good idea."

"For city folks we're turning into quite the farmers," Peter mused.

"Wouldn't it be wonderful if the meals for workshop participants came from what we grow and raise here?" Elizabeth said hopefully.

Looking up from her book, Ruby agreed, "I think that's where we're heading."

"This is all fine and good but the more we take on, the less time we have for the reasons we came here," John emphasized. "Christopher, when is the last time you spent an afternoon working on your textbook? I know I haven't either, so don't get me wrong. I enjoy what I'm doing on the farm but I don't want to get sidetracked from what I think I should be doing."

"Oh, that's the problem," Elizabeth jested. "John's thinking again."

"Okay," John quipped, raising his arms, "I surrender my logic and reason."

"You know," Peter said, "there's truth in that. If I've learned anything it's to trust my gut. It's taken me five years to let go of what I think I should be doing—and doing what I want to do. And you know something, I've never been happier."

"I've really enjoyed the people coming to the workshops," John agreed.

"We've gotten pretty good at it, too," Elizabeth added. "Never thought you'd be teaching the value of community-based living, did you, John?"

"Or herbal remedies along with art instruction," John teased her.

"I get your point," Elizabeth laughed. "It's interesting to look at where we've been. I wonder where we're going."

∞

Another seven years passed on the planet.

"Hold steady," Michael directed.

"There's nothing else we can do," Miriam declared, "but wait and watch."

"In the centuries that we've been guardians of this planet, I've never seen such a storm," Michael grimaced, as he watched the North Atlantic below him, seething in what would become known as a category six hurricane.

Reading his thoughts, Miriam reminded him, "We can't intervene. We can only assist."

Turning to the team prepared to assist those who would not survive the storm, Michael commanded, "Take your stations!" Throughout the night, those upon the ships watched as the land was barraged by the fury unleashed by humanity's ignorance and abuse of nature. Michael was notified of an eight point five earthquake in Asia and the simultaneous eruption of a volcano in the South Pacific.

"The earth is fighting back," Miriam stated.

"It's begun," Michael whispered.

She put her arm around him. "They're not alone. They're just not aware."

Michael nodded in agreement. "It's their greatest challenge—and their only hope."

∞

John slammed the door against the cruel wind and declared angrily, "You can't fool with Mother Nature! Sooner or later this was bound to happen." The windows rattled, reminding them the fury outside was just a thin sheet of glass away.

"Are the animals secure?" Elizabeth questioned.

"Yeah, if the barn roof doesn't blow off," he responded. "I hope we don't lose the bridge. Another foot and it'll be under water."

"Should we take the cars across?" she asked, half-panicked.

"Too late," he answered. "I wouldn't trust it. The footings could be gone. We'll just have to wait it out."

The wind whistled across the chimney as the flames chaotically interacted with the varying changes in wind direction and speed. She could hear the hiss of steam from the onslaught of water attempting to invade the chimney.

Huddled in the middle of the room, she asked, "Do you think the others are okay?"

"I'm sure," John comforted. "It's necessary for them to stay and protect their homes."

Elizabeth thought of Christopher's home across the now raging stream—he seemed so far away. A chill of desperateness went up her spine with the realization that if the bridge went out, they would be isolated. Silently she prayed that the newly planted seed would not be washed away. In her head, she heard John's voice, "Too late." She quietly resigned herself to the fact that they would need to replant.

Falling fitfully asleep in John's arms, the howling winds faded from her mind. She woke to a knock on the door. It was Christopher, Peter and Ruby standing in the early morning light attired in raincoats and hip boots. The rain and wind had stopped. The air was humid as the three laid their raincoats over the porch railings and their boots by the door. In two sentences, all of Elizabeth's questions were answered.

"The bridge survived," Christopher reported. "The barn is standing and the animals are okay." Elizabeth hugged Christopher for his good news—and the three of them for just being there and being alive.

John sighed in relief, "I'll put some coffee on."

Elizabeth placed a few logs on the embers to rekindle the fire. Turning to Ruby, she uttered, "It must be horrible on the coast!"

"Hey," John yelled from the kitchen, "the electricity's off!"

"We'll have to rough it," Elizabeth called back. "Get the old pot, we'll boil water over the fire."

The last remnants of the storm vanished from the sky. Over the next few days, reports of the destruction, flooding and death along the seaboard verged on the cataclysmic. Elizabeth stood in the waterlogged field, wondering how long it would be before they could plant again. She had insisted that John and Peter go into town immediately and get more seed. She was sure all the locals had suffered as they did, and seed would be at a premium. As she stood ankle deep in mud, she made a promise to herself that they would always set aside a portion of the harvest for the next year's planting.

∞

"She's a good listener," Michael affirmed. "Little does she know, it's probably one of the most important decisions she'll ever make."

Miriam nodded in agreement.

Three months passed on the planet below.

∞

John intently read the headlines of the paper. "Well, it's official," he declared. "We're in a recession."

"I could have told you that," Elizabeth grimaced. "You just have to go in town to the grocery store or to buy gas."

"At least we have gas and groceries we can buy," he retorted. "You know, 'The Storm' raked the coast for five hundred miles. They still don't even have shelters or enough food to feed the homeless."

"John, we're so fortunate. I wish there were something we could do."

∞

"You are—and there is," Miriam whispered to Elizabeth.

∞

"What did you say?" Elizabeth asked.
"I didn't say anything," John responded.
She said a silent prayer for all those who were suffering.

Ascension

Chapter Ten

Preparation

Elizabeth awoke from her thought-walk to a crowded Council Chamber. In human terms, it had been only a few moments since she, John and Christopher had stood on the pinnacle but, in a dimension without time, she had reexperienced the eons which had led them to this day.

Regaining her bearings, she looked around at her companions. John and Christopher were busy in conversation while Michael was focused on the great ships encircling the planet. He had invited representatives from each of the ships and numerous individuals from the planet to participate in the final preparations. Those returning to the planet would not remember, but an inner knowing and subconscious remembering would guide them through the upcoming events.

The conversation and laughter among friends did not distract Elizabeth from her contemplation and awe of the profoundness of what was about to take place. Her thoughts were interrupted by a woman's voice. "Elizabeth! My friend, Elizabeth, it's so good to see you."

At first Elizabeth did not recognize Katrina and her husband, Charles. Before she could collect her thoughts, the woman took her hand and excitedly asked, "How's Stephen? How's my little Stevie?"

In a flash of realization, Elizabeth grinned, "He's doing great! He definitely keeps us busy but we love him dearly."

"We miss him so much. We're so grateful he has you and John to love him." Katrina paused and with a mischievous smile confessed, "You know, I was the one who guided you through the woods to find him."

Understanding lit Elizabeth's face as she gave Katrina a hug. Now she knew who the lady in the woods had been. Her mind drifted off to a warm spring day a year and a half ago. Surrounded by her friends and immersed in her work, life was good. Even though nearly fifty refugees had found their way to this hideaway in the mountains, neither John nor Elizabeth fully realized that a wave of humanity was heading in their direction.

"Elizabeth," Ruby asked, "do you think I need to peel more potatoes for dinner?"

Elizabeth looked into the pot Ruby held for her inspection and answered, "No, I'm sure that's enough." As she turned to leave the dining hall, she added, "I'm going outside."

It had been a beautiful spring day and they had tilled the garden in preparation for planting. Elizabeth thought about going down to inspect what had been done. She had become known for her "green thumb," as everything she touched seemed to thrive. John always consulted her about when and where to plant in order to assure a bountiful harvest.

Standing on the first step of the dining hall, Elizabeth paused for a moment, deciding whether to stroll down to the garden or relax on the front porch of the main house. She could hear John and the men in the distance putting their tools away in the barn.

Her thoughts were interrupted by Christopher's friendly greeting from his porch across the brook. "Yo, Elizabeth!" he called, waving his arm.

She turned and waved at him seated in his rocking chair reading in the late afternoon light. As she turned to go toward the meadow, something caught her eye. She thought she saw a woman in a long white dress just on the edge of the woods near the main house. She looked twice in hopes she might see her again. She did not recognize her as one of the residents of the community. If the woman was going for a walk, she was in the wrong place. There was no path in that area and the terrain was steep and overgrown. Elizabeth saw what she thought was the flash of the woman's white dress between the trees and decided to investigate.

As she approached the edge of the forest, she saw the woman looking over her shoulder as if inviting her to follow. Elizabeth thought it was strange yet, instinctively knowing it was safe, began to follow her into the woods. The woman was almost out of sight as Elizabeth entered the forest and she wondered how the woman could move so quickly up the steep slope overgrown with brambles and littered with fallen limbs.

"Where's she going and why am I following her?" Elizabeth asked herself incredulously.

As if she had heard Elizabeth's thoughts, the woman turned and beckoned her to follow. It took some effort to keep up with the woman who seemed to glide gracefully and easily up the steep grade. Far less graceful, Elizabeth climbed over fallen logs, caught her jacket in blackberry brambles and tripped in a tangle of kudzu. The mysterious woman smiled at the disheveled Elizabeth and disappeared deeper into the woods. Brushing off the dirt and regaining her balance, Elizabeth's eyes searched the forest, trying to catch sight of this strange apparition. She wondered if the woman had been a phantom of her mind since she was nowhere to be seen.

Shrugging her shoulders and turning to start the trek back down the mountainside, Elizabeth's descent was interrupted by the sound of whimpering. At first she thought it was a small animal which had been injured. She listened intently to hear what direction it was coming from. It sounded very close. Working her way further up the steep embankment, she reached a small knoll and looked around. About ten feet away, she saw something huddled against a tree. Cautiously approaching, instead of finding a little four-legged creature, she found a two-legged little boy—dirty, clothes torn, tears streaking his muddy face, wet and shivering from the cold.

Elizabeth gently reached down and picked up the forlorn child. The boy held her tightly as she cradled him in her arms. Maneuvering through the rough terrain, she moved gracefully as she carried her sweet burden. For a fleeting moment she thought of the mysterious lady who had led her to this child, wondering who she was and if they would ever meet again.

"Indeed, you will," a small voice within her whispered.

Unknown to Elizabeth, Katrina and Charles watched from far above as she carried her newfound treasure out of the forest and into the light.

"Thank you. Again, thank you." Katrina offered what she had—her simple appreciation for the gift Elizabeth had given her son. She continued, "I can't wait to hold him again. I've touched his heart and whispered to his soul to let him know I am near. But it isn't the same as holding him in my arms."

Tears welled up in Elizabeth's eyes as she remembered the long nights holding Stephen, rocking him as he cried himself to sleep. She was not sure if her tears were of sorrow for the pain he had experienced or for the reunion which was about to occur. Katrina, Charles and Elizabeth conversed, loving parents speaking of their little friend playing on the planet below.

"I wish," Katrina whispered, "he knew I never left him and that I've always cared for him and loved him."

Charles put his arm around his wife and reminded her, "Today he'll know. Today he will know."

"Yes," she said as she kissed Charles on the cheek, "it's just a matter of hours but it feels like forever."

Katrina took Elizabeth's hand in hers. "I have one more favor to ask. Will you tell him I love him?" Elizabeth nodded and tightly embraced her.

The great ships maneuvered in unison around the planet, each radiating soothing, healing energy to Earth and its inhabitants. Michael was thankful he had sent a message throughout the universe when his friends had become enmeshed in the lower vibrations of this new dimension. A great armada of love had responded to his call for assistance. Lightbeings from throughout the galaxies had gathered around this small speck in the vastness of the universe. It was a doorway into a new dimension, into a new awareness of themselves and where they dwelt.

For thousands of years, the great armada had surrounded Earth and participated by offering its inhabitants the opportunity to awaken to their oneness with each other and All That Is. A chasm had been created by those seeking to remember and those striving to forget. The clash in consciousness had become critical. The internal conflict in the minds and souls of humanity had created environmental and sociological effects upon the planet which would soon render it uninhabitable. Both Earth and humanity would need a period of time for healing.

The greatest moment in the history of the universe since the threshold of free will was about to occur: the doors on the darkness of forgetting would be forever closed by the light of awareness of All That Is—and the oneness that comes from that realization. This was not some arbitrary moment in which to take action. It was an event created by their friends, the inhabitants of the planet below. They would soon be reaching an energetic moment, a crossroads, when they would individually make an eternal choice. The moment of choice between eternal remembering or eternal forgetting was fast approaching—a moment conceived eons ago when free will had chosen to forget.

Michael thought-talked with the captains of all the ships and invited them to join him in the Council Chamber. In the twinkling of an eye, a multitude of shimmering lights appeared and took their places at the crystalline table.

"We've held our positions," one of the captains reported. "We've begun the process of lowering our vibrational field in order to be in resonance with the inhabitants for the evacuation process."

Michael added, "And we continue to focus energy on the planet."

All was in readiness. Michael sent a command to the great engines of the ships. "Hold steady."

All the universes stood in awe of this moment. A hush fell upon the Ships of Song which surrounded the radiant jewel of Earth. Beings from every galaxy, every universe, every dimension had gathered in focused thought. In one great moment of giving birth, the fragment of pink granite which had been placed in the center of the council table began to glow, bearing evidence to the transformation which was occurring on the planet below.

The Council had gathered and the meeting was about to begin. Elizabeth took her place with Christopher on her left and John on her right. She felt refreshed and refocused by her thought-walk. She savored the journey she had just taken as one might enjoy sitting around a table with friends after a sumptuous meal.

Michael began the meeting. "Welcome, thank you for coming." He gestured around the room to the thousands who had gathered. "Each of you stands here in the knowingness of who you are and of your rightful place in the universe. These great ships, created by your consciousness, have assisted you to explore All That Is by exploring this planet."

As Joshua stood to speak, each in the room saw him in their own way: to some, he was the man known as Jesus; to others, Buddha, Mohammed or Confucius; to the ancients, Yahweh, Ishtar or El Shadai. What their brother, Joshua, symbolized to each of them was the perfection of who they truly were.

"Welcome," Joshua smiled broadly, echoing Michael's greeting. "Welcome home. Home is not a place, it's a state of consciousness. It's neither the planet below nor this Council Chamber. One is home when they are in conscious awareness of All That Is. Over the centuries of human existence, we have sought to utilize every philosophy, every religion and every belief system to remind humanity of this truth."

Elizabeth absorbed every word and was profoundly moved that humanity would again be aware of their oneness with All That Is. Her mind reviewed what she had experienced in her thought-walk. She remembered gliding over the precipices, waltzing on the waves of the wind and dancing with the dolphins. She recalled her marriage in consciousness with the great rock by the sea. Taking a deep breath, she understood how the density of their vibrations had allowed them to know forgetfulness.

From her experience, she had come to realize that forgetfulness was like a tear in the fabric of Universal Consciousness. It was because of this tear that the void created from the absence of love could be known; unmended, the tear would become larger and larger. The moment was quickly approaching when the tear would be mended through humanity's awakening and the passage through it would be closed forever. Those who chose to forget would be reminded no more. The void would again become still, for there would be no one to stir it.

Michael's voice brought her thoughts back to the Council

Chamber. "The pathway home is love," he reiterated. "You will soon return to the planet to participate in the ascension of humanity into the consciousness of All That Is. You are but one part of a vast gathering of humanity preparing for this event. We've been speaking to you in your dreams, in your thoughts and in your visions in order to prepare you for this day. We have given you signposts and milestones to show you the way on your journey back to who you are."

"You, and your friends like you, are eternal travelers exploring yourself," Michael continued. "Like a child who comes to know it can walk, only then does it realize the cradle was a stepping stone. With that realization, the child has the courage to throw its security blanket aside and explore its world. Today, humanity will cast the blanket aside and step out of its cradle into the vastness of the universe as pure expressions of All That Is."

Michael concluded and invited the captains of the other ships to the control room for a final briefing. It was a complicated procedure and he wanted to be assured everyone understood the final adjustments in the tonal frequencies of the *Ohm*.

The others mingled, greeting old friends and sharing their thoughts about the coming events. Many reminisced about the challenges they had faced and their excitement about the great adventure still ahead.

"Imagine," John whispered in Elizabeth's ear. "Imagine an Eternal Dawn of consciousness, a world without darkness."

Overhearing them, Christopher added, "A world where the light of who we are never fades."

"It's beginning," Elizabeth whispered.

"It began," John reminisced, "the moment we stepped foot on the planet."

A seed of awareness had been planted in the consciousness of each inhabitant of the planet. Those who had chosen the path of oneness would hear the melody which resonated with their souls and they would see the ships. Those who had chosen otherwise would neither hear the song of the universe nor the call of reunion. In fact, they would never miss those who journeyed to the ship because they would not remember them.

This moment of revelation had been well planned. Ever since the star travelers returned to the planet in the form of humanity, intense energy had been infused into the consciousness of the planet and its inhabitants to begin the awakening. Signs in the skies, symbols in the grain fields, scientific discoveries, cultural evolution, philosophical thought, ancient prophecies and awareness of life on other planets were all pointing the way to this day. Humanity was on the verge of the most profound revelation of its existence. Nothing in known history would approach the impact of what would occur this day. Even the discovery that the earth was round or that it revolved around the sun would not come close. Humanity was about to embark on a new adventure. The only ticket needed was respect, honor and love for All That Is.

Earth was also rejoicing. There was a hope for things fresh and new. The ships sent gratitude to Mother Earth for her assistance and patience. She knew that she was about to return to her original beauty. She had given birth to many children and now awaited the return of her youth and those she loved, transformed beings aware of All That Is. The Eternal Dawn breaking upon the planet would usher in the pinnacle of human consciousness—the New Heaven and the New Earth.

Those on the ships were like parents waiting for their child to awaken on Christmas morning, knowing their own joy would be increased by sharing in the happiness of the child. The Council Chamber was electric with anticipation and wonderment of what was about to occur. Those in the great room were delighting in remembering old friends who would soon be coming home. All those who had "died" were excited, knowing their loved ones would soon know that they were not dead at all. The illusion of death would forever be cast aside when their friends awakened in consciousness. The reality of eternal existence would again be known.

Michael's voice could be heard over the hum of conversation, announcing it was time to return to the planet. Previously, at the thought of returning, Elizabeth would brace herself as if going out into a cold winter night—but today was different. The promise of remembering forever was close at hand.

For the first time in eons, she saw herself spiraling downward through beams of golden light as she experienced the sensations of pure thought and energy. She spiraled into denser physical form and felt her feet lightly touch the ground.

She laughed, remembering and relishing the first time she had descended to the planet and had ended up to her knees in the earth.

Chapter Eleven

The Return

A cool breeze carried the delighted squeal of a child up the mountain, startling Elizabeth out of what she thought was a daydream, unaware she had ever left the pinnacle. What had she been thinking? I can't remember, she thought. She looked at John and Christopher who were stumbling over their words while attempting to make sense out of their conversation.

The lantern still burned like a lighthouse overlooking the valley. She reached over and extinguished it. The glow behind the gray clouds in the east betrayed that the sun had now risen and the gray haze overhead held a hint of blue. She wondered, Could we see blue sky today? She searched her mind trying to recall the last time she had seen a cloudless blue sky. About two weeks ago, they had had a break in the clouds for about a half hour. Maybe we'll be lucky, she thought, glancing at the threatening dark clouds accumulating in the east. Perhaps not.

"Luck," Elizabeth questioned aloud, "is that what life's all about? And if it's a game of chance, who's dealing?" The weight of their plight again descended on her shoulders. Imperceptibly, her posture slumped under the burden.

"Oh, yes. I remember what we were talking about," Christopher was saying, catching Elizabeth's attention. "We were trying to figure out how many cows to stop milking."

John nodded in acknowledgment. "That's not going to solve our immediate food problem. We can't depend on game. The wet summer has taken a toll on their food source, just as it has on ours. Remember the buck we shot last week? He should have had a thick layer of fat for this time of year. If starvation doesn't get them, the cold will."

Elizabeth grimaced. "Maybe they'll be lucky."

John gave her a quizzical look.

"Are we just trying to beat the odds," Elizabeth asked, "against a game we can't win?"

Appearing startled by her words, John stood up and walked toward her. "It'll be okay, Hon," he said as he put his arm around her.

"How do you know that? Do you know that?" she interrogated him.

His only response was to pull her closer.

"I can't figure it out any more." Tears streamed down her face. "I've…we've done everything, everything we can, yet it doesn't seem to help." She turned and looked out over the valley, now free from its blanket of fog. "We can't stop what's out there from affecting what's in here," she said, her arm sweeping toward the encampment. The words startled her and silently she repeated them, "We can't stop what's out there from affecting what's in here."

She paused. Out there—the world, she thought. In here—my soul, placing her hand on her heart. I can't control out there. But only I can affect in here. She gathered all her courage and murmured, "I'm safe in here."

"What?" John asked.

"I am safe now." John held her even closer. Elizabeth smiled, knowing John thought it was his embrace which made her feel safe. But she knew she had discovered a truth which would set her free from her fears: a sanctuary no one or no thing could intrude on. For a moment, it was as if the world had lost its sting. No matter what the winter had in store, she deeply desired to remember what she had discovered. The only place of refuge in the cold winter ahead may be in the warmth of the sanctuary within her own being.

A strange thought, almost a whisper, passed through her mind. "From in here," the voice continued, "you create out there."

∞

"Message sent," Michael declared.

"Message received," Miriam smiled.

∞

Encouraged by her thoughts, Elizabeth felt secure enough to leave the pinnacle. In some unknown way, her sanctuary high above the encampment had rejuvenated her and given her strength.

"I think it's time we get back," she suggested. "It's getting late."

"Oh, right, I'm in charge of the wood detail today," John remembered.

The three began the steep descent back to the encampment. Elizabeth watched the sunlight dance on the autumn leaves turned brown by the frost as she listened to the sounds of laughter, dogs barking and clanging pans rising from the community below. She could see the rooftop of the dining hall through the heavy green boughs of pines. With each careful step, the sounds of the encampment grew louder and the aroma of wood smoke stronger. These filled her being with a sense of contentment and peace seldom found in this chaotic world. The encampment was her home and those who lived in this valley, her family.

The encampment was perfectly situated, nestled in a V-shaped valley, high enough in the mountains to escape summer's heat and also be protected from cold winter winds. The stream of pure cool water that cascaded down the mountainside and through the fertile valley almost equally divided the property. This had become a life-giving gift which provided a reliable source of fresh water to quench the thirst of man and beast alike. Its journey slowed as it gracefully meandered through the meadow, offering easy irrigation for the crops. The stream marked the boundary between the agrarian aspects of the community where the barn, animals and crops were located, and the cluster of buildings that made up the community of people. The only connection between these two areas was the single-lane wooden bridge whose log planks clattered in announcement of any approaching vehicles.

The farmhouse was tucked high in the grove of trees at the head of the valley. A large and inviting wraparound porch offered a panoramic view of the encampment and its activities. The main house, as it had become known, was the headquarters for this burgeoning community and provided living quarters for John, Elizabeth, Stephen and those who had become designated as staff. Its accommodations were simple but luxurious in comparison to the cramped quarters of the other buildings. The generous front parlor provided a quiet, comfortable place for counseling and consoling those who needed a respite from the clatter and confusion of the community. The spacious country kitchen, designed by Elizabeth, had become the center for canning and baking, and the house's spacious cool, dry stone cellar provided ample food storage.

The dining hall, in which the daily meals for the community were prepared and served, was located in the multipurpose activity center originally constructed for conducting and housing workshops. It was a white framed building, with multiple paned windows and forest green shutters. The largest building on the property, it provided over five thousand square feet of desperately needed space. Though adequate in size for its original purpose, it was woefully inadequate for their present needs. It had become the focus and heart of the community, a place where people gathered around a warm fire to nurture their bodies and soothe their minds. The dining hall included an open, industrial kitchen and a seating area which comfortably held fifty. The other half of the building consisted of bathrooms and a dormitory which had housed up to forty workshop participants. The dining hall was now needed to provide meals for three times as many people, and the dormitory housed half again as many.

Christopher, Ruby, Peter and others had built homes which were now bulging at the seams in an attempt to provide adequate housing. In addition, numerous tents were erected to accommodate people as they found their way in from the trail.

Of the thirty-five acres which made up the property, about ten were level enough for gardening and planting crops. A small herd of milk cows roamed the pasture. The horses were allowed to graze in the meadow when they weren't working. The remainder of the animal population consisted of goats and chickens who roamed freely.

Ruby and Peter were busily working in the kitchen, aware that soon the dining hall would be filled with hungry people. Cooking had become an art since the past summer when the community had permanently lost electricity and they had brought up the old wood stove from the barn. Peter had become the master and unspoken champion of flipping pancakes on the stove's well-seasoned iron griddle. He began to pour the rich batter onto the hot grill. The aroma filled the air with a feeling of warmth and welcome as some of the one hundred fifty residents began to converge upon the dining hall. Peter was often teased that his pancakes were the best alarm clock the encampment had.

Ruby jumped as the dining hall doors flew open. Nine-year-old Stephen, bigger than life, burst into the room yelling at the top of his lungs. "They're here! They're here!" he screeched.

For a moment there was stillness in the dining room, until people realized it was just Stephen and continued their break-fast conversations. "Stephen! You know better than to yell in here!" Ruby admonished.

Words were spewing out of his mouth in an attempt to convey his message, "They're...they're here...their car broke down..."

"Slow down. Slo-o-o-w down. Who's here, Stephen?" Ruby asked deliberately.

"Th-e-e-y're here." Stephen said slowly, delighting in his imitation of her.

Ignoring his mimicking and starting to become exasperated, Ruby demanded, "Who's here?"

"Ah, to understand the mind of a nine-year-old," Peter quipped. Ruby threw him a scowl.

Seeing her expression, Stephen carefully chose his next words, "Your friends are here."

"Who?" Ruby interrogated, losing patience.

Stephen paused and wrinkled his eyebrows. "Wait a minute. Wait a minute, I'm trying to think," he said in his defense. Peter turned away to conceal his laughter.

"M-i-chael. No, no, um...Mica!" Stephen blurted.

"Mica?" Ruby said questioningly. "Mica and Helena?"

"Yup, that's them!" Stephen nodded. His message delivered, he bounded over to get a stack of pancakes.

"End of the line, buddy, like everybody else," someone directed.

"Aw, man," Stephen whined. "Don't I even get a reward?" His shoulders slumped as he walked to the end of the line.

Ignoring him, Ruby looked dumbfounded at Peter. "I wonder what happened?" she questioned as they both headed toward the door to find their friends. Before they had taken ten steps, the door opened and Helena and Mica, carrying their daughter, Emily, stumbled into the room. Ruby and Peter gasped in horror at their appearance. They looked cold, hungry, disheveled and in shock.

With tears in her eyes, Ruby approached and gave Helena a gentle embrace, whispering in her ear, "You're safe now." Helena smiled, but her expression of appreciation could not hide her tears of exhaustion and despair. Ruby glanced at Peter with a thousand questions in her eyes. He inconspicuously put his finger to his lips, communicating to her, "Not now." Ruby nodded in agreement. The most important question had already been answered: her friends were alive and safe. This was a time for nurturing and not questions. She scurried off to find blankets for them as Peter led them to a table by the fireplace.

As Ruby returned with the blankets, she focused on the stark image of Mica and his family huddled in front of the crackling fire. She could only imagine what had occurred to create the sharp contrast between this scene and the last time she had seen them in New York. Helena had prepared a sumptuous feast for them in their Upper Eastside penthouse. It was an evening filled with laughter, memories, hopes and promises to visit in the future. Ruby quickly dismissed the thought of what would have occurred if Mica had not made his "inspection" of the encampment. Now that there was no longer any means of communication with the outside world, would they ever have found the encampment? Probably not.

Peter handed Mica and Helena steaming cups of tea. Holding the cup tightly to warm his hands, Mica looked up appreciatively and whispered, "Thanks."

Peter nodded in acknowledgment and returned to the kitchen for the pancakes Ruby was dishing up. "I don't think I've ever heard him thank anybody," he told her.

"What?" Ruby inquired.

"Later," Peter responded. "It must've been pretty bad." Taking the plates Ruby held, Peter asked, "Should we send somebody up to the pinnacle to get Elizabeth, John and Christopher?"

"No," Ruby replied, "they'll be down soon enough. There'll be more than enough time. Let's give 'em the quiet time they need."

As the breakfast crowd diminished, Peter and Ruby relinquished their responsibilities to the cleanup crew. Approaching Mica and Helena, Ruby asked, "Would you like to lie down for awhile? You can use our room."

"No, we'd just like to sit for a bit. And she's asleep," Helena responded, looking down at Emily in her arms.

"I'm beyond sleep." Mica's tone betrayed his hidden anguish. "And when I do sleep, I have nightmares." Helena put her free arm around her husband. He looked away as tears welled up in his eyes.

An awkward silence ensued as neither couple knew what to say or what to ask. Ruby's deep concern and curiosity got the best of her. "It must've been awful. Are you okay?" she softly questioned Helena.

"It didn't happen overnight," Helena began. "We just weren't willing to acknowledge it."

"It was the damn weather," Mica exploded. "Even we can't control that, though God knows we've tried! God—that's a joke!"

Stunned by Mica's anger, Ruby knew better than to attempt appeasing him.

"We thought we were the masters of the universe," Mica continued. "I guess we've been put in our places, and a helluva place it is! It's all gone—what's the use anyway?"

"We've had some really tough years," Helena offered apologetically. "It was a domino effect. When the weather went bad, the rest was just a matter of time."

Ruby's mind swirled with images of how humanity had abused the earth. Now the earth was fighting back. She needed to let go of her anger and judgement of people like Mica, whom she felt were to blame. Her conflict, though, was that she gladly participated in the services, products and conveniences they hawked. Who was the victim? Who was the villain? Or were they the same? One thing was for sure: none of them had done anything about it.

As if doing penance for her thoughts, Ruby said, "I'm glad you're here. We'll find you a place." Looking directly at Mica, she whispered, "It'll be okay."

∞

Upon the great Ship of Song, Michael and Miriam watched their friends on the planet below. Giving Michael a peck on the cheek, Miriam said, "I have things to prepare," and headed out of the room. As she left the Council Chamber, she thought-walked through the ravaged planet. She felt the oceans and their great storms and placed her hand upon the quivering faults to soothe the Mother's labor pains. She touched the heart of each inhabitant and, like a mother comforting a child awakening from a nightmare, she whispered, "You are safe. You are secure. We are with you."

Michael, turning to Charles and Katrina, said, "Soon they'll never again feel pain. Never again will they feel loneliness. Never again will they experience limitation. No more sickness and no more death."

Charles nodded in agreement, but Katrina's attention was on her little boy bounding across the wooden bridge to meet Elizabeth.

∞

Elizabeth, John and Christopher had worked their way down the mountain to where the path started to level out. Sounds of children playing and dogs barking sifted out to greet them. As they approached the clearing which opened onto the encampment, Elizabeth spied Stephen playing with their dogs, InkSpot and PolkaDot. The sight of him warmed her heart. "Good morning!" she yelled across the stream.

Hearing her, Stephen bounded toward the bridge to meet them, yelling at the top of his lungs. What was he saying? She wasn't sure. Stammering and stuttering, Stephen finally reached them.

"Stop! Take a breath, Stephen," Elizabeth urged. He continued to try to speak between his gasps for breath.

"Stop! Take a breath, I mean it," she again warned. Surrendering, he became silent and regained his breath. Elizabeth squatted in front of him, looking him square in the eyes. Stephen looked as though he expected to be scolded. Instead, with a big smile on her face, she whispered, "I love you. And you know something, your Mom loves you, too." With that she gave him a big hug.

Stephen tolerated the hug for about as long as a nine-year-old boy could and whispered back into her ear, "I know." He wiggled out of her embrace and declared, "They're here!"

"Who's here?" John asked.

"Mica and Helena! You know, Ruby and Peter's friends."

Elizabeth's sense of well-being disintegrated with the rush of fear traveling up her spine. A wave of nausea washed over her. Why had they come? She and John had pleaded with him not to repossess the property. Surely he must understand that with the economy in a shambles and the university bankrupt, the retirement fund was in litigation. Things would work out with the fund, if he'd just wait a bit.

"When did they get here?" John questioned Stephen.

"Just before breakfast," Stephen quickly responded, obviously glad to be the bearer of information. "While you guys were up there," pointing toward the pinnacle. "Hey, what do you do up there, anyways? Can I go sometime?"

"Maybe sometime," Elizabeth responded absentmindedly. Her thoughts focused on her greatest fear—Mica had come to take the property back.

Realizing he could again be the bearer of news, Stephen turned around and raced ahead, his jacket open and shoes untied.

She watched Stephen sprint across the wooden bridge as the boards clattered under his feet. He again was on a mission to be the first, this time to tell Ruby and Peter that he had been the first to tell John and Elizabeth of the arrival.

Seeing the expression on Elizabeth's face, Christopher questioned, "What's wrong?"

"The mortgage…" John began.

"Oh. Do you think he would…? Would he dare?" Christopher cautiously asked.

"I don't know," Elizabeth answered. "I hope not. He hasn't been very sympathetic to our requests."

"He must realize that for the last six months it would've been difficult to get him a payment—even if we'd had the money," Christopher responded.

"What could he do anyway?" John questioned. "Everybody's in default and there isn't a legal system that would bother."

"He could take over if he wanted," Elizabeth said emphatically. "Or worse, he could throw us off the property. Remember when he surprised us with that inspection. He tried to take over the construction, and we were paying the mortgage then. Imagine now that we aren't, what he'd be like." She stammered, "I won't be under the direction of Mica!"

"Aren't you jumping the gun?" Christopher admonished.

"Maybe, but I don't think so," Elizabeth retorted. "I've never felt comfortable around him. I hope having him hold the mortgage isn't coming around to, pardon my expression, bite us on the butt!"

"I bet his business associates watched theirs," John responded sarcastically.

"If he's here to stay, he must not have watched his," Elizabeth smirked.

"I think you're both being a bit critical," Christopher reprimanded. "Since he's here, he's probably in the same boat as the rest of us."

His words jarred a sense of compassion for how far Mica would have had to have fallen to end up in this valley. "Well," Elizabeth conceded, "we'll see."

Walking across the wooden bridge, Elizabeth made out Stephen's voice in the dining hall announcing their arrival, and Ruby's voice as she scolded him for yelling.

As Elizabeth entered the dining hall, the image of Mica as a broken man so startled her that without thinking she wrapped her arms around him and said, "We're glad you're here." His cold stare jolted her. He was the picture of hopelessness and anger rolled into one. She wondered if he could be saved from the pit into which he had fallen—or even if he could be reached. Her instinct was to recoil; her heart was to embrace.

Elizabeth softly asked Helena, "Are you okay? Is there anything we can get you?"

"No," Helena responded gratefully. "Ruby and Peter have taken good care of us."

Elizabeth chose a chair next to Helena as Ruby handed her a cup of tea. "What a beautiful little girl you have," Elizabeth stated.

"Thank you," Helena whispered.

"I see you've met our adopted son, Stephen," Elizabeth continued.

"I don't think I remember Mica mentioning him," Helena replied.

"No, he arrived after Mica's last visit." Anticipating Helena's next question, Elizabeth continued, "I found him in the woods, alone."

Helena took a deep breath. "Times have been rough, haven't they?"

"Yeah, they have. But you're safe now and welcome," Elizabeth reassured.

Out of his silence, Mica whispered, "Thank you."

Chapter Twelve

The Encampment

The dining room had become quiet as the last stragglers cleared their dishes and headed toward the door. The only sound that could be heard was the clattering of dishes being washed. Ruby had returned from "tucking" Mica, Helena and Emily into bed. The friends sat quietly near one of the large windows. Mica and Helena's arrival had surprised and shocked them all.

"To see him in that condition," Ruby stammered, "is almost more than I can bear."

Peter added, "I'm stunned. I'd never have thought he would have come."

"What else could he do?" Ruby continued. "Where else could he have gone?"

"He seems so lost," Christopher interjected.

"And broken," Ruby agreed.

Mica's appearance at the encampment threatened Elizabeth's sense of security. She reaffirmed to herself that what is outside cannot affect what is inside. Yet Mica seemed not only to have lost what he had, but who he was. The thought frightened Elizabeth. In some inexplicable way, she felt he represented their greatest fears within themselves, putting salt in a wound already raw from a chaotic world.

"Are you okay?" John's voice intruded upon her thoughts.

"I'm fine, just thinking," Elizabeth responded.

As if Ruby were reading Elizabeth's thoughts, she said, "I don't get it. I don't understand it."

It seemed to Elizabeth that Mica and his family could be the proverbial straw that broke the camel's back. His presence was a witness to a collapsing world in which no one was immune to the chaos. Elizabeth remembered how Mica had touted that he was prepared for anything. His portfolio was diversified, his retirement secure and his penthouse and Hamptons home paid for. Elizabeth recalled how she, too, had once seen her life in a neat little package.

Thinking aloud, she muttered, "How do we survive the winds of change?"

The question seemed to startle her friends.

"What did you say?" John asked.

"What do you do when nothing around you is stable?" she continued, almost pleading. "Where do you stand so you're not swept away?"

After an awkward silence, Elizabeth continued. "Is this what any of you expected your life to be like? Or what you'd be doing? Is this the world we expected to leave to our children?"

"No," Ruby whispered.

"Is the goal simply to survive—or even to survive well?" Elizabeth inquired.

"I've always believed that challenges are to help us grow," Christopher responded. "They cause us to reach deep within our beings and find our strengths."

"Well, this is one helluva challenge," John interjected.

"So, it must be a 'helluva' lesson," Christopher retorted. "I think that's the key—if we can understand the lesson then we can understand the change."

Ruby asked, "It would seem then, that we all have the same lesson. In fact, everyone in the world has the same lesson."

"You know," John offered, "it's really not any different than it's always been, except for one thing—it's happening all at once." They looked at him questioningly. "Think about it. Haven't we all faced changes in our lives? A loss of a job, a home?" Glancing at Elizabeth, he whispered, "A child? Haven't governments fought before and finances collapsed? Hasn't the world faced drought, floods, volcanoes and earthquakes before? We're acting like it's the end of the world."

Seemingly annoyed, Christopher challenged. "So what's your point?"

"The best way to understand something is to understand its parts. We're overwhelmed by the whole picture. We need to look at the little things. We can identify what we're to learn from the changes in our lives."

"If I can't figure out what's going on, how can I figure out the questions?" Peter insisted.

"Whatever challenge you're facing is the teacher of the lesson to be learned," John answered.

Elizabeth piped up. "Mine today is trust. All day I've wanted to be afraid. Our conversation on the pinnacle about the coming winter. Mica's arrival threatening my security and confirming the world really has fallen apart. I've had this ongoing battle in my mind between hope and despair." She realized she had always felt that way. "That's always been my challenge, this is just a different set of circumstances."

"What happens if we ignore the lesson?" John questioned.

Elizabeth responded, "From my experience, it doesn't go away, it only gets bigger."

"What happens once we learn the lesson?" John inquired.

"We know it," Christopher answered.

"And it goes away," Elizabeth added.

John concluded. "And we don't have to study that subject anymore."

"I'd like to know who planned the curriculum," Christopher declared.

"And the syllabus," John interjected.

"But," Elizabeth stated, "we chose the school." Her mind wandered from the conversation to the encampment, suddenly realizing there were chores waiting for them. "Food for thought," she said, getting up from the table.

"Oh, right!" John jumped up. "The wood crew's waiting!"

Turning to John, Elizabeth whispered, "Love you," and gave him a kiss. "Have fun."

John smiled. "Always, on both accounts."

"Bye," Ruby chirped as she left to help the kitchen detail clean up from breakfast.

As Elizabeth walked down the steps and toward the main house to work in the canning detail, she turned and threw an unseen kiss to John who was now on his way to the barn with Christopher. She tried to rationalize why she had chosen this "school." She guessed that she must have a lot to learn since her challenges were many.

Their discussion had left her with an odd feeling—that either none of this was real or it wasn't important. She felt torn between her growing concerns and an underlying sense that all was well. Even the chores of the day in preparation for the coming winter seemed unimportant. But she wasn't going to bet on a hunch and change the camp's priorities.

Closing the heavy wooden door of the main house, Elizabeth hung her jacket on a hook and headed for the kitchen. She remembered designing it with Ruby and deciding, at the last minute, to add a wood stove. "Good thinking," she thought as she entered and saw Martha boiling bottles on it while Trisha peeled rich orange pieces of pumpkin.

"Hi! I'm here!" Elizabeth called.

"Hi," the women sang in unison.

"How can I help?" Elizabeth inquired, grabbing an apron off the pantry door.

"You can help me cut up the pumpkins," Trisha answered as she handed Elizabeth a knife.

As she gingerly began peeling the heavy leather-like skin off a pumpkin, Elizabeth was appreciative of the mundane task to distract her. All her cares and worries seemed to fade away as she felt one with the women as they laughed and worked.

"We should make some pies," Elizabeth blurted out, much to her surprise. She immediately dismissed it as one more of those jumbled thoughts she seemed to be having today. The pumpkin was far too precious to frivolously use now rather than saving for Thanksgiving. To Elizabeth's surprise and before she had a chance to recant, the women eagerly agreed and Trisha hurried into the pantry to get flour and pie pans.

Surrendering with a chuckle, Elizabeth thought, Oh well, the dye is cast. Let them eat pie.

John spied the wood detail waiting for him as he and Christopher approached the barn. The crew hoped they would not need to go too far today, although it had become commonplace to go deeper into the woods to avoid cutting live trees.

Joining the men, John announced, "We'll take the truck today." The crew stared in amazement since they had been using the wagon and horses in order to conserve fuel. "Who said that?" John thought, realizing it was too late to recant. The men had already begun loading the truck and returning the horses to the barn. Was he becoming reckless? He questioned himself, yet he could not shake the feeling there was no longer a need to conserve. Where it came from, he didn't know.

"It's going to be a good day," Ernie chuckled, loading the truck.

Christopher's mouth was still open in utter amazement at John's instructions. John couldn't resist. "Better close it before you catch a fly," he snapped as he hopped into the passenger seat.

Christopher was now grinning mirthfully. He slapped John on the shoulder and kidded his friend, "Well, Mr. Personality, you certainly know how to win votes."

By now, John was simply amused by the situation and waved to Christopher as the truck drove away. Bouncing along the dirt road, John wondered, "What have I done?"

Though he did not understand it, deep down inside he knew it was okay to consume the precious fuel.

Christopher headed toward the wooden bridge leading to his home on the far side of the stream. He stopped for a moment to soak in the panoramic view of the encampment, noticing how it seemed to be so active yet so peaceful. It felt as if the camp were enveloped in a blanket of tranquility, yet he sensed laughter in the air. Unable to make sense of this dichotomy, he decided the camp exhibited the most organized disorganization he had ever experienced.

As he continued walking, his thoughts were jarred by a finger poking him in the small of his back. "Guess who?" a voice demanded.

"Stephen!" Christopher called out, annoyed at being startled.

"I'm not Stephen! I'm a spaceman and I've come to take you home," he said in a deep, pretend voice. "See," as he pointed to a large circular cloud overhead, "that's my spaceship."

Christopher did not bother to look up at Stephen's "spaceship." If he had, he would have seen a brilliant white circular cloud about fifteen miles in circumference.

If he had been observant he would have realized it was not moving at all.

If he had been even more observant, he would have noticed that above the cloud the sun was beginning to penetrate the gray shroud of pollutants which blanketed the planet.

It was ten o'clock and too early to start lunch, so Peter and Ruby decided to take a walk. As they strolled hand-in-hand across the wooden bridge, Ruby took a deep breath and turned to Peter, saying, "Even the air feels fresh today. Look at the light, it's beautiful. If I get some time later, I might come back out and draw."

"That's great," Peter said, putting his arm around her waist. "I'd love to see you enjoying your art again."

Ruby reminisced, "Remember how we used to sit in the park and talk as I drew?"

Peter smiled in acknowledgment and glanced up, "Look," Peter said excitedly, "I swear I can see the sun trying to peek through the haze!"

"Haven't seen that in a long time." Ruby mused, "Maybe it's a good omen."

"Hey, I've got an idea," Peter clamored. "Let's pick up your pastels from the studio and go up to the pinnacle."

"Oh! Do you think we have time?"

"Sure, we have more than enough time 'til lunch."

It was as if time didn't exist for them. Carefree, like children on a holiday, with Peter carrying the pastels and Ruby holding the drawing pad under her arm, they began the climb up the steep path to the pinnacle. Singing along the way, they reached the clearing and found they were not even winded from the climb.

Ruby sat on Elizabeth's favorite log. It had been a long time since the two friends had sat together drawing the spectacular landscape. She positioned the pad in her lap and reached for one of the pastels as Peter ceremoniously opened the case of well organized colors for her.

Looking up, Ruby uttered, "Oh, Peter! Look, the mountains are so clear today!"

"It's beautiful," Peter whispered, "and brighter than it's been in a long time. And look," he said pointing at a large white cloud directly overhead, "I can't remember seeing one that white."

"Look at how perfectly shaped it is," Ruby observed. "It looks like a fine silver tray." She paused, her thoughts cluttered, as if trying to remember a distant memory. Somehow, though, it didn't seem important to remember right then.

They spent what seemed to be hours in deep conversation, talking about the past, commenting on which pastels perfectly picked up the hue of that mountain or the sky, and about their hopes for the future. Without fully understanding, they felt the future was full of promise.

A blanket of stillness lay across the encampment, enveloping it in an atmosphere of security and safety. From a bird's eye point of view, the encampment normally looked like an anthill of activity, yet today there seemed to be a rare tranquility and serenity. The fears and anxieties of the community overstressed by personal pain and loss seemed calmed by the cool breeze which rustled through the autumn leaves, and hearts were lightened by the unusually bright day. The drifting leaves, coaxed loose from their hold by the wind, seemed to whisper, "Lay your burden down," as they gently settled upon the earth. Nestled in the fold of a great mountain chain which protected them from stronger winds, the encampment had become their home. The "seeds" which had blossomed in this valley from turmoil and strife had born a rich harvest of compassion, caring and love.

Today, for some inexplicable reason, the weary minds, broken hearts and dashed dreams disappeared into a buzz of conversation, laughter and hope. Both John, on the wood detail, and Elizabeth, in the kitchen, had noticed the raised spirits. It was nearly noon and neither of them had been called upon to be judge and jury in an erupting argument or counselor to a grieving and distraught refugee. Today there was a welcome peace.

As John hauled a large branch out of the way of the wood choppers, he noticed how the men worked easily together, laughing and joking as they swung their axes against the standing dead wood. The hollow thud of falling axes and the rattle of quivering branches echoed throughout the forest. John brushed the debris off his gloves and flannel shirt as he observed a lawyer, teacher, doctor, student, preacher, factory worker and salesman, with their sleeves rolled up and sweat running down their foreheads, working together for the common good. Men who in another "world" might never have known each other, or even cared to, had become close friends. Their bond was the joy of being alive, chopping wood for their very survival with not much more than the shirts on their backs. Like the sap that once flowed through the maple just felled by the crew, life and its meaning had been boiled down to its pure essence by the fires of change which rumbled across the land. The wonder was that the essence of life was just as sweet and just as pure as the lifeblood of the maple.

John soaked in the laughter of his companions along with the warmth of the day. He relished this moment of harmony and peace, whispering silently his hopes that it would never end. Much as he wished that the men's cheerful spirits were because he brought the truck, he knew it was something more, but he did not know what. Always one to question why and to worry about when the next shoe was going to drop, John made a conscious decision to simply accept without question this overall sense of well-being. Wiping his forehead with his shirt sleeve and combing pieces of bark out of his beard, he dismissed his questions. This simple act of acceptance allowed him to appreciate the meaning of the moment. Men chopping and gathering wood—good men, honest men who cared for and loved their families. He was glad to know them—and glad they were his friends.

He watched as one of his friends in worn jeans carried an unusually large load of wood to the truck. Ernie's young face was flushed from the exertion and nearly matched the color of his fiery red hair. Victoriously dumping the load into the back of the truck, he stamped his feet to dislodge woodchips and sawdust from his clothing. Ernie took a ladle of cool water from the barrel and stole a moment of rest, quietly enjoying the day. Looking up and catching John observing him, he acknowledged him with a friendly smile before returning to his task.

John grimaced, remembering what some of these men and their families had endured to taste this essence of life. It was a nightmare beyond his wildest dreams and he wondered if he could have survived so well. John remembered when Ernie, his wife and their two little girls had arrived at the encampment. Ernie had been a lawyer in South Carolina on his way up in the corporate world. He had lost his home, his livelihood and, more tragically, his eldest daughter in the devastating floods of the previous spring. It brought tears to John's eyes as he remembered Ernie holding the tattered and water-stained picture of her. Their lives shattered, they ventured toward the relative safety of the mountains with their dog and what little they could salvage from the flood and pack into their van. They had left for the mountains with little money and had run out of gas. Ernie confided in John that he had traded the family dog for a few gallons of gas. He told the girls the dog had run away when they stopped for gas. John shuddered to think what had become of the dog. Hopefully not dinner.

To shake himself from his thoughts, John looked up and said to no one in particular, "Man, it's warm!"

Having removed his wool shirt, Ernie yelled back, "And it feels great!"

Startled by the unexpected response, John gave a casual salute back in acknowledgment. The faint outline of the sun filtering through the haze was directly overhead, which meant lunchtime, and John's stomach growled in agreement. "Lunch," he yelled.

As if rehearsed, the men simultaneously stopped their work and headed for the truck, wiping their hands on their pants and handkerchiefs as if remembering their mother's admonition to clean their hands before eating. Reaching into the back of the truck, John brought out the baskets of sandwiches and dried fruit which had been prepared that morning by the kitchen crew. As he turned back to grab one of the buckets of water, Ernie wedged in saying, "I'll get that for you, John. Go sit down."

"Let's enjoy this while it lasts," said Teddy, a twenty-year-old college linebacker, grinning as he propped his shirt under his head for a pillow. John knew Teddy enjoyed the work crews because fitness was important to him. When not working he gathered anyone he could for a game of touch football. He was probably hoping the weather would last and the wood be chopped quickly so there would be time for a game.

"Hoping for a game if we finish early?" John asked him.

"You betcha!" Teddy eagerly replied.

John smiled and teased him, "How are you going to play football when it snows?"

Teddy retorted, "I'd play in ice skates if I could."

Ernie agreed, "Bet you would." The men laughed. It was a bet they all agreed he would not lose.

A real sense of camaraderie had emerged from this shared task. Sprawled out on the green grass to catch the warmth of the sun, these men relaxed as if they didn't have a care in the world.

And for a moment, as they enjoyed their lunch, they truly didn't.

Elizabeth returned the large canning pot to its place in the pantry and dried her hands on her apron. She had enjoyed herself, laughing and even singing with the women on the canning detail. They had shared stories about their children, their husbands and their lovers. It was girl talk, a time of sharing deep feelings and profound insights. She felt that in the last three hours she had come to know these women more than she had in the last two months—and they her. Today she had become one of them—no longer the one who provided shelter, she had become one who shared it with them. Their chores faded away into play, and in that childlike state, undistracted by the burden of exacting responsibility, Elizabeth was able to clearly comprehend the magnitude and magnificence of what she and John had created.

Stepping out onto the porch, Elizabeth stretched her arms as if to accept the warmth of this wonderful day. The glow of the sun behind the haze warmed her body as the glow of friendship had warmed her heart.

Hearing Martha walking out onto the porch behind her, Elizabeth said without turning, "It's the warmest it's been in a long time."

Martha nodded in agreement. "Maybe the promise of a gentle winter," she added hopefully.

They stood in silence enjoying the warm breeze dancing through their hair. As Elizabeth's hand smoothed back her long hair, she surveyed the encampment. It was unusually quiet and had a pastoral feeling. It was an image she would have liked to capture on canvas if she could find the time. "Maybe later," she thought.

They could see InkSpot and PolkaDot playing and jumping on the hill past the barn. Martha chuckled. "You'd swear it's spring. Look at them."

Elizabeth agreed. "They think so." She mused, "All we need is a blue sky to make this day perfect."

"Let's hope it happens," Martha added wistfully.

As Elizabeth stood on the porch, the sharp fragrance of evergreens floating on the autumn breeze brought back childhood memories of Christmas. Just fifty feet away, the stream sang as it bounced over its rocky course on its way to the meadow. Down in the barn, she could hear a chicken cackling, laying its share of the main course for tomorrow's breakfast. The muffled banging of pots and pans in the dining hall made Elizabeth suddenly think of lunch.

At that very instant, Stephen came bounding out of the double doors of the dining hall. "Lunch!" he yelled. "Lunch! Come and get it!"

Martha smiled at Elizabeth. "I don't know what we'd do without him."

Elizabeth laughed. "He doesn't know what we'd do without him."

Like two girls on their way to a picnic, they walked hand-in-hand along the path to the dining hall. Elizabeth mused, "Maybe after lunch I'll paint a little."

As they entered the dining hall, Christopher passed them with a heaping plate of food. "Better hurry before it's gone," he teased.

"Where does he put it all?" Martha asked. "For someone who can't weigh a hundred thirty pounds, he eats like a horse."

Christopher turned around. "I heard that. I burn all those calories with my brain cells," he exclaimed with a toothy grin.

"You'd better do a lot of eating quickly," Elizabeth quipped. "I think your brain needs some food."

Giggling, Elizabeth grabbed two trays, handed one to Martha and stepped back to let her go first. Martha motioned Elizabeth ahead. Insisting that Martha go first, Elizabeth stepped behind her. Ruby, who was distributing lunch, laughed as she observed these antics. "You two remind me of a cartoon from my childhood where two chipmunks always insisted the other go first and, in effect, they went nowhere."

Surrendering, Martha went on ahead. Elizabeth tore off a long-anticipated piece of freshly baked bread. Its aroma had drifted throughout the encampment during the morning, teasing her appetite. Voraciously, she took a bite of the still warm bread, unable to wait until she sat down. Filling her plate with greens and vegetables and pouring herself a cup of tea, she headed over to sit down with Christopher. Instead, she stopped short to view the room, intentionally waiting for Martha to sit down and hoping there would be a place for her at their table. To her delight there was one place left and Martha motioned her to join them. Elizabeth winked at Christopher and turned to join Martha and the others who welcomed her with enthusiasm. She felt more at home today with her family than she had in a long time.

$$\infty$$

High above the planet, the armada of great ships hovered in silent vigil. Michael observed his friends and companions, and took pleasure in the joy and acceptance they were feeling. His mind returning to the duties at hand, he turned to Miriam. "I must go. It's about time and I must verify all is in order."

He again surveyed the planet and whispered, "I hope they know how much they're loved."

"They'll know, my love. They will know," she said reassuringly. She sensed his body quiver and realized he was silently weeping for his friends.

It was the tears of a parent for a prodigal child, for the pain the child had suffered and for the joy the child was about to experience. "It's been too, too long, my love," he said as he turned and hugged her.

It was the first time since the entrapment of consciousness

in the third dimension that Miriam had seen Michael with tears in his eyes. She thought, "We have, indeed, come full circle."

Knowing her thoughts, Michael smiled and wiped the tears now flowing from his eyes. As the warrior of light that he was, he straightened his great frame and walked forward into the Council Chamber to prepare for the ascension of humanity.

∞

In the encampment below, there was a slight mist falling. A few unseen drops of rain fell like tears unnoticed on the flagstone steps leading to the dining hall. One such "tear" fell directly on Stephen's head as he went out to play before school resumed.

Inside, Elizabeth quickly consumed her lunch. She must have been hungrier than she thought. She had eaten every morsel on her plate and now rested in the company of friendship. She had not realized how hungry she was for both. Now sated with both food and friendship, her mental list of afternoon tasks faded away as a surprising thought crossed her mind—to take a nap.

Giving herself permission, she stood and said her goodbyes. Placing her dish and cup in the sink, she turned to Ruby and said, "I'm going up to the house for awhile if you don't need me for anything." Ruby nodded, acknowledging that all was fine.

Elizabeth stepped out of the dining hall, surprised to see that it must have rained during lunch since the flagstone path to the main house was splattered with the remnants of rain-drops. She took a deep breath. A blanket of warm air lay across the valley, belying winter's approach as she walked briskly to-ward the main house. Her thoughts were of John with the wood crew and about what a wonderful day it was to be outside. The warm sun caressed her body as she slowed her pace to savor its warmth. She unfastened her jacket as a gentle breeze again tossed her hair, adding to the illusion of early spring. She glanced at her watch. Nearly one thirty. She would have enough time to rest before John returned. She almost expected to see the tulips she had planted near the porch of the main house peeking up through the rich dark soil. If it weren't for the now rare sight of a flock of geese heading south for the winter, there would have been no evidence this was not a spring day.

As she reached the steps of the front porch, she glanced at the tulip bed—just in case. As she stepped onto the porch, she turned for one final look at the encampment to assure herself it was safe to take a nap. The unusual serenity and tranquility which permeated the encampment confirmed that all was well and only enhanced her decision to rest. She could hear the birds singing as she closed the wide plank oak door and hung her jacket on the post. She realized just how brightly the sun was shining as she needed a moment to adjust to the darkness inside the house.

Elizabeth decided to let in the fresh air and the songs of the birds, and headed into the living room to open a few windows. As she lifted the sash and propped a stick under the heavy frame, she noticed the crisp shadows of the porch railing marching across the oak floorboards. She was tempted to go back outside to see if the sun had fully emerged from the haze. If she had, she would have seen five of her tulips beginning to poke their heads above the ground.

Before heading upstairs, she opened a few more windows throughout the first floor. Trisha and Martha entered. Elizabeth turned to them and said, "I'm going up to rest for awhile. Would you keep an eye on things for me?" They nodded and scurried into the kitchen to put the next batch of pumpkin pies into the oven. Pumpkin pie was always a big hit and they wanted to have more than enough.

Elizabeth reached the second floor landing and walked down the spacious hallway to the front of the house to open the hall window. She stood for a moment between the two rooms she and John had saved for themselves. To the right, she saw their comfortable featherbed inviting her. To the left was their sitting room, a gift they had given themselves, a sanctuary—theirs alone. "They can have all the rest," she and John had agreed, "but this is ours." At first, John had felt a little guilty because of the crowded conditions, but Elizabeth was aware that not only survival but sanity was important in providing sanctuary—and they jokingly called this their therapy room.

She opted for the sitting room and her overstuffed chair. As she covered herself with a throw and snuggled into a comfortable position, she was surrounded by her favorite books, photographs and mementos. It was her treasure trove, more precious to her than a king's ransom. This room not only provided her a place of solitude and a reminder of when things seemed more sane—it was a remnant, the last vestiges of days gone by and the life that she and John had intended to build with each other.

As she drifted off to sleep, her eyes fell upon the painting of the valley she had done from the front porch before any other houses or the dining hall had been built. She observed the deep, lush green of the trees and the muted reds of the weathered barn. The sky was deep blue and the clouds white. What caught her eye most was that she had painted an almost perfectly round cloud in the foreground, as if it were hovering overhead. Curious, she thought. She had never noticed it before and failed to remember even painting it.

She had often sat in this room and played her favorite music but now, as if they knew there was no electricity, the birds serenaded her to sleep. The encampment remained unusually quiet and its occasional noises did not intrude upon her peace or distract from the birds' serenade. Her conscious thoughts merged with her dreams as she drifted into a deep sleep.

Lounging with the men in the warmth of the unusually bright day, John savored each moment of his lunch break. Hands behind his head, he leaned against a tree. He glanced up at the faint outline of the sun through the haze and saw that it still looked like high noon. "Boy, time is passing slowly today," he thought.

Pulling his hand from behind his head, he looked at his watch and was startled to see that it was well after two o'clock. Alarmed that they had taken a two-hour lunch break, he jumped up and called to the men, "We've got to get this load on the truck. It's after two and it'll be dark by five!"

He was the only one who seemed to be in a rush, but the men obliged and loaded the truck with the last pieces of wood for the day. Teddy's suggestion for a touch football game when they got back to camp was definitely an incentive.

Christopher entered his home and pulled open the curtains to let the sun spill into the makeshift classroom his living room had become. He had been the obvious choice for the encampment's "schoolmaster." He always enjoyed the role of teacher and the opportunity to inspire young minds thrilled him. He knew today would be a challenge as he watched the children linger in the warm sun on their way to school. As each child arrived, he greeted each by name, a reminder of his professorship at the university. Unlike many of his associates, he felt knowing each student by name was important.

Stephen came bounding in, yelling, "Hey, teach!" and flopped into Christopher's favorite chair. It was the first time since his morning ambush of Christopher on the bridge that Stephen had seen his victim. "I was only playing, really," Stephen declared, hoping to make amends. Christopher's smile assured him that he had been forgiven but the wave of his hand told Stephen he had better move.

School was not a full-time occupation in the camp, but all

agreed that whatever the world was or was to become, education was important. Christopher's task was to ensure that each child could read and write, in addition to understanding both math and science. Interwoven throughout the curriculum was the importance of mutual honor and respect for all living things.

Christopher was pleased the children looked forward to his classes; he knew he had a knack for making learning fun and turning lessons into adventures. Since he had traveled extensively, he often interspersed his own experiences into the lessons. The children always enjoyed his vivid descriptions and interesting personal stories. He hoped it left them feeling as though they themselves had been there. Stephen often asked Christopher to talk of the time when he, Elizabeth, John and a student, also named Stephen, had collaborated on their research project and traveled to such faraway places as Stonehenge, Easter Island, the Andes and the Giza pyramids.

As he scooted Stephen out of his chair, Christopher decided to do something different. He had been prepared to give a reading lesson, but something told him to tell a story instead. He decided to tell the children about an ancient myth he had discovered during the research project. "I've decided to tell you an adventure story," he proclaimed. The "oohs" of the class echoed their interest as they moved closer so as not to miss a single word.

At the same time, across the encampment…

Elizabeth snuggled into her favorite chair, prepared to dream…

Christopher leaned back in his favorite chair, prepared to speak…

Elizabeth surrounded by her books of earthly wisdom…

Christopher surrounded by the open books of young minds…

Waiting to be written upon….

Christopher closed his eyes for a moment to collect his thoughts. Silence fell over the room as the children became aware he was about to begin. "A long time ago when the world was very young," he started, "before anyone lived here, before there were any animals or birds, the earth was just a baby, newly born. Far away at the very center of creation, there were beings of light who knew they were one with everything. They were eternally happy. They laughed and sang as they flew like the birds of the air. They played with beams of light as you might play with a basketball. They were adventurers and travelers. Since they were one with everything, they wanted to explore everything and, as a result, come to know themselves better. They didn't have school because they learned by experiencing."

One of the children quipped, "I wish I was them. Not having to go to school and everything." The rest of the children readily agreed in chorus.

Another added, "I wish I could fly."

"You can," Christopher responded. The children were startled by his response and became just a little more intent on what he would say next. "One day they decided since they were so happy and had such a wonderful existence that they wanted to share it. They wanted to take what they knew to the far corners of the universe. You know how you feel when you know something special and you want to share it?" Christopher asked, looking around the room. The children nodded in agreement, especially Stephen.

"So with their thoughts, they created great ships to travel in which were propelled by the energy of their love. The great ships didn't sound like a jet plane or the truck in the barn when we start it up. Their ships sounded like music, like an *O-h-m*."

He could hear the echo of the children imitating the resonant sound. The room seemed to hold that note longer than one would expect and a little chill went up Christopher's spine.

When the room became still again, Christopher softly added, "It was a song made by the sound of people loving each other."

"Cool," one boy piped up.

"Real cool," Stephen added.

Christopher smiled, "C-O-O-O-L."

The children giggled.

"These wonderful beings who lived forever traveled the universe and stopped off to visit many places. You'll never guess where they went."

"Jupiter," one boy yelled.

Another, "Saturn."

"The North Star," was heard from the back of the room.

"You're all correct. They visited all those places," Christopher said approvingly. "But guess where else?"

The room was silent.

"Earth," Christopher answered triumphantly.

"Wow, where are they now?" the children asked simultaneously.

"They are right in this room," Christopher said seriously.

A chorus of voices asked, "Where? Where?" as the children looked around.

Stephen, always the clown, stood up, turned around and lifted the couch cushion he had been sitting on. With great exaggeration, he peered underneath it, shook his head and plopped it back down on the couch, declaring, "Nope. Nobody's here!"

As he sat back down, Christopher gave him a mockingly serious glance. "Well, let me tell you more of this story." Slowly and deliberately, he said, "I know that you know everything—everything in the universe is connected. The trees, the animals, the stars, the moon, the rocks and people—all are one," he said pausing after each.

"And special!" one of the children echoed.

"And special," Christopher repeated in agreement. "When

these great travelers arrived at Earth, they wanted to experience Earth completely."

"How'd they do that?"

Christopher answered, like any good teacher, with a question, "What is your body made of?"

"Water."

"Blood."

"Hair."

"Guts!" Stephen added.

Another piped up, "Minerals."

"Ah! Minerals such as salt and calcium?" Christopher nodded. "Do you think your body could be made of the same things as the earth?"

They all thought for a moment. "Yes!" was the resounding answer.

"But I don't get it," Stephen protested. "Where did the space men go?" He was being quite serious but the other children laughed.

"We didn't go anywhere," Christopher smiled and softly spoke. "You and I are those star travelers. Do you remember who you are?"

There was a hush in the room. Then slowly, individual smiles of knowingness spread across the children's faces. Accepting that, the children wanted to know the answer to a more important question. "What happened? Why can't we fly now?"

One of Ernie's daughters angrily protested, barely able to speak. "It doesn't seem like a great place to me. I haven't seen any of these loving beings you're talking about flying around. And if we're so magical, bring my sister back!"

As she wept, Christopher moved over to comfort her. Sorrow was not alien to the children. Silently, they all shared her grief and looked to Christopher, hoping he had the answer. With emotions far greater than his words could express and in the most gentle and loving voice, he gave the most honest answer he could. "We forgot."

Elizabeth stirred from her sleep, pulling the blanket around her chin to ward off the cool breeze flowing through the open window. Half conscious, she watched as the shadows of the curtains blowing in the breeze danced on the wall in front of her. Too awake to fall back asleep yet too asleep to get up, her mind drifted in and out of consciousness—lingering in the state where reality and fantasy become one. The dancing floral curtains became children dressed in bright, crisp new clothes. The flutter of the material became their laughter as they skipped and played. The lush green of the trees beyond her window became the garden in which they played.

As Elizabeth drifted into a deep dreaming state, her vision became more real and she became one of the children. They saw a beautiful garden beyond a gate and entered, skipping and giggling. They watched the butterflies, played with the flowers and studied the rocks. Happy and carefree, they ate the fruits of the garden. All the children played and played but the more they played, the more they began to hurt themselves. Elizabeth grimaced in her sleep. They began to trip over the rocks they studied and prick their fingers on the thorns of the flowers they tried to pick. Their hair became disheveled, their clothes muddied and torn. This beautiful garden no longer seemed like such a fun place to be anymore.

They had become lost in the garden and could not find the gate to go back home. Their friends and neighbors around the garden heard them crying. They came running to see what was wrong and how they could help. Some went into the garden after them, only to get lost themselves. Others went in to show them how to play but forgot. Some of the children became so angry that they threw stones at those who came to help. As a result, they began to feel the garden more a prison than a playground—and they became sadder and sadder.

Soon their parents heard them crying and looked down on their children. They reached down from the sky, lifting each of them up, lovingly holding them, wiping away their tears and assuring them they were safe. The clothing of each child became new and crisp again. Their parents showed them that the garden was a wonderful place to play and how not to get hurt.

Elizabeth awoke and wondered what the strange dream meant. Staring at her Native American dreamcatcher hanging by the window, she sat still until her body caught up to her awakening mind.

The children asked Christopher, "Why did they forget? How come?"

"They had become so-o interested and believed so-o much in what they saw that they couldn't remember anything else," Christopher explained. "Take Hermie for example."

The children looked over at their guinea pig as Christopher walked over to his cage. "This is Hermie's world. He was born in this cage. He's lived his entire life in this cage or in this room, whenever we let him out to play. This is his world. Hermie thinks he has seen everything and there's nothing more. He has what he needs—his food and water. He doesn't know anything about the outside world, even though that's where guinea pigs naturally live. His mom lived in a cage. His dad lived in a cage. His grandparents lived in a cage. He doesn't even know the outside exists, much less want to go there."

"Let's take him outside," they shouted. "Let's show him what he's forgot!"

Christopher agreed.

∞

Michael and Miriam smiled as they looked down upon the encampment. They watched the children playing with Hermie as he munched a blade of grass on Christopher's front lawn.

With no bars to hinder his exploration and the gentle guidance and protection of the children, Hermie was free.

"Free at last!" the children exclaimed.

Little did the children know that they, too, were free.

Chapter Thirteen

The Visit

Now fully awake from her afternoon nap, Elizabeth stood and stretched. She became aware that she heard no dogs barking, no children playing, not even a dish clattering in the kitchen. She would have sworn no one was there and she looked out the window to assure herself everything was okay.

She observed what she thought to be the sun shining through the haze and was surprised that it still remained so high in the sky. She wondered if it was possible that she could have slept for only a few minutes. Looking at her watch, Elizabeth saw that it was almost four. A momentary chill of fear crept up her spine and left her feeling uneasy. Concerned that things seemed a little too strange, she decided to go to the dining hall, the encampment's center of activity, and see what was going on. She hurried down the stairs and grabbed her jacket as she headed out the door.

As she reached the bottom step, she heard men laughing and saw John turning the corner by the grove of trees near the barn. He was waving goodbye to the men and she heard him yell, "Have a good game!" as the men headed toward the meadow. Elizabeth's anxiety melted away as John turned and saw her. She waved and gestured toward the dining hall. Responding with a thumbs up, he headed for the wooden bridge.

She slowed her pace to await his arrival. As he approached, she noticed that he seemed happier than usual, especially since he was just coming back from a work detail. As John rounded the corner of the dining room and met Elizabeth on the flagstone path, she looked radiant and beautiful. It was as if they were suspended in a moment in time before the world had gone mad. They hugged each other longer than usual and, for a moment, their sanctuary seemed as if they were the only ones there.

As they walked hand-in-hand up the steps, they heard Christopher's voice echoing across the stream, "Hey, you love birds!" he called, waving from his front porch.

Seeing them, Stephen announced, "We're taking Hermie on a field trip!"

Elizabeth smiled at Stephen. Gesturing for Christopher to join them, she yelled, "Tea's on." Responding with a wave, he started to collect Hermie and the children. John and Elizabeth sat on the dining hall steps to wait for him and laughed hysterically at the kids attempting to corral Hermie as Christopher was attempting to corral the kids. Finally, with Hermie safely back in his cage, Christopher led his troops across the wooden bridge and dismissed them. The children could be heard calling out their goodbyes to "Mr. Christopher" and their requests to take Hermie out on a field trip again.

The children scattered and Christopher, looking somewhat beleaguered, turned the corner of the dining hall. Elizabeth chuckled at his appearance and he responded with a wry smile, "I'm not as young as I used to be."

Elizabeth entered the dining hall feeling awake, refreshed and uplifted. The image of Christopher, the professor, now the teacher and custodian of prepubescent children, tickled her. She wondered who was teaching whom. Christopher had never been married, swore he never would be, and declared he would never have children. Always watch what you resist because it will persist, she reminded herself.

Before she had time to contemplate what she herself was resisting, her words became more prophetic than she would have liked. There sat Mica, alone at a table in the middle of the dining hall. Any place they sat would have been within his earshot and not to have joined him would have been awkward. Elizabeth felt intruded upon by him. Mica made her feel uneasy and his presence affected her sense of well-being. She felt trespassed upon. These thoughts and feelings which swirled in her head created both confusion and anger.

She sat down across from Mica and politely offered, "Were you able to rest?"

"A little," he responded.

"Would you like something to eat?"

"No, thanks. Peter got me leftovers from lunch."

An awkward silence ensued until Christopher joined them as John went to the kitchen to prepare some tea.

"Hi. Where's Helena?" Christopher inquired, as he pulled up a chair.

"Still sleeping," Mica reported. "This has been very difficult on her."

"And difficult for you, I'm sure," Christopher responded, not mincing his words.

Pausing, Mica nodded in acknowledgment and turned his head away.

Elizabeth only became more frustrated. Her thoughts were now a mix—not only of confusion and anger, but compassion. She wondered if it was Mica who made her uncomfortable, or her conflicting thoughts. In some inexplicable way, he challenged her emotionally, mentally and, even, spiritually. How, she questioned, could one man intrude into her innermost places and threaten her sense of well-being? Who had given him the key?

She wanted it back. She wanted to understand. She questioned why for years she had been able to protect her sanctuary from a chaotic world, yet was now incapable of shielding herself from the anxiety this one man caused her. What was she resisting? Whatever it was, it was now sitting in the middle of her valley, annoying her more each moment! She pleaded for an answer to her conflict.

Her thoughts were shattered by John's voice from the kitchen exclaiming, "Oh, my God!" As she blurted out, "What's wrong?" he sprinted toward the entrance and she followed him in anxious pursuit. As she reached the door, he was already on the bottom step greeting an extremely elderly couple.

He assisted the man up the first step as Elizabeth reached out to the woman. By that time, Christopher was standing on the top step, astonished at seeing the couple. Elizabeth motioned for him to move out of the way.

After the couple were seated comfortably by the fire, the old man acknowledged Mica, who was a few tables away, with a nod. Christopher grabbed John's arm and escorted him back to the entrance. "I don't remember seeing them on my way over here," Christopher whispered. He walked down the steps, glanced around the corner of the building and stated, "No car!"

"They couldn't have walked!" John said emphatically. "They could hardly make it up the stairs!"

Christopher shrugged his shoulders and raised his eyebrows dumbfoundedly as they headed back into the dining hall.

"What can I get you?" Elizabeth asked the elderly couple.

"Just a little tea if you don't mind, dear," the old woman answered.

Elizabeth looked at the elderly man who only shook his head and said, "Nothing, thank you."

Returning to the room, Christopher asked them, "How did you find us?"

The old man turned and responded, "We followed the lights."

"Hmm," John surmised, "you must have seen the camp-fires." The old man smiled.

Still curious, Christopher inquired, "Did you come far?"

"Not too far," the old man replied.

"Never too far for a good cup of tea," the old lady added, smiling as she took the steaming mug from Elizabeth.

"It must have been a difficult journey," Christopher continued, pressing for information.

The old man looked at him with a knowing smile. "Many miles, many years." His enigmatic answers left Christopher befuddled.

Elizabeth wrapped her coat around the shivering woman. "Thank you, dear," the old woman said softly.

"Let's get you something to eat. What would you like?" Elizabeth urged, observing their frail bodies.

The old man waved his hand again, "Oh, no, no, you have so many to feed."

John insisted, "There's more than enough."

Christopher whispered to John, "How does he know we have many to feed?"

Overhearing them, the old man replied, "It's obvious."

Christopher's embarrassment was evident.

It didn't matter to Elizabeth how they knew, she felt safe in the old couple's presence. She glanced at Mica who was staring intently at the old couple.

The old woman patted Elizabeth's hand and softly assured her, "It'll be okay. You'll be okay and he'll be okay." Elizabeth wondered if her thoughts had been that obvious. "Remember," the old lady continued, "nothing outside of yourself can affect you unless you let it in. You hold the key." Elizabeth silently questioned, yet marvelled at the old woman's intuition. She felt as if she knew the old woman yet was aware they had never met.

"Rebecca's Place! What a wonderful name," the old woman commented. "It must be your daughter's."

Not even questioning how she knew, Elizabeth smiled in acknowledgment and prayed she would not ask how old her daughter was.

The old woman remained silent.

"John!" Elizabeth stated, "We must find them a room."

"Oh, no, no," the old woman said, taking Elizabeth's hand. "Thank you but this will be plenty. We're not staying, we're just passing through."

"Passing through? What do you mean," Christopher stammered incredulously. "You're not staying?"

"We're just passing through. We have a place to stay," the old man reiterated. "We'll be there before dark."

Elizabeth quietly surveyed the locale around the sanctuary in her mind and could not imagine where they could be going that they could reach by nightfall.

"We've heard of your great hospitality and decided to experience it for ourselves," the old man continued.

"What?" Christopher blurted out loud.

As if the old man had read his thoughts, he looked at Christopher and said, "You told us, my friend."

Christopher was disarmed by the old man's response yet admitted, "You look vaguely familiar but, for the life of me, I can't remember where we've met."

"You'll remember soon," the old man promised.

Deliberately changing the subject, the old woman commented, "This cup of tea was worth the trip." Elizabeth smiled appreciatively.

"Come my love," the old man said holding out his hand, "it's time for us to go."

"You can't be serious?" Christopher insisted.

"Yes," the old man said patiently. "We've received what we came for."

"But it'll be dark soon," Elizabeth protested.

"Not yet," the old woman responded kindly.

"Oh," the old man said, reaching into his pocket and pulling out a small velvet bag, the color of the night sky. "I have something for you. A gift for your hospitality."

"No!" Elizabeth exclaimed.

"Yes," the old man whispered as he gently opened her hand and placed the bag in her palm. "This is for you," he said. "It's yours."

Elizabeth did not understand and to her surprise did not question. She simply accepted the old man's graciousness. She untied the string which closed the velvet bag and emptied its contents into her hand. It was a fragment of pink granite. The very sight of it generated an inexplicable rush through her body. She rolled it between her fingers to feel its texture. It was hers, the old man had declared. It felt very familiar, as if it had been part of her childhood rock collection. Could it be a fragment of the pink granite embedded in her fireplace? If it was, how would they have it? How would they know whose it was? Could the old man have been the stoneworker who had expertly laid the pieces of stone together? Leaving her questions unanswered, Elizabeth focused on the old couple. Do I know them, she questioned, and why do I think I should?

She returned the granite fragment to the bag and put it in the pocket of her slacks. The old man winked at her, only confusing the issue. The couple began to walk toward the door, saying their goodbyes. Resigned to the fact that they were leaving, Christopher and John helped them down the stairs.

"Please let us drive you somewhere," Elizabeth begged.

"No, no," the old woman replied, "we'll find our way."

"At least tell us your names," John pleaded.

"My name is Michael and this is my wife, Miriam."

At that moment, Stephen came barreling around the corner of the dining hall at full speed, brandishing a snake as he chased two terrified girls from his class.

"Stephen!" Elizabeth screamed.

"Stephen! Stop!" John scolded. "Come here!"

Stephen stopped short and dropped the snake as the girls screamed away. He was caught! "Oh, man," he murmured, hesitantly approaching them as the snake slinked away.

Elizabeth bit her tongue, seeing the situation as almost comical but needing to be dealt with seriously. "That's no way to play with your friends," she reprimanded. "You're going to apologize to them and to our guests."

Stephen looked around questioningly. "What guests?"

"These guests, Michael and Miriam." John turned and pointed into empty space.

Stephen stood and watched the three adults turning around in circles, as if they were looking for a lost coin. Stephen again questioned, "Who?"

"Oh, never mind," Elizabeth stammered. "They…they must have…Oh, just go play and don't do that again."

A mixture of shock and relief flooded Stephen's face, but he quickly regained his senses and scooted off to find his snake.

The serene presence of the strange couple was now replaced with the rattling of dishes from the kitchen, people laughing in the dining room, dogs barking, children playing. The encampment had become alive and noisy once again.

Fearful the visit had been a hallucination, Elizabeth reached into her pocket to see if the velvet bag was real. Indeed, it was. She pulled it out and swung it in front of John and Christopher as if to confirm that they were not completely crazy. Not a word was spoken; none of them knew what to say. None of them fully comprehended what had occurred.

Eventually Elizabeth said, "Let's have that cup of tea."

John, close behind her, quipped, "This is how it all started."

Christopher peeked around the corner of the dining hall, watching to double check that the old couple was not walking down the road. They were nowhere to be seen. Shaking his head, he followed Elizabeth and John inside.

The dining room, which Elizabeth was sure had been empty except for Mica who was now walking toward her, was filled with activity. Watching his approach, she absentmindedly over-filled her cup of tea. Her mind was in a daze as she gingerly carried three steaming cups over to the table where John and Christopher sat in silence.

Mica followed her to the table where the three were sitting. He stood above them, expressionless. The awkward silence and the image of Mica towering over her forced Elizabeth to invite him to sit down. He pulled out the chair closest to her. She hoped her recoil was not noticeable. Mica reached into his worn brown tweed sports jacket and pulled out a folded legal document. Its sky blue outer page was faded and stained with dirt. A rush of panic invaded Elizabeth with the realization that it was the mortgage on the property. Bristling with anger, she thought, Here it comes! Her defenses up and ready for battle, she gave him a steel cold glare.

Mica, though, seemed not to notice; his eyes were cast down at the table. Shaking his head as if answering "no" to an unheard question, he spoke in a quivering, barely audible voice. "I fought and struggled to maintain what I had, yet I was unable to save it. I sought to protect what I owned and it was devoured. The harder I tried to keep it, the more it slipped away. All I have left is this piece of paper, a remnant of what I had. Yet look at you."

He raised his voice, more in questioning than anger. "You don't struggle to keep what you have. In fact, you give it away. I've watched you today," he said, glancing at the three of them. "It seems the less you hold on, the more you have. I fought to save my home—and I have none. You give yours away—and you have shelter. You know I hoarded food—and I'm hungry. You freely feed all these people—and you have enough to eat. I couldn't even feed my family or myself. I believed only in myself—and I am alone. You," he looked directly at Elizabeth, "believe in everyone—and your heart and your home are full."

Pausing, Mica's voice lowered to a whisper. "I came here to take back the only possession I have left—this property." Tears began streaming down his face. "But I fear I would lose my own soul. I want what you have. I'm sorry. I'm sorry for myself. I'm sorry for what I have done to my family. You know, the old couple showed me what I must do."

Elizabeth thought of the stone in her pocket.

Mica handed Elizabeth the worn document, the last vestige of Mica's collapsed empire. "It's my gift to you, in thanks for what you have given me today."

Elizabeth looked questioningly at him.

"Hope," Mica answered her unspoken question. He embraced her and left as silently as he had come. John, Christopher and Elizabeth sat dumbfounded.

Elizabeth watched Mica's thin frame disappear into the dormitory and wondered if it was her imagination that he seemed to be walking taller. She questioned which was the greater miracle—Mica or the elderly couple—and what miracles could possibly lie ahead.

Finally Elizabeth suggested, "Let's take the tea to go." John and Christopher readily agreed and the three headed toward the relative solitude of the front porch of the main house. Claiming her favorite rocking chair, Elizabeth sat rolling the stone, still in its bag, between her fingers, hoping to discover its meaning and origin.

Elizabeth surveyed the encampment as if to assure herself she was not dreaming. "The brightest day I've seen in awhile," she observed absentmindedly.

"And the warmest day," John added, as he took off his jacket. "Hopefully, it's the sign of a short winter."

"Or maybe no winter at all," Christopher teased.

"What do you mean?" Elizabeth shot back. Hoping Christopher might have some insight into the strange events of the day, she turned to look at him. What she saw was Christopher simply pointing his index finger upward at the golden glow behind the haze. "What time is it?" he inquired.

John glanced down at his watch and reported, "Just past four thirty."

"The sun's a little high in the sky for late afternoon in November, wouldn't you say?" Christopher asked pointedly.

A rush of excitement ran through Elizabeth, surprising herself how open she was to the possibility of mystery and magic. She questioned where her practical side had gone.

Having made his point, Christopher leaned back in his chair and resumed rocking.

"I knew today was special!" Elizabeth exclaimed. "What do you think it means?"

Adding to the intrigue, Christopher questioned, "Who was that couple and where did they go? In fact, where did they come from?"

John rejoined, "You know it's said we entertain angels without knowing it."

"Do you think it's possible?" Elizabeth asked hopefully.

"I think anything's possible," John replied. "It certainly was a strange occurrence."

"It did happen, didn't it?" Elizabeth blurted.

"You have the stone to prove it," Christopher declared.

Elizabeth removed the granite fragment from the bag and held it in her hand. Though part of the mystery, it gave her a sense of safety and security. The stone seemed to offer her hope, as if this little treasure held a long forgotten promise. As she rolled her fingers across it, a picture flashed through her mind, an image of something she could not quite comprehend. She sat as still as the stone, attempting to grasp the elusive image.

"What's wrong?" John questioned. "Are you okay, love?"

"I just had the strangest thought," she replied.

"What was it?" Christopher quizzed, hoping she had insight into the evolving mystery.

"Oh, nothing, just silly thoughts," she said, slightly embarrassed. "I think we're all being too childish. It's a luxury we can't afford," she exclaimed, fearful of being disappointed.

"Is it childish or childlike?" John replied. "In a world gone mad and without meaning, all we have is childlike hope."

"A respite from reality is okay with me," Christopher mused. "So tell us your strange thoughts."

She hesitated and then cautiously began. "I've been sitting playing with the stone in my hand and had the strangest feeling." She paused and stared at it between her fingers. Straining to express her feelings accurately, she continued, "It felt like my whole body was touching it. No…No…That's not quite it. I felt like I was inside the rock. No. I got it…I am the rock!" She had nothing more to say or to add. She could neither remember anything else nor make sense of it.

The two men responded with silence. Finally, Christopher spoke, "Maybe what we think is real is only imagined. And what is imagined is real. Who's to say?"

"That's the most confusing thing I've ever heard you say," John retorted indignantly.

Christopher's words taunted Elizabeth, as if invoking some

forgotten truth she was unwilling to acknowledge.

"No, think about it. What is reality? And how do we determine it?" Christopher asked in a professorial manner. "I told the children this afternoon about what we learned on our travels."

"What travels? The research project?" Elizabeth raised her eyebrows.

"About humanity's travels through history. No, more like the universe," Christopher added. "Humanity's travels through its own self-awareness."

John nodded his head in agreement. "And humanity's multi-leveled evolution. That's what we set out to prove with the research project."

"Ah, *The Holographic Nature of Humanity: Myth, Magic or Mystery?* They weren't too fond of that paper we published," Christopher cynically interjected. "They weren't willing to accept or even seriously consider the conclusions."

"I'm not sure it was the conclusions they wouldn't accept," John responded, "rather that they were afraid of the unknown. Human history is not as simple as it seems and more universal than commonly acknowledged."

Christopher shared the story he had told the children and the ensuing experience with Hermie. "That was the icing on the cake for me. They really got it," he said enthusiastically.

"I wonder when someone is going to let us out of our cage," John grimaced.

"Or worse," Christopher emphasized, "that the door is already open and we refuse to go outside."

"I think without the belief in something beyond what is seen, we won't even look for the door," Elizabeth said wistfully.

"Perhaps," Christopher contended, "the willingness to accept the possibility of magic and miracles is the key which unlocks the door."

Tears welled up in Elizabeth's eyes as she remembered believing in magic and miracles as a child. The world, its trials, and its pain had taught her not to trust or hope. What had she become? Whatever it was, she didn't like it. The thought taunted her. Yet perhaps she had unlocked the door. She had gone to the pinnacle this morning searching for something she did not understand.

"Thank you, Christopher, I needed to be reminded."

"No," Christopher responded, "I feel we've all been reminded today."

John whispered, "I wonder who the old couple was."

"I wonder what they were," Christopher replied. "Are we afraid to remember what we believed?" Not waiting for an answer, he continued, "Maybe now, more than ever, is the time to believe that there's more than just what we perceive."

"You may be right there," John responded. "What we perceive hasn't gotten us very far."

"I wouldn't be that critical," Elizabeth suggested. "I wonder if we're just seeing one side of a coin and it takes both sides to make sense."

"Common cents, c-e-n-t-s," John quipped. They all laughed.

"Well, if I had some 'common cents,' I'd start over again," Christopher volleyed.

"Maybe that's what we're doing—starting over," Elizabeth added.

Christopher agreed. "We're definitely down to basics, aren't we?"

"And the basics aren't that bad, are they?" Elizabeth concluded.

Suddenly, Elizabeth remembered the sun and looked into the sky to see if it had moved. She hoped to confirm the magic they all felt. To her disappointment, the dense cloud cover had returned. It was so thick she could no longer see the glow of the sun. Her heart sank as she studied the colors of the encampment which had now become dull and muted. The day looked like any other day and the dusk like the herald of any other night. The magic was gone and seemed as elusive as her memory of what she had hoped to find on the pinnacle.

"Is this a bad joke? Or just a bad dream?" she asked in frustration.

Christopher said philosophically, "If it's a joke, we'll forget it. If it's a dream, we'll awaken."

Elizabeth watched Stephen running across the bridge toward the barn. She smiled as she recalled his narrow escape from punishment, thanks to the abrupt exit of their guests. Maybe they were Stephen's guardian angels. God knows he needs two! Wherever or whoever they were, may they be with him now, she prayed, acknowledging her uneasy feeling as he disappeared behind the barn.

Stephen played as he went, throwing rocks and picking up sticks, swinging them in the air. He was paying no attention to where he was going. But suddenly he realized the familiar sounds of the encampment had faded away. He had moved deep into the forest, further than he had ever gone. In a terrifying moment, he realized he was lost.

Fear filled his young heart as Stephen relived the days when he had wandered in the woods after his parents and younger brother had been ambushed by a gang. The sound of the shots which had stolen them away rang in his mind and helplessness and guilt flooded over him. He remembered hiding behind a fallen log crying, "Mommy! Daddy!" The terror of the long nights in the woods returned as his eyes filled with tears. Not knowing what to do or where to go, he was afraid he would be alone in the darkness again.

A rustle in the woods startled him and he panicked. Screaming at the top of his lungs, he pleaded for someone from the camp to hear him. He called out in the advancing darkness for someone, anyone, to come to his aid. In the distance, he heard someone calling his name. "Over here!" he yelled as he began stumbling over the fallen limbs and rocks toward the voice. Someone from camp must've heard me, he thought.

Stephen heard the voice again, this time more clearly, and he wondered who was coming for him. As the voice grew louder, he strained to determine who it was. It was a woman's voice. Maybe Elizabeth, he thought. But it didn't matter, someone was coming for him!

He could barely see through his tears as he stumbled through the woods listening for the voice to guide him. "This way, Stevie." He stopped short. Only his mother had called him by that name. Could it be possible?

He wiped the tears from his eyes and ran in the direction of the voice. He never seemed to be fast enough to catch up with it but he was sure it was the same voice which had led him before and it would lead him again to the camp.

"This way, Stephen," the gentle voice said. It seemed louder than before. He picked up his pace.

"Over here, my love," the voice continued. "Stephen, Stevie, over here."

He dashed toward the voice, yelling, "Mommy! Mommy!"

"This way," the voice responded.

He scrambled up a small embankment on his hands and knees. The voice seemed to be coming from there. On all fours, he reached the top and found himself looking into the face of a beautiful woman surrounded by golden light.

His mother lovingly put her hand out to take his. She was not quite sure if her son recognized her. She gently said, "Stevie, I would never leave you alone."

And in the twinkling of an eye they were gone.

∞

Stephen danced where only those with childlike hearts may, in the Council Chamber on the great Ship of Song.

Chapter Fourteen

The Gift

Alone with her thoughts, Elizabeth wondered about magic and the meaning of it in her life. Was it synchronicity? Or the movement of something unable to be comprehended out of the corner of your eye? Was magic, in truth, reality? And what we perceive reality to be, indeed an illusion? Perhaps miracles would give deeper meaning to what she and the others sought to express. Possibly magic was the term given to those inexplicable events and circumstances in our lives—the unseen hand or the unheard voice which guides us to just the right place at just the right time for just the right miracle.

What would have happened if she hadn't been invited to participate in the research project? If Rebecca hadn't died, would she be sitting on this porch? Would Stephen's voice be echoing through the encampment if she hadn't gone for that walk at that very moment? Who was the woman who guided her to him, or was there no woman at all? Who was the odd couple who gave her this gift? Could it be that magic and miracles are the language of the universe? Was what she called magic simply the evidence of a world beyond her perception, and miracles, proof of its existence?

Elizabeth looked into the night sky and whispered, "I believe. Whoever you are, wherever you are, I know you are there. Thank you."

A warm breeze whisked across her face and she felt as if someone had passed through her very being. She wondered how many miracles she had missed. She questioned if it mattered at all and decided that magic exists only in the moment and this moment was magical.

"Wake up, wake up, Elizabeth," John gently coaxed, tapping her on the shoulder. His words seemed strangely familiar to her. "You've been a long way off."

"Oh, just daydreaming," she answered absentmindedly, fiddling with her long hair.

Peter and Ruby came up the stone steps to join them. Ruby chose the remaining rocking chair as Peter straddled a straight back chair. "So what's up?" he asked pointedly, signalling the group he wanted a serious discussion,

Christopher baited Peter, "Why do you ask?"

Peter looked at Ruby and began. "Well, Ruby and I have just come back from a walk down past the barn to the stream…"

"It was such a beautiful day," Ruby interjected.

"It's been so busy," Peter continued. "We had no more than laid our blanket out on the grass…"

"You know that spot down by the bend in the river where the grass is so green and soft?" Ruby interrupted again. Elizabeth nodded, remembering with pleasure many quiet moments there, skinny dipping and basking in the sun.

Peter began again. "We had no more than laid out our blanket and stretched back to absorb the warmth…"

"We both must have fallen asleep," Ruby again interjected.

Peter added emphatically, "And we both had the same dream."

"Isn't that strange?" Ruby exclaimed, "To have the same dream and at the same time? It must mean something."

Now trying to hurry the story, Christopher pushed Peter, questioning, "So what's the dream?"

Peter and Ruby looked at each other as if silently deciding who would begin. On whatever level the decision was made, Peter started. "I dreamed..." He corrected himself. "We dreamed we were floating like eagles over the mountains."

"But it wasn't like now," Ruby added, unable to contain herself. "There weren't any buildings or roads."

"That's true," Peter acknowledged, "everything seemed very pure and untouched. As we soared through the sky, we saw you, Elizabeth, and you, too, John. At one point, I remember you diving into the water and playing with dolphins."

Christopher raised his eyebrows. Elizabeth leaned forward in her chair.

"And I was dancing with the trees," Ruby added with a smile, "and you, Elizabeth, you were studying a rock." Everyone laughed except Elizabeth who was attempting to remember something as she fingered the precious gift in her pocket.

"It seemed so real." Peter paused and then, as if to convince himself, continued, "It must have been a dream."

"And that's not the best part. All of a sudden...all of a sudden," Ruby repeated for emphasis, "we were in a great domed room with a brilliant light on the ceiling."

Christopher, Elizabeth and John were in rapt attention. Each was intrigued by this dream which sounded so familiar, yet none of them could quite remember ever having had that dream themselves.

Peter continued, "And the three of you were there and hundreds, no thousands, of people from all over the world. We seemed to be in a meeting. What it was about I'm not sure," Peter hesitated.

Ruby took this opportunity to jump in, "We were in council, discussing…" She stopped short with a look of surprise. "I thought I'd remember…"

"Hmm. I felt today was special. That's why I dragged you guys out of bed before dawn to go to the pinnacle," Elizabeth said thoughtfully. "At first, I didn't get it. I thought we were going to the pinnacle to see something, or find something." Elizabeth contemplated, "To my disappointment, the dawn was like any other. I felt let down and confused."

John and Christopher nodded their heads in agreement.

"In some ways, the day was like any other, yet in others, it was much more," Elizabeth continued. "In retrospect, as I look over my day, I think I understand why I felt drawn to the pinnacle this morning. The invitation I heard in my mind was to let the magic in. We responded and our day has been magical."

"I wonder," Christopher spoke thoughtfully, "if magic is just a reality we are not yet aware of."

"How often have we dismissed the wonderment of a mystical experience by declaring it unreal and thus denying ourselves the paradise it holds?" Elizabeth pondered, "We've become too grown up. I think I understand why we must be like little children."

The group fell silent. There was truth in her words.

Speaking of children, Elizabeth wondered, Where has Stephen run off to?

∞

From the great Ship of Song that hovered above, Michael and Miriam watched as the sun set over the encampment. Michael nodded to himself, pleased the ship's presence had gone undetected. Unknown to the inhabitants on the planet, time was no more. It had been ushered out on a quiet afternoon, much like an unwelcome guest in the palace of kings.

Michael and Miriam joined the captains of the other ships in council. They gathered around the great table observing a holographic image of the planet. All thoughts were focused on that image as they discussed how to proceed. Michael turned to Joshua and their gazes met. No words were necessary as they remembered a planet once glorious in its newness, now scarred and befouled by her own children. Today, Earth wept as she pushed her young from the nest. Her only hope was that they would learn to fly and someday return to her again.

Hearing their thoughts, Miriam comforted them. "Earth will heal with time and love. We have been the hummingbird who has taken nectar from the flower. Remember, it's that same act which creates the opportunity for rebirth."

Michael addressed the assembly. "There has never been a greater challenge in the history of the universe than what we have faced here. There have been times in our exploration when we have faltered, been unclear or even stumbled, but we have never forgotten who we are. We see ourselves as pieces of a puzzle which create one grand picture."

"It's that interrelationship which makes us one," Miriam added.

Michael responded, "Our friends on Earth not only didn't know they were a piece of the puzzle, they didn't even know there was a puzzle."

A young man clothed in a golden robe entered the room, dazzling all with a smile which betrayed his present incarnation. "It's a lot like a touch football game," Stephen offered without being asked. "First you have to be a team and then understand the rules of the game so you can win." He stood behind Michael, smiling at his contribution.

Nodding in agreement, their attention returned to the holographic image of Earth above the center of the table. It now presented a planet transformed, emerald green set in a sea of blue. Gentle winds blew across her face and birds sang again in her trees. The oceans teemed with life and the streams ran clear and clean through the valleys. Majestic mountain peaks rose through the clouds, as if praying to the heavens.

Stephen knew it was time for him to return. His work was not yet done.

Michael nodded in agreement and in the twinkling of an eye, Stephen spiraled down to the very spot where the golden woman had stood.

∞

Straight as an arrow, Stephen ran toward the encampment, yelling as he came out of the woods, "Hey, everybody! I've got something to tell you!" His trauma in the woods had been overshadowed by his excitement to share this wonderful experience.

Elizabeth was the first to hear Stephen's unmistakable holler as he ran across the lawn toward them. Stomping up the porch steps, he tried to catch his breath and speak at the same time.

"Slow down," Elizabeth cautioned him, "slow down, Stephen."

Turning to John, Christopher whispered, "He's either gone crazy or he's had a vision. Knowing Stephen, either's a good possibility."

After numerous tries between sips of water, Stephen got out enough of his story to say that he had been playing in the woods and had gotten lost. He had seen a beautiful woman who had told him which way to go. They listened intently, careful not to dismiss it as his imagination.

Before they could respond, his friends called him. "Stephen! Come, let's play."

"Let's play a game of touch football," Stephen yelled to them. An odd look came over his face as he wondered why he had said that. He knew it was getting too dark to play it. Shaking his head, he looked back toward those on the porch, collected his thoughts and said, "Bye! See ya later." As he started down the stairs, he thought, Touch football? Why does that seem important?

Elizabeth watched as he ran off to play. She could hear the children laughing and giggling in the shadows. They must be playing hide 'n seek, she thought. Stephen's voice bellowing, "I'm it," confirmed her suspicions. It seemed like things were getting back to normal. The encampment was bustling again. She could hear the children playing and the cows calling to be milked.

Martha and Trisha emerged from the house and studied the group sitting on the porch. "You all look like you've been thinking way too much," Martha declared. "I've got the remedy for that. Some cold milk and fresh biscuits will fix you right up." With great relish, she set down a plate of hot biscuits with butter and strawberry preserves. Trisha followed with a pitcher of cold milk and mugs, proudly stating, "This should hold you 'til dinner."

A chorus of thank yous greeted this unexpected picnic.

"The night is so beautiful. Tonight would be a great night for a campfire," Elizabeth suggested. "We could have singing and dancing. I think it would be good for us all."

"And we could decorate," Ruby said excitedly. "Let's make it a party. But what should we celebrate?" She paused. "I know! Let's have a birthday party, a birthday party for everyone! I know a lot of birthday parties have been missed this year."

Elizabeth smiled. "A birthday party! That sounds perfect!"

The idea caught on at once. Ruby jumped up, grabbed Trisha and Martha and headed inside to plan the extravaganza. The men, already discussing the bonfire, headed down to the pasture on the far side of the barn. Elizabeth was sitting alone on the porch.

Word spread quickly as the sounds of the encampment

joined in a chorus, creating a mood of celebration. Elizabeth could hear the women laughing and talking in the kitchen, as the men called for hands to build the bonfire. It was as if she was listening to an orchestra, each instrument adding its own unique contribution to the whole, creating a melody which soared into a symphony. She could hear the children singing "Happy Birthday," the song echoing off the mountains as if all the world was celebrating.

∞

Miriam and Michael smiled.

Joshua hummed the "Happy Birthday" tune.

The encampment had unwittingly begun the celebration of the birth of a new age.

Truly, it was to be a Happy Birthday.

Chapter Fifteen

Happy Birthday

Elizabeth listened to the last strains of the song reverberating off the mountains. She sat alone on the porch and observed the encampment as she rocked rhythmically to the babbling brook's accompaniment. The encampment was full of activity and excitement. The celebration had brought out the child in each of them. She was intrigued by their inventiveness, imagination and cooperation. The farmer, banker, homemaker and physicist were as excited as children over building a campfire and decorating the dining hall.

As she observed her world, Elizabeth contemplated the pathways of her life—the many roads she had traveled, as well as the dead ends she had endured. Each, she hoped, contributed to her only request—to understand herself better and to make a meaningful contribution to the world in which she lived. She wondered, now over half a century from her birth, if she was nearer her goal.

Pulling the velvet bag from her pocket and gently spilling its contents into her hand, she studied the pink fragment lit by the lantern hanging from the porch. It seemed to glow against the darkness. It hinted of a secret she wished to know and of answers to her questions. Quizzically, she thought, why would this stone hold such meaning? She had many stones more beautiful and more rare in her collection. Was it the mysterious way in which it was delivered? Or was it a key to a long forgotten memory? She again searched her mind to remember if she knew the old couple. No, she remembered neither them nor the stone.

Her thoughts of childhood immersed her in memories of a more innocent time. A distant memory, long forgotten from her past, emerged of when she would lie in her bed at night and see a man and woman calling to her. She could not have been more than eight or nine but the memory was as vivid as if it had happened today. "Today," she blurted out loud, "that was them!"

"Who?" came from the kitchen.

"Oh, nothing. I'm just talking to myself." Why had they returned? More importantly, Elizabeth thought, why had they left? She remembered how safe she had felt in their presence. And the stories they had told her of times long ago!

Her mind blossomed into a meadow of vibrant memories. Thoughts swam through her mind in a flood of imagery. She remembered as a child being taken into a great domed hall and shown things that she could now only vaguely recall.

"The rock, the rock!" she again said out loud.

Trisha scooted from the kitchen to the front door to see if she was okay.

"I'm okay," Elizabeth reassured Trisha. "I do my best thinking when I talk to myself."

"You know what they say about those who talk to themselves," Trisha teased.

"You may be right," Elizabeth chuckled as Trisha turned back to the kitchen.

Alone again with her thoughts, Elizabeth held the fragment

tightly against her heart. She did not understand why she knew, but she knew the answer was in the oneness she felt with this piece of granite. To know this rock was to more fully know herself. To become one with everything around her was to know herself completely. The magic that she sought was held in the secret recesses of oneness with All That Is.

She recalled, as a child, walking with the old couple in her dreams and wondered if they were dreams at all. She questioned if the imagination of children was imagination at all, or rather fading memories of a reality soon to be forgotten.

She thanked the unknown voice which had called her to the mountaintop this morning. She thanked herself for heeding the invitation. She thanked the madness in the world which had led her to the magic which now permeated her life.

How complex she had become. Yet what was important was very simple.

She prayerfully looked up and said, "Thank you."

For the first time, she dared to step back long enough to realize how arduous this journey had been. It seemed safe to let her guard down, for she felt strong enough to catch herself if she fell. Looking over her life and the choices she had made which led to this valley, she knew she had been guided by some invisible presence into the awareness of her own power. She had depended on her career for abundance, her religion for spirituality, her government for security and order. When these external forces were taken away, she had discovered her own true self.

∞

Upon the great ship, Michael reveled in his friends' celebration. "Deep thoughts, my love?" Miriam asked.

He continued to observe his friends. "How I wish I could

have protected them from the pain and turmoil they have endured. But I would have stolen their most precious possession—themselves."

"And what would they have learned if you had stepped in with the answers?" she inquired. "Would they have grown from your act of intervention? Would they have greater understanding and awareness of who they are?"

Miriam put her arms around Michael as he looked out into the universe. "It's true," he acknowledged, taking a deep breath. "It's a journey they needed to walk themselves. I have felt like a parent watching our children taking their first faltering steps, wanting so to protect them from falling and getting bruised. Yet if they were ever to run, they would first need to stand."

"And then to dance," she smiled, observing the celebration below.

"And fly," he smiled, anticipating their friend's ascension.

$$\infty$$

The celebration was about to begin. The dinner bell rang in the encampment, awakening Elizabeth from her reverie.

$$\infty$$

Upon the great ship, Michael and Miriam danced in celebration around the council table. Their friends were about to come home.

$$\infty$$

On the planet below, Elizabeth, John and the others danced in celebration around the bonfire.

Near them, but unnoticed, an old man and woman danced

in and out of the moving couples, blending so well they appeared to be just a smile on the face of the night.

∞

Unnoticed, the song of the great ship kept harmony with the celebration.

∞

Exhausted from the dancing, Elizabeth and John collapsed onto a log bench, laughing with their friends. Elizabeth giggled as she watched Stephen dance with one of the girls he had earlier terrified with the snake. Overwhelmed with the beauty of her life, her friends and this valley she called home, she discreetly wiped a tear from her eye.

People began to head off to the dining hall and soon only John and Elizabeth remained lounging around the bonfire. Delicious aromas floated through the air, tempting them to head to the feast, but they lingered to bathe in the deliciousness of the moment. The crackling of the fire, the sound of distant voices mixed with music, and the low thudding of pine trees knocking together in the night wind were the only sounds to be heard.

The wonder of how rich her life had become filled Elizabeth's mind to overflowing. It was hard to imagine that it could be even more wonderful, yet she had a deep feeling that all of their lives were about to change in some dramatic way. The moment was exquisite and she stood back, observing the masterpiece of her life through the eyes of an artist. The many choices of her life had each led to this moment. How different, she wondered, would her life have been had she chosen another path? Or would all the paths have led her to here? Whatever the answer, she was thankful for the choices which had led her to this precious now.

John reached over and, squeezing her hand, inquired, "More deep thoughts?"

She nodded. "Contemplating the pathways of my life."

"Never thought the quickest way from point A to point B was going around in circles," John quipped. They both laughed.

Elizabeth was jerked back to the present by Stephen's hands coming up from behind and covering her eyes. He whispered in her ear, "Guess who?"

Pretending not to know, she answered, "Um…an angel?"

"No! It's Stephen!" he screeched as he uncovered her eyes and leaned over her shoulder, smiling. She reached behind her and, pulling the rascal onto her lap, proceeded to tickle and hug him. Stephen squealed with excitement as he kicked and screamed at the attention. He finally escaped victoriously from her onslaught by threatening to wet his pants if she didn't stop.

Giving her a big hug, he said, "Dinner's ready and we're celebrating my birthday!"

"Really?" Elizabeth responded.

"So that means I owe you a birthday spanking!" John teased, pretending to stand up.

"No way!" Stephen giggled as he ran off toward the dining hall, stopping far enough away to be sure that he could outrun John. Turning around, he stuck out his tongue and wiggled his hands by his ears, daring John to come get him.

"I'll get you later." John teased. "Better watch out!"

Elizabeth and John continued to sit in the glow of the fire's embers, serenaded by the music and laughter coming from the dining hall. The autumn wind made its own music as it moved about in the tree tops. The two lovers, alone by the fire, gave each other the gift of the realization of the fullness of their love and life. Lost in one another, they perceived the glow in the night sky to be nothing more than the full moon through the haze.

"You know what I have come to realize, Elizabeth?" John asked softly as he put his arm around her. "We are on the dawn of finding ourselves and you know what? When I find myself, I'll find everything I perceive I've lost."

She whispered in his ear, "Do you know what I'm thinking?"

"Yes," he answered softly.

"I wonder what she would have been like?" Elizabeth said wistfully. "Our little girl. She would have been a young lady now." For a moment they held their silence. Though Rebecca had lived only an hour, it seemed that she was the guide who had brought them together. When Elizabeth told John of her pregnancy, it became the catalyst causing them to acknowledge their love and commitment. This little soul, having never had the opportunity to take her first step, or call out "Mommy" or "Daddy," had given them the greatest gift of all—the recognition of their love for each other.

Elizabeth wept openly. John cried silently by her side.

∞

Upon the great Ship of Song, another couple held each other in love.

Michael put his arm around Miriam. "Good job, Rebecca." he whispered.

She smiled in response.

∞

Regaining her composure, Elizabeth observed, "It seems sometimes when we're the least sure of the way to go, God sends an angel to show us the way."

John responded, "I guess that's the magic."

The great ship now shone through the highland mist, softly lighting the valley nestled deep in the mountains. The light was bright enough that the color of the grass was clearly visible and the white of the buildings in the encampment was luminescent.

Elizabeth turned to look at the small clusters of people eating and enjoying themselves, scattered about the gentle slope between the dining hall and the main house. InkSpot and PolkaDot were making the rounds looking for handouts. In the dining hall, the musicians took turns playing their various instruments, delighting the audience with their performances.

"What a gift," Elizabeth sighed.

John agreed. "This is such a wonderful place and we have so many loving friends."

"Speaking of friends, I think we should join them," she said getting up and holding her hand out to him.

As they walked arm-in-arm toward the dining hall, Elizabeth shared her appreciation for what she had come to know. "I have searched for a long time to find that place called home. I know I have finally found it."

John, gesturing toward the dining hall, asked, "Is this home?" Taking the same hand, he placed it over his heart and asked, "Or is this home?"

Elizabeth glowed as she whispered, "Isn't it wonderful when they are one and the same?"

John acknowledged his agreement with a smile and a squeeze of her hand.

"I've come to realize the only pathway home is love," Elizabeth thoughtfully continued. "Where there's love, I'm home. Home is the union of where I am and who I am."

"Actually, they are one and the same," John added, "two sides of the same coin."

"Love, in some unexplainable way, unites the creation— where I am, with the creator—who I am," Elizabeth responded.

In the light of realization, John said, "I think that's why many define God as Love."

Glancing toward her friends, Elizabeth acknowledged, "I think there's a mystery here. Each of us is like a grain of sand in a desert. Once the grain of sand remembers that it is part of a greater whole, it no longer needs to fear the winds of change."

Chapter Sixteen

The Beginning

The great ships hovered around the planet like silent sentinels guarding a treasure long ago forgotten. The moment had arrived and Michael knew the time was now. The time was ripe. The harvest was ready.

The physical ascension of humanity into the awareness of All That Is was about to take place. The evacuation would not be done by locale, but by energetic resonance or, it could be said, vibrational consciousness. Each of the inhabitants would ascend to the ship which most harmoniously resonated with their being. Hearing the invitation in greatest harmony with them, they would be guided to the appropriate ship. When the time came, in the twinkling of an eye, the great ships would move about the planet in unison sending forth their unique vibrations of Universal Energy.

Each inhabitant who had even the tiniest spark of love or respect for All That Is would be drawn into the skies. While Earth healed, they would spend their "days" in integration, learning and remembering their true identity. Each would ascend to their own level of conscious awareness, where they would be taught by those they considered spiritual teachers. All beliefs and philosophies would be represented; each would hear the message of the oneness of All That Is in a way that they would understand and accept. The great question of human existence would be answered with each individual's recognition of their unique contribution to the puzzle, thus revealing the tapestry of existence. When they and Earth had healed, they would return again to paradise, never to forget.

Never before had Michael given a command which so touched his heart. With Miriam at his side, he declared, "Begin!"

For a moment, the great ship seemed to quiver as it shifted its vibrations into the lower octaves of the third dimension and began to sing a new song in harmony with the planet's lower vibrations. Michael and Miriam felt the gentle downward movement through the atmosphere and the ship's adjustment to the gravitational pull of Earth.

Michael was aware that as the ships lowered their vibrations, they would become vulnerable to the laws of physics, such as gravity. Their increasing density would cause them to be detected by the planet's electronic surveillance systems. The unison and synchronicity in which this celestial armada descended would be seen as a malfunction and the operators would likely not react. Even if they chose to react, the great ships would not be vulnerable to their attack.

When the ship hovered over the Jordan two thousand years ago, the skies were not littered with the satellites which now bounced off the ships like bugs off a windshield. Already, numerous communication links had malfunctioned and were being investigated. Those who would remain on the planet because they had not chosen the path of oneness would observe this phenomenon and see it as a glitch on their radar screens and a solar storm which had disabled the communication satellites.

Michael knew they would be visible to the naked eye. In order not to create fear or confusion, they had decided to camouflage the ships in clouds until the moment of ascension. Now hovering close to the planet's surface in silent vigil, they were the midwives awaiting the birth of humanity into self-awareness. Cloaked in the clouds, the great ships waited for their children to take flight.

∞

Elizabeth and John continued walking arm-in-arm toward the wooden bridge leading to the dining hall. They were startled by the brightness of the encampment and they looked up to see if the moon was full. A chill of excitement ran through Elizabeth as she saw a clear, star-filled sky with one gigantic billowing cloud directly overhead.

"What could possibly have happened that would have cleared the sky?" Elizabeth turned to John and said, "We must make sure everybody sees this. I don't know how long it's been since we've seen the stars." As they hurried toward the bridge, she turned her attention from the star-filled sky to the people milling around, laughing, talking and eating. She was amazed no one else seemed to notice the phenomenon.

"Look!" John said pointing to the hair on his arm. "It's standing straight up!"

"It feels like a chill in the air," Elizabeth commented, "but I think it's more electrical."

"Is that cloud a thunderhead?" John asked. "It almost feels like lightning."

"I don't know." Elizabeth looked around. "I hear the wind but I don't see a single tree moving."

Reaching the bridge, Elizabeth and John stopped and listened to the water of the mountain brook dancing softly beneath their feet. Inexplicably, they lingered, no longer in a hurry to leave this panoramic view of the encampment and join their friends.

The dining hall was full and the overflow of celebrants had spilled out onto the lawn. Stephen squeezed his way through the packed room to announce to those outside that it was now time to sing "Happy Birthday" and cut the pumpkin pies.

As the last strains of "Happy Birthday" echoed off the mountains, the people in the dining hall thought those outside were holding the last note. Those on the lawn thought those in the dining hall had continued to sing. To all it seemed like a soft "ooouuuh," the sound a mother might make to lull her child to sleep.

Elizabeth and John knew differently. From their perspective, they were aware that the sound was not coming from the encampment. It was coming from every direction, as if the mountains were singing. The melody crescendoed into a resonating *Ohm*.

Why in that moment Elizabeth thought to herself that a shepherd boy was singing, she did not fully understand. She wondered if the melody was being heard by her ears or by her soul. It was obvious that everyone in the encampment now realized that the song was coming from the heavens, as they noticed people on the lawn staring and pointing toward the sky.

Simultaneously, Elizabeth and John looked up. They stood in rapt attention as they saw the great wheel within the wheel hovering majestically overhead. A myriad of memories awakened in Elizabeth's mind. The air was electrical and their bodies felt weightless as they were immersed in music and held in love.

Just as the thought crossed her mind that they should go and be with the others, a brilliant light of inexpressible love flowed out from the center of the wheel and enveloped the entirety of the encampment. It was brighter than midday and not a single shadow could be seen. There was no darkness. A great presence could be felt. Elijah's chariot of fire had returned.

What brought tears to John's and Elizabeth's eyes was not the overpowering presence of love but the vision of Stephen being held by Katrina and Charles. There were now over four hundred individuals milling about the encampment—two hundred fifty of them having just arrived from the stars. Everyone either saw a loved one who had "died" or a spiritual teacher they trusted, assuring them that all was well—and welcoming them to paradise.

Joshua turned and gave a knowing smile to Elizabeth as he stood talking with Mica and Helena. An exhilaration spread through Elizabeth's being as she remembered her promise to Mica in the Atlantian Council Chamber. She had come back! In that instant, she experienced the intertwined threads of individual expressions which make up the tapestry of life and tell the human saga. She could feel, deep within the recesses of her soul, the darkest corners being lit with the light of understanding and the imprisoned thoughts of her mind being set free. She recalled her lifetimes of experiences. It all made sense: each life she lived and each person she met was an integral part of the puzzle of her existence; each adversary, a teacher to challenge her to excel; each obstacle, an opportunity to become strong. Every individual she had encountered on her journey of awakening had prompted her to move forward—be it with a kind word or an aggressive act. Every act, no matter how despicable, ultimately would move humanity toward its destiny. She had compassion for all those who had offended her and forgave herself for those she had offended. They were just classmates in the schoolroom called Earth.

Every individual who stood in this now illuminated valley and in the myriad other "valleys" now illuminated throughout the planet were in their own process of remembering. She real-

ized humanity's pain was created by the struggle with the unconscious awareness of who they truly were and who they were
destined to become. The chaos which had gripped the world
for the past decades had been the labor pains of the birth of a
new species. Humanity would never be the same again, for indelibly imprinted upon their conscious mind was the truth of
All That Is.

Still standing on the bridge, Elizabeth and John witnessed
humanity and eternity becoming one. Their emotions over-
flowed as the song of the universe, the *Ohm*, echoed off the
mountains. In slow motion, they saw what appeared to be
tongues of fire forming above the heads of each person and then
enveloping them completely. Once enveloped, the flame turned
into a spiral of light which ascended upward toward the ship.

And in the twinkling of an eye, they were gone.

Elizabeth and John stood silently viewing the now empty
encampment. The bridge on which they stood seemed to span
time and eternity.

They were startled as Christopher emerged from behind the
dining hall. They walked to join him as he stood alone on the
once crowded lawn. The three stood in silent knowingness. The
great ship hovered overhead as if patiently waiting for them to
say their goodbyes.

There was nothing for the three of them to say to each other
as they stood in the tranquility and serenity which comes from
understanding. What could they add to what they had seen and
what they had remembered? The encampment was quiet and
Earth had become still. The only evidence of this supernatural
event was the great Ship of Song overhead. Even the glow from
the ship was now more like a moonlit night than high noon.

InkSpot and PolkaDot thought they had arrived in doggy
heaven as they devoured a smorgasbord of goodies now left un-

attended. Elizabeth eyed Hermie's cage, now on its side with one scared guinea pig recovering from being dropped when Stephen saw his parents.

Elizabeth leaned over and picked up Hermie's cage in order to free him. She eyed InkSpot and PolkaDot, assuring herself they would not consider him dessert. As she started to open the cage, she stopped short as a thought went through her mind. She smiled and whispered to herself, "I wonder…"

And in the twinkling of an eye, the cage was empty and InkSpot and PolkaDot were gone.

John, Elizabeth and Christopher now stood alone in the stillness of their own thoughts. Elizabeth noticed the candles in the dining hall were flickering as they were about to go out, and the bonfire was now but a glow of embers in the distant meadow. The encampment felt like an empty nest from which its young had just taken flight. She swore that she could still hear the laughter of the children and the voices of her friends. She was joyful at their leaving and happy for the journey which lay ahead for all of them.

But this had been home. It had been a good place to be and her heart was a bit melancholic. She slowly looked around one last time to make a lasting impression upon her mind which would endure for eternity.

Her mind, again, became a kaleidoscope of images. She smiled, remembering John as the wild-haired prophet standing waist deep in the muddy waters of the Jordan. Her mind welled with remembrances of both of them in the Council Chamber in Atlantiana where they had argued their case. A deep breath of excitement filled her being as she recalled the great Council Chamber on the great ship to which they were returning. Reverently, she remembered merging her very being with the granite rock on the shores of Atlantis. She brushed her foot against the grass to acknowledge her desire to have made a ripple in the sea.

An awareness awoke within her as she realized why humanity had come—to unite the creator and the creation. In this endeavor, they had obtained the best of both worlds and had merged into a new species. A new dimension had been created and there was a New Heaven and a New Earth. The garden gate had now been swung open and they again were able to walk in the cool of the evening with the creator. She stood in the clarity of understanding that all of humanity's experiences were building blocks in the pyramid of their beings on which rested the capstone created from the Eternal Now of their existence.

Christopher approached his friends and gave them a hug. He glanced up at the great ship suspended in the heavens above them. Ezekiel had called it the "wheel within the wheel." Humanity would realize the glowing lights were a reminder of home.

"It's time for me to go," Christopher said. "You were the first to come to this beautiful valley. It's fitting that the two of you be the last to leave." As if some unseen ear had heard and some unheard voice commanded, Christopher spiraled up to the ship.

Earth was still and seemingly uninhabited, reminding Elizabeth of when she had first come to this planet. She remembered the gift she had been given and who had given it. Profoundly moved by the realization that this was the very piece of granite she had taken from the planet as a symbol of this adventure—she knew what she must do. The circle now complete, it was time to return it home.

She reached into her pocket and placed the contents of the bag in the palm of her hand. Holding the pink granite toward the heavens in a sign of offering, she gently placed the gift at her feet and looked around the encampment for one last time. She knew someday she would return. Just as birds return to the nest when full grown—they would return to this planet again.

She and John heard the *Ohm* gently and sweetly calling them. They felt weightless as they saw tongues of fire swirl above their heads. Their beings sang in harmony with the melody of the ship. They stood facing each other as they felt their very souls lifting them from the earth.

Elizabeth and John took flight as the birds of the air into a sky which no longer knew time or space. As they rose out of their beloved valley, they could see the light of a new day glowing in the distant sky.

Together, they glided over the mountains they called home and the sea where they had once danced with the dolphins. As they soared through the billowing clouds into a perfect blue sky, they looked down upon a reborn world. The mountains were green and the valleys lush, the waters ran clear and the stars shone brightly, awaiting the great cities of golden light which would soon sparkle with the dawn of a new day.

Knowing that it was now time to join their friends, Elizabeth and John bid farewell to the planet and entered eternity as they spiraled upward as one light into the great ship.

The Eternal Dawn had begun.

Omega

In the night of my forgetting,

I called to myself to awaken from my slumber,

to greet the Eternal Dawn of self-awareness and recognition.

I looked upon all that I created and saw that it was good.

About the Authors

Patricia & Stanley Walsh-Haluska
are currently living in the South
and are traveling extensively
doing research for their next book,
The Eternal Dawn.
It is scheduled for publication in early 2001
and will continue Elizabeth and John's exploration
of the holographic nature of human existence.

Patricia and Stanley are available
for speaking engagements and
can be contacted through
Destiny Press, Inc.

See you on the ship!

Ships of Song
Order Information

Internet: Order from our secured line at
www.destinypressinc.com

Fax: Fax order form to (888) 577-9121

Mail: Mail order form with check or credit information
to: Destiny Press, Inc.
Distribution Department
P. O. Box 1906
Birmingham, AL 35201-1906

Number of books _____ X $13.95 per book   =   _____

Tax (Alabama residents only add 8% sales tax)   +   _____

Shipping $3 + $1 each add'l book ($10 max)   +   _____

TOTAL _____

_____
Credit Card Number (Visa, MasterCard, American Express)

_____   _____
Expiration Date   Cardholder Signature

_____
Name (exactly as it appears on card)

_____
Address

_____
City   State   Zip Code

_____
Phone   Email

Orders generally ship within 48 hours.